Elizabeth Mary Dobell

Ethelstone, Eveline and other poems

Legends of the castle and tales of the village

Elizabeth Mary Dobell

Ethelstone, Eveline and other poems
Legends of the castle and tales of the village

ISBN/EAN: 9783337174248

Printed in Europe, USA, Canada, Australia, Japan

Cover: Foto ©Andreas Hilbeck / pixelio.de

More available books at **www.hansebooks.com**

ETHELSTONE, EVELINE

AND OTHER POEMS

OR

LEGENDS OF THE CASTLE AND TALES OF THE VILLAGE

BY

ELIZABETH MARY (FORDHAM) DOBELL

AUTHOR OF "VERSUS A WOMAN, PRO WOMEN, A MAN'S THOUGHTS ABOUT MEN, AND OTHER ARTICLES," ETC.

LONDON

C. KEGAN PAUL & CO., 1, PATERNOSTER SQUARE

1881

PREFACE.

THESE Poems were written under many vicissitudes, some only the other day, some in years gone by; some in a solitary room in an old Manor-house; some in the green lanes of Hertfordshire and Surrey, some in the wide corn-fields of Cambridgeshire—some by the seashore—and some, in the happiest of all places to the author—in a London library, by London lamp-light, surrounded by the roar of London life, and with the sweet companionship of a sympathetic fellow-worker.

84, HARLEY STREET.
  December, 1880.

CONTENTS.

		PAGE
A Farewell to Odsey	... ...	3
The Evening Star	... ...	6
The Good Physician	... ...	9
Dirge of the Red Indian Warrior	... ...	14
Ethelstone (*A Legend of the Castle*)—		
Introductory Lines	... ...	18
Canto I.	... ...	19
Canto II.	... ...	29
Canto III.	... ...	39
Canto IV.	... ...	49
Canto V.	... ...	64
The Lost Star	... ...	79
An Appeal to France	... ...	82
A Letter to ——	... ...	85
Impromptu Lines on hearing of the Hopeless Illness of ——		87
Thoughts in the Chamber of Death	... ...	89
Eveline (*A Tale of the Village*)—		
Canto I.	... ...	95
Canto II.	... ...	108
Canto III.	... ...	121

THOUGHTFUL MOMENTS.

The Graves of Three Brothers	... ...	139
To Dr. ——	... ...	142

		PAGE
LINES TO MY LOVE	... ...	144
OLD-FASHIONED PRAISES BY A LOVER OF SUMMER	... ...	146
TREASURED MEMORIES	... ...	148
DESPAIRING WORDS ...	... ...	150
IMPROMPTU ADDRESS TO CALUMNY ...	... ...	153

POEMS BY THE "SAD SEA WAVES."

NEAR THE HOARSE WATERS OF THE DEEP	... ...	157
THE FISHERMAN	... ...	162
ENGLAND'S DAUGHTER	... ...	164
THE FISHERMAN'S BRIDE	... ...	166
MURMURS BY THE "SAD SEA WAVES"—		
Murmur I.	... ...	171
Murmur II.	... ...	173
Murmur III.	... ...	175
BY THE WHITE CLIFFS ...	... ...	177

A FEW SONGS OF LIGHTER HOURS.

THE SPITEFUL BEE ...	... ...	181
THE WAY WE LIVE NOW ...	... ...	183
MOAN OF THE DISCONTENTED	... ...	188
A YOUNG GIRL AMONG THE CHESTNUT TREES	... ...	190
IMPROMPTU LINES ON "MY UNCLE"	... ...	192
THE SPURIOUS CRITICS ...	... ...	194
HAPPY THOUGHTS ...	... ...	197
PADDY'S INVITATION	... ...	200

FRAGMENTS OF AN OLD LEGEND—

Introduction	... ...	205
Canto I. ...	... ...	207
Canto II.	... ...	220
Canto III.	... ...	234

CONTENTS.   ix

OCCASIONAL PIECES.

	PAGE
The Mother's Farewell	249
The Student's Garret	251
Lines to ——	255
The Dying Girl	257
Love! there are Days	259
The Home of my Childhood	261
Dreams of the Past	263
The Mother and her Three Daughters	265
The Brother Spirits of Death	267
More Happy Thoughts	273
A Boundless Empire; or, La Calomnie—the Mighty Empress	275

A FEW SCRAPS WRITTEN BETWEEN THE AGES OF TEN AND SIXTEEN.

	PAGE
Dying Words	279
The Mother's Lament	283
A Thought	286
L'Histoire se Répéte	288
Peaceful Reflections	289
Moorish Burial Chant	290
Question and Answer	292
A Reflection	294

CONCLUDING VERSES.

	PAGE
Lines to ——	297
To Woman	299
Morning and Evening	300
The Veil of Night	301

A FAREWELL TO ODSEY.

THE EVENING STAR.

THE GOOD PHYSICIAN.

DIRGE OF THE RED INDIAN WARRIOR.

B

A FAREWELL TO ODSEY.*

[By one who, passing from the platforms of quiet country life to unknown backwoods in New Zealand, was never heard of again. There
was much reason to believe that J. F. was lost in a remarkably violent
tempest, while sailing round the coast.]

FAREWELL—a long farewell !

ERRATUM.

In Note to "A Farewell to Odsey," page 3, read, "*Supposed*
to have been written by one," etc.

Farewell—a long farewell!
Ere yet a month hath rolled its course away,
Ere many setting suns have lit thy dell
With the deep purple of departing day,

* This and a few others only of the following poems have already
appeared in print.

A FAREWELL TO ODSEY.*

[By one who, passing from the platforms of quiet country life to unknown backwoods in New Zealand, was never heard of again. There
was mnch reason to believe that J. F. was lost in a remarkably violent
tempest, while sailing round the coast.]

FAREWELL—a long farewell !
For me, when evening's tranquil hours are o'er,
The watch-dog's surly bark, the far sheep-bell,
Shall wake the echoes of thy woods no more !
I leave thee, sunny as thou art and fair,
I leave thee to thy calm, unbroken rest,
My step will rouse no more the timid hare,
Or scare the brooding partridge from its nest.

Farewell—a long farewell !
Ere yet a month hath rolled its course away,
Ere many setting suns have lit thy dell
With the deep purple of departing day,

* This and a few others only of the following poems have already
appeared in print.

I shall be far, far absent, and for me
The curlew's note will henceforth sound in vain ;
The fox may haunt the wood or grassy lea,
But step of mine will scare it not again !

　　　　Farewell—a long farewell !
I shall think of thee when the spring returns,
Recalling oft-times the sweet, tender spell
Of thy rose hedges and thy greenwood ferns.
I shall think of thee when the swallows come,
And when thy fairest flowers are in their prime,
Not *then* shall I forget, forsaken home,
How beautiful thou art in summer time !

　　　　Farewell—a long farewell !
Full many a happy hour I owe to thee,
What time the gentle dews of evening fell
On lowly flower-bell, or on lofty tree ;
And birds were hushed in copsewood and in dingle,
And voices died upon the summer air,
While the deep shades of evening seemed to mingle,
And veil the earth for thought, for rest, for prayer.

　　　　Farewell—a long farewell !
I shall remember thee, too, when the night
Full heavily hath fallen, and the swell
Of worldly feeling dies—as with the light—

When, poring o'er some wild or thoughtful book,
Through brightening starlight, when the flitting bat
Told of the deepening hour, with dreamy look
Beside mine ivied casement I have sat.*

        Farewell—a long farewell
To them and thee, and when again we meet,
What shall have been no prophet can foretell,
Nor how the pulses of our hearts may beat.
It may be when the feeble hand of age
Hath rung o'er Hope's young grave his dreary knell. ·
Ah me! that future, weird, mysterious page
I dare not seek to read.—Farewell! Farewell!

* This was a beautiful old window, surrounded by ivy, in the western
aspect of Odsey House, where J. F. lived.

THE EVENING STAR.

STAR of the evening ! from our deep blue seas
Thou'rt passing, with thy beautiful, pale ray,
From mossy haunts, and noble forest trees,
And castled crags, and ruins wild and gray.
Yet linger for one passing moment more
O'er scenes of beauty thou hast loved of yore.
Though leaves are fallen now and flowers are dead,
And summer, with its glorious skies, hath fled,
And summer, with its evening song of birds,—
Oh, linger yet to hear my last sad words !
  For I have loved thee ; for thy smile hath been
Upon me in my hours of thought and prayer,
When twilight glimmered o'er the wild wood scene,
And voices died upon the summer air,
And hearts were melted by the softened sound,
Or by the thrilling hush of all around,—
Then have I prayed beneath those silent skies,
My soul were freed from all its earthly ties,
That I might follow in thy train, and see
The glorious Footsteps of Eternity !

Through the long hours of night, when others slept,
And I my solitary watch have kept,
When strange, unfathomed thoughts awoke in me,
And dreams and hopes of things that might not be,
Wild and mysterious as the stirring strain—
Aye ! wilder, and as incomplete and vain—
A tempest's powerful spirit may awake
From deep and thrilling harp-strings, ere they break ;—
Oh, then, when the brain's passion-dreams were o'er,
Each vision stern Reality had crushed,
And I could wish that Feeling were no more,
That the deep voice of Life and Thought were hushed ;—
Then hath thine image met me, so above
All the base conflicts of this mundane spot,
Breathing of peace, of gentleness, of love,
Of future worlds, of things which perish not.
Alas ! I can but grieve that thy soft light
Must vanish from my yearning, wistful sight,
Perchance to shine on fairer scenes than these,
More glorious than *our* dells and plains and trees!

I owe thee much, fair Star ; for thy pale ray
Hath often turned my heart from earth away ;
And through the long twilight, when mists have hung
Full densely o'er the pinewood and the hill,
And the weird stillness of the hour hath flung
A shade of sadness on my spirit —still
One faithful heart has watched for thy calm smile
To glimmer through the storm-cloud's heavy pile !

O light eternal ! when my aching head
And weary heart are resting with the dead,
May my last hour of peace and quiet be
In some lone spot where thou mayst shine on me,
In some green wilderness, some untrod wild,
Where thou art gleaming, and where God hath smiled !

THE GOOD PHYSICIAN.

An aged man sat musing on the past,
Recalling patiently each recollection,
Upon whose pale and furrowed brow was cast
The shade of many cares and much reflection.
Alas! too early had those eyes grown dim,
Too early had that slender form been bent,
For life had been a busy scene to him—
A task in which his energies were spent.

A night was falling round him, like the sleep
Of Eastern waves when evening is declining,
And Heaven seems o'er the world His watch to keep,
And stars by myriads on the seas are shining—
So calmly on the city's depths it fell!
Unless the dull wheel of some carriage rolled,
Far distant, drowsily, or some deep bell
The passing hour from a cathedral tolled.

Musing he sat, recalling, as a dream,
The image of a young, aspiring boy,
Pacing the streets at morn's most early gleam,
With footsteps light and bright eyes full of joy.
It might be with that vision in his heart
Of future years our childhood only knows,
With which too oft in later life we part,
And think of, as a phantom, at its close!

More than a dream, in truth, of brilliant fame,
Of high renown, glowed in that ardent mind;
All youth's proud hopes of love, of wealth, of name,
Were his; but even then with these combined
Were nobler aspirations, strong, and yet
Growing more daily strong, as he began
To comprehend the task before him set—
To comfort and to heal his fellow-man!

That energetic figure bent, at length;
That boy's rich hair was scattered now and gray,
For since that dawning time of youth and strength,
Near fifty years had rolled their course away;
And with the calm but deep regret that age
So often brings, he sat reviewing it,
Perusing once again that mystic page
On which the stories of our lives are writ!

How had those high aspirings been fulfilled?
How had those lofty dreams been realized?
Had that young heart been early checked and chilled,
Its efforts failures, its proud hopes despised?
Did he, too, in thus picturing his past life,
And calling back its hours of joy and pain,
Feel he had waded through a sea of strife,
Like many men, to find his labours vain?

Alas! whate'er our efforts may have been,
There still must have been much in which we failed;
Much guilt and sorrow all who live have seen,
Against which naught of human power availed.
And since that youth had left his parents' hearth,
He, too, had often grieved above the fall
Of those bright futures, round our earthy path
Built, fondly cherished, and then wept, by all!

Ah! marvel not, then, that those fleeted years,
In giving up again each past event,
Blinded his sad eyes with unwonted tears,
And deeper shadows to his pale brow lent.
But, conquering soon that tender grief, he turned
From phantasies he long had seen depart,
To other hopes with which his soul had burned,
That came back, even as sunlight, to his heart!

He did a lone and narrow room recall—
A single lamp that half illumined it,
A table, like that room, confined and small,
Whereby a student oft was wont to sit;
And where, with books and papers round him piled,
He used to study, with a mind untired,
Until the star of morn upon him smiled,
Or, in its socket, his dim light expired.

No useless learning that which he pursued,
No idle lore engaged his leisure then,
No wild ambitious hopes his mind amused,
Untouched, by him, the poet's glowing pen.
Or, if aught visionary could allure
That meditative brow from sober thought,
No *selfish* dream at least was his—that cure
For maladies deemed fatal might be wrought.

Then, as he pondered, there arose again
Remembrance of that student's later life.
He saw him bending o'er the couch of pain,
He saw him, where disease and death were rife,
Applying all the powers that he possessed
To rescue, from a sad or early grave,
His fellow-creatures—or to give them rest
And passing comfort, if he could not save.

Oh! he, the just and the upright, who can
Look back thus on his active life, and feel
He had dealt rightly by his fellow-man,
And if he failed, yet ever sought to heal;
How must his heart such recollections cheer,
Gilding the very pathway to the tomb;
To him the thoughts of death can bring no fear,
And age, though premature, can bring no gloom.

So felt that aged man, as he looked back
Upon the path he had from childhood trod,
And hoped that his had been no useless track,
But one that was approved of by his God.
And thus, though tottering on the very brink
Of man's last home, with a contented breast
He could wait patiently the hour to sink,
At peace with all men, to his last long rest.

DIRGE OF THE RED INDIAN WARRIOR.

Go to thy rest !
Not where the tall and calm magnolias bow,
Slowly and solemnly each snowy crest;
Beneath the violet-grass we lay thee now !

Not where the pine,
With dreary sighing, echoed back thy tread,
When forest-dwellers made beneath its shrine
The ancient sleeping-places of their dead.

Not where the stream,
Beneath the arching wild-vine whispers low,
With spirit voices, when the sun's last beam
Falls where it bathes thy warriors' dust, we go !

To thy dark bed
We would not that sad music's wail should come,
Nor see men bow the plumed and glittering head
In stately march to the deep-sounding drum.

They mock us well !
With drooping banners, and the hollow sound
Long pealing from the battlements, to tell
That thou, our brave, at last has ransom found !

We do not weep !
Thy brothers have no tears to shed for thee ;
Smiling we gaze upon the dreamless sleep,
The fetters broken and the captive free !

Hither we bring,
Ere yet the earth on thy cold brow we lay,
Thy boy ! for one wild moment here to cling,
In love's first sorrow to thy lips of clay.

Bend low and near ;
Nor sigh nor moan must break our chief's repose.
Yet, boy, in thy young heart be written here
A deep and burning memory of his foe !

ETHELSTONE:

A LEGEND OF THE CASTLE.

C

O! tell me a tale of the days of old,
When maidens were lovely and knights were bold,
And life, with its dull and dreary prose,
Was brightened by praise of the lily and rose.
Ah! what in these modern days avails
So much of *pretentious* moral tales!
Enough of the Pharisee (not the Saint!),
Enough of the Hypocrite's blighting taint,
In the daily paths of our lives we see—
So a tale of the old Romance for me!

ETHELSTONE.

Canto I.

Grey Hall of Ethelstone! far out at sea
Benighted vessels steer their course by thee;
Tossed on the surges in the fading light,
When nearer objects only mock the sight,
Thou, built upon the summit of a hill,
Through unseen danger guid'st the pilot still.
Fair may thy bowers have been, O Ethelstone!
Merry with voices silent now and gone—
Bright was thy dwelling on a former day,
Filled with the forms that since have passed away,
When, deep in leafy groves, the flowers sweet
Bent down at the light tread of childish feet.
Now, when the shades of night enshroud the earth,
Dim are thy lights, and heard no more thy mirth;
Though ever, at the same late, lonely hour,
Is lit a lamp in Lady Ethel's bower,
Who, scarce emerged from girlhood, and yet pale
With thought, awaits her absent lover's sail;
And thus, through many years, is seen to keep
Her faithful watch o'er the Atlantic deep.

Sole heiress of a wealthy sire
She sits unsought and silent there ;
And looks, as though the hope and fire
Of youth, were quenched in early care.
For Ethel has her mother's eyes,
Her mother's voice, and pensive brow—
That mother, once so worshipped, lies
Forgotten with her kindred now.
And he who worshipped her bears not
The slightest mention of her name ;
Dark and unhappy was her lot—
A broken heart, an injured fame.
But, oh ! in comfort rest thee here,
Below the earth's long-hardened crust,
For slander shall not reach the ear,
Or falsehood wring the heart of dust.
And if, poor wife and mother, Time,
That sometimes even rights the dead,
Hath proved thee innocent of crime,
And planted lilies o'er thy head—
It matters little now to thee,
Sleeping beneath the cypress tree.

There, near the mother, rests the son
One dying of neglect, and one
Was lost 'mid all that most endears
The memory of our youthful years.
The father who so rarely smiled,

Yet brightened, when his favourite child
Drew near, and all that wealth could give
Was fondly lavished on his path ;
Yet, Heaven ! thy chastened sons must live !
And by his solitary hearth
The grey-haired parent sits alone,
Though all that cheered his heart is gone.

Untended is the once gay hall,
The play-ground now is desolate,
And grass and nettles, rank and tall,
Grow up and choke its wicket gate ;
The moping, discontented hound
Howls in his kennel, night and day—
He misses the accustomed sound
Of voices, calling him to play ;
And sparrows in the chimneys build,
And ivy climbs the walls at will ;
The ancient courts, that once were filled
With childhood's laugh, are cold and still ;
Long spider's-webs are on the wall
And ceiling of that little room,
Where tiny bed and playthings, all
Are left to dust, and damp and gloom.
Poor Ethel ! all her tender care
Soothes not her parent's sorrowing mind ;
Made harsher still by his despair,
He bids her hence, in tones unkind—

She turns from him her mournful brow,
But where is she to wander now ?
Not underneath the chestnut shade,
Where, with the lost one, oft she played

Two weary years have passed away
Since that most sad, unhappy day ;
And down beside the bubbling spring
Where first the primrose glads the sight,
And where the fairies form their ring
And revel in the moon's full light,
Beneath the twisted, scented thorn
Sits Ethel, in the light of morn.
And one, whose bright and rapturous gaze
The glorious Hope of youth betrays,
Whose eyes so often search for hers,
Too eloquent interpreters !
Is near her, sketching her sweet face,
Her form of elegance and grace.
It matters little whence he came,
Nor yet what titles graced his name;
Whatever was his heritage,
His brow was like an open page,
Whose characters, distinct and bold,
Spoke there the spirit, warm and true—
Why care, then, Reader, to be told,
How ranked he in the world's cold view ?

Fairest of all the fairy spots
That here th' admiring gazer sees,
Where hawthorns grow in rugged knots,
And shed their blossoms in the breeze;
And where, beside the mossy creek,
The water-wagtail builds her nest,
Or wild bee, humming, comes to seek
The flow'rets that she loves the best,
How suited to a scene like this!
To those whose voices love and bliss
So soften, that the timid hare
Wakes not among the Meadow-sweet,
But slumbers even at Ethel's feet.

Fondly and long the lover lingers
O'er each fair line his pencils trace;
There must be magic in those fingers,
So like, so truthful is that face.
First Love! sweet Love! ere yet the world
Hath chilled us with its prudent creed,
While yet the living page is furled
We afterwards so sadly read,
Beneath the stars there cannot be
An earthly joy compared to thee.
O happy youth; with hope elate,
Thy heaven appearing near to view,
Thy soul aspiring to be great,
Thy heart resolving to be true,

How is thy breast with rapture moved,
As, veiled by twilight's friendly hours,
The graceful form of thy beloved
Meets thee among the greenwood bowers!
And wandering homeward through the vale,
While sheep-bells tinkle from afar,
Thy lips still breathe the same fond tale,
Beneath thy favourite evening star;
Still promising that life shall be
As tranquil as that tranquil night,
When even the Night-jar seemed to thee
A Nightingale, in thy delight.
Yes—hope that *thou* mayst realize
This glorious promise of thy heart;
But, ah! thy brother's mournful eyes
Have long since seen *his* dream depart.
He sits beside his lonely hearth—
Cold—cheerless—loveless—desolate—
Returning on his homeward path,
None fly to meet him at the gate;
She, once the idol of his youth,
Even she hath left him there alone,
His model once of Love and Truth
To cheer a stranger's home is gone!

Awhile, with hearts that warmly beat,
Untroubled by an evil doubt,
By changing lights the lovers meet,

Forgetful of the world without.
A little time that dream dispels,
As Ethel's faltering footstep tells,
Her tears, and scarce coherent speech,
One night, upon the sandy beach;
While looking dim and on the wane,
The moon sets slowly on the main.
This hour they part; ere breaks the day
Her lover will be far away.—
" And yet I kneel not at thy feet
To take the oaths that others swear,
To vow, that never voice was sweet,
That never form but thine was fair "—
Said Ernest, in a tender tone,
Pressing her hand within his own.
" No; Heaven has given to thee the charms,
Beside which face and form are vain,
That make the clasp of these frail arms
More binding than the strongest chain.
The soul that lights thy gentle eyes,
The tender kindness of thy speech,
Have taught me more of Paradise
Than all that priest or pastor teach.
If I am poor and lowly born,
I think thou lov'st me more, not less;
When others speak of me with scorn,
Thy dark eyes swim with tenderness.
Once loved, once deeply loved by thee,

I know I cannot be forgot;
Whate'er my future lot may be,
This worst of fears will haunt me not.
Such perfect faith thy love hath taught,
That I have sometimes fondly thought,
None who inspired so firm a trust,
Could have been formed in kindred dust!
And now I leave thee, love, for Rome;
Alas! I shall be long from home—
Though only till my labours earn
For thee so bright and wide a fame,
That, when in triumph I return,
Thy father shall not scorn my claim.
O Heaven! this hour instructs too well
The heart that knew not grief before;
Too dear for words or looks to tell,
One last embrace, one more—one more!"

"Farewell."   That last embrace is o'er—
But motionless upon the shore
Still Ethel, cold and pale, remained,
Each nerve of hearing wildly strained
To follow still her lover's track
By each faint foot-fall echoing back.
Yes! he may trust her, if we may
Trust any on our earthly way:
Though, through her eyes there often smiled
The meekness of a very child,

The strong attachments veiled below
A universe could scarce o'erthrow.
While tranquilly there dwelt within
The heart that worshipped without sin,
Such faithful, truthful, pure belief—
Such trust in him she loved—her tears
Were only those of simple grief
In parting from him, though for years.
Not what the world would call a saint,
But grief had taught her self-restraint.
The fluttering breath, the timid sigh,
Heard when her lover's step was nigh,
The voice, so tremulously sweet,
Betrayed how that warm heart could beat.
But passion was subservient still
To higher powers—to nobler will.
It could not slave so pure a soul,
Whose high affections sought a goal,
A Paradise wherein to live,
That passion has no power to give.
They who would think to lightly sound
A mind so temperate—truthful—wise—
A love that had no human bound,
Yet learned not thoughtlessly to prize,—
These careless triflers little think
How silently, link after link
Was joined, to form that loving chain,
That life shall never break again ;

For rather, with a gentle pride,
A mind so modest seeks to hide,
From those that gaze with mocking eyes,
The joys for which it lives and dies.

Canto II.

" Far, in the calmest hour
Of night, the clear, shrill piping of a bird,
Resounding from some wreck of Roman power,
Oft on the high surrounding hills is heard.
For o'er the fallen warrior's buried crest
It builds its lonely, unmolested nest.

" The statue from its niche
Hath been dragged down and trampled in the dust;
The brazen image, and the palace, rich
With carving, left to rapine and to rust.
These, and the rifled tomb and grass-grown fane,
Are all that now of Roman pomp remain.

" Rome, when her blood-stained hand
The flag of Death and Victory unfurled
Above the fair homes of some ravished land,
Looked, spoke, and felt, the conqueress of the world !
The wreath of laurel binds no more her brow ;
Proud empress say, where are thy triumphs now !

" Tread reverently—thy tread,
O wanderer ! is on her mighty dead.
Yon wild flowers, with their bells of beauty, hide

The monument defaced—the column's pride.
Men raised them there to tell a tale to us,
Nor dreamed posterity would read it thus.

        "O mortal! if a boast
Of human greatness e'er thy lips defiles,
Remember Rome! her nation's conquered host,
Her noble cities, heaped in ruined piles.
So learn humility; for here below
No wiser lesson human hearts may know."

        Thus mused an artist, as the day
        Closed o'er him on the Roman plains,
        And sadly cast upon his way
        The shadows of their vast remains.
        For who, with thoughtful step, has pressed
        The ground where heroes take their rest—
        Where, cumbering the unconscious soil
        Of radiant spring, lies heaped the spoil
        Of temples, human hands prepared
        As dwellings fitted for a god—
        Oh! who, in human shape, has dared
        To tread the ground that Cæsar trod,
        Nor thus reflected, as the light,
        By brilliant stars and planets cast,
        Gave greater magnitude by night
        To these grand records of the past!
        There—at that hour—the very wind

Sighs forth, from tombs and emptied urns,
Those solemn lessons that the mind
So tardily and sadly learns.

Near the rapt gazer, where the mound
Is raised above the bones of those
Who rest, however once renowned,
In indiscriminate repose,
Reclined a Roman girl, whose face
Recalled, by its fixed, earnest gaze,
Those characters of Roman race
So rarely seen in modern days.
Her haughty brow, her lofty mien,
Might well have graced a Roman queen!
And yet she wore no broidered vest,
Her robe was neither rich nor wide,
But simply as a peasant dressed
She wandered forth at eventide,
To gather, with her brother's aid,
The sleepy herds, that idly strayed
And cropped the pasture, as it grew
O'er tombs whose history none can trace !
Or slept among the flowers, nor knew
How memory sanctified the place.

Descendant of a noble line,
Her fortunes with the past were gone;
Her task was now to tend the kine—

This daughter of an ancient throne!
Forgetting never, as her slow
And stately steps, at break of day,
Or at the sunset's parting glow,
Pursued her lone, inglorious way,
That through her young and restless veins
Flowed blood of those who scorned the chains—
The mean and ignominious crimes,
That mark the race in later times.
So, living only in the past,
The shadowy sadness of her eye
Confessed her spirit overcast,
By mourning for a time gone by,
Embittered by the sense of shame
Now clinging to her country's name.

Formed in a different mould from hers,
Her brother was a bright, young boy,
Who had the warm, free pulse that stirs
With every passing grief or joy.
That evening, resting at her feet,
His own within his sister's hand,
He mused on dreams, as pure and sweet
As those we steal from fairy-land:
Or raised his large and lustrous eyes
To count each star that lit the skies,
And seemed a careful watch to keep
Above this kindred world, that lay

Enraptured on the breast of Sleep,
Forgetful of the parted day.
So peaceful was the air, that she,
Who seemed so often sad of soul,
Sat rapt in some sweet reverie ;
And yielding to that hour's control,
She, who so often sang with fire
The heroes of her native land,
To-night awoke her silvery lyre
Ere long, with hesitating hand ;
While passionate, and with a swell
Of tenderness, in her most rare,
Her flute-like voice arose and fell
To some Æolian dream-like air ;
Though something might the ear have caught
Of bitter self-reproachful thought,
That mingled sadly with the sigh
Of her voluptuous Italy.

  " I hear thee, O my heart !
Thou hast aroused me with a sudden start ;
And turning from the tombstones, damp and gray,
I look up, dazzled by a new-born day.

  " Trembling with unknown fear,
Bewildered by a new and sweet delight,
Strange melodies are wafted to mine ear,
Strange worlds are dawning on my troubled sight.

D

"Rome! beautiful in chains,
Most god-like phantom of thy former state,
I thought my heart was buried in thy plains,
Or marble as the statues of thy Great.

"I wake thee not again,
Thou mournful lyre, with Rome's imperial lays;
I must attune thee to a softer strain,
And crown thee now with roses, not with bays.

"Thy reign of pride is o'er—
O Roman daughter! boast thyself no more;
Descendant of the noble and the brave,
Alas! thou, too, art suppliant and a slave.

"Bend lowly, then, thy knee;
There is a goddess greater than thy Rome,
Whose slightest sigh shall have more power o'er thee
Than all the pæans of thine ancient home!"

Lifting her glowing face to heaven,
Such queen-like sadness o'er it spread,
Even Ethel almost had forgiven
The eyes that there seemed riveted.
Then, with a trembling hand, once more
Marcella struck her lyre, but now
Her song was fainter than before,
And sung with an averted brow.

" Tell me if thou hast loved,
O Saxon!   Something in thy kindling cheek,
Thy flashing eye, thy frame so strongly moved,
Confesses what the lips are last to speak.

" Know'st thou what 'tis to feel
Such sweet enslavement of the heart and brain,
That thou, transported, wouldst not shame to kneel,
And kiss the fingers riveting thy chain ?

" See if thy firmer hand
Can tune my disobedient lyre aright.
My touch is faltering, and can scarce command
The melody of its full tones to-night."

ERNEST'S REPLY.

" Fairest of Roman daughters !
    Far across the sea,
Where England breasts the blue Atlantic waters,
One faithful heart is watching now for me.

" Not her's the southern eye,
    So languishing and bright—
'Tis rather like the mildness of a sky
Touched by the morning's first, celestial light.

"Full many a weary year
　　Her heart hath kept its plight,
While summer bloomed and autumn leaves grew sear,
Or angry tempests woke the winter's night.

" But, idol of my heart—
　　Most precious life ! no more
Vain, worldly obstacles our fates shall part ;
The weariness of thy long watch is o'er !

" For soon I see again
　　My native sunny isle,
Its cottage homes, its sheepfolds on the plain,
Its rivers, gleaming in the sun's calm smile.

" O fair Marcella, thou
　　And I no more may meet ;
Yet oft shall I recall thy noble brow,
Thy brilliant eye, thy voice so rich and sweet."——

He fancied that he heard the sound
Of weeping, but he was alone ;
He paused, and looked in vain around—
Marcella—Flavius—both were gone.
Far o'er the distant hills arose
The moon, but looking sick and pale,
And shining through her misty veil,
Like one subdued by secret woes.

And Ernest watched her with a sigh—
His mood was changed—he knew not why;
But suddenly there seemed a weight
To press upon his heart and brain;
He felt as though some ghostly Fate
Moved sullenly across the plain.
Fortune had favoured his career—
His path to glory had been clear—
He stood a victor where, of yore,
A conqueror had stood before.
Yet sorrowing voices seemed to fill
The future with a dull despair—
A face, whereon was seen the chill
Of Death, seemed gazing through the air;
Recalling, to his fevered mind,
The voice and face of one he loved.
They were but fancies, scarce defined,
And yet his very soul was moved.
Oh! oft, in after troubled years,
Returned that night of spectral fears,
When, musing on his distant home,
He stood upon the plains of Rome!

   O'er the bent flowers and dewy grass
A voice of warning seemed to pass;
Faint as the sound of some far bell
That catches yet eludes the ear—
Sad as the tolling of a knell,

It mocked yet filled his heart with fear.
" O thou ! " it murmured, " whose light tread
Profanes the precincts of the dead—
Who grasp'st at all within thy reach,
Forgetful what the past might teach—
Fond, foolish youth, shall grief and change
For ever to thy heart be strange ?
Shall joy and pleasure be the words
That wake alone thy heart's deep chords ?
Must all the past portentous signs,
All wisdom elder minds impart,
Be lost within the light that shines
Round some fond idol of thy heart ?
Alas ! how little can thy gaze
Have read of what the wise are shown,
How little learned of human ways,
To call one single heart thine own !
Far wiser thou, to stop and pray
Beside some tombstone on thy way."

Canto III.

His steps are on his native shore,
'Tis England welcomes him once more.
There is the grey old dwelling yet—
Yon lurid sun, so soon to set,
Shines redly on the ivy leaves
Now clustering o'er its very eaves ;
And there the casement, so well known,
Where Ethel used to sit alone.
Full many weary years have passed
Away, since Ernest saw her last ;
And yet he pictures her as bright
As in that hour of hope and bliss,
When first the trembling, loving light
Of her pure eyes encountered his ;
More timid than the first pale ray
Of starlight kissing now the bay,
Ere yet the sunset's gorgeous smile
Hath faded quite from rock and isle.
And pausing where lay heavily
Deep shadows, both of rock and tree,
Fond, dreamy memories, that thrilled
Not less than hopes of future years—
The eyes of Ernest slowly filled

With tender and delicious tears.
There, where the shore is smooth and low,
'Twas there they parted years ago,
With heavy hearts, oppressed with sorrow;—
'Twill be their trysting place to-morrow!
But, ah! he stood not there alone—
Upon a broken, mossy stone
Sat one whose gaze seemed calmly fixed
Upon that distant point of sight,
Where sky and sea seem intermixed,
And melt and mingle in the light.
The moisture of the ocean air
Unbound her long, luxuriant hair,
The winds played gently with each tress,
As she sat mute and motionless.
But, when she heard his footstep's bound,
She sprang up with a frantic cry,
That wrung his heart, as though the sound
Were not of joy, but agony;
Then, shrinking from his touch, she bowed
Her pale wild face, and wept aloud.

One moment's glance had shown that face
So strangely marked by sorrow's trace
He scarcely knew it for her own—
Hope, joy, youth, beauty—all were gone.
" How changed thou art! I did not dream
So great a grief awaited me;

When dark my future hopes might seem
I never thought of change in thee."
Said Ernest, in the weary tone—
The dull, unbroken voice of one
Too stunned by sudden grief to show
That grief in outward signs of woe.
" Thou wert to me as some fixed star,
That still shone brightly, though afar;
A steady beacon in the dark,
That gleamed when other lights had died,
By which I steered my trembling bark
O'er the fierce breakers of life's tide.
How changed thou art to meet me thus !
It had not been in earlier days;
Yon blue sky, bending over us,
Had then less softness than thy gaze.
I do not mourn thy faded cheek—
'Tis not of change like that I speak ;
It was not for thy girlish brow
I loved thee, or could love thee now.
Oh ! if one smile, one tender smile
Could light thy altered face awhile,
It were more beautiful to me
Than sunbeam to the pilot, tossed
Upon some strange, tempestuous sea,
His anchor gone, his rudder lost.
Alas ! thou art so sadly changed
That even thy heart has grown estranged.

"Speak to me! if thou hast forgot
Our parting on this very spot;"
He added, in a tone more wild;
"If I have only been beguiled
By falsehood—if thou wouldst deny
The vows exchanged in fonder hours—
Forswear them! I will ask not why—
Forswear them! even in sight of bowers
Beneath whose listening trees I heard
Those mute lips breathe the first, fond word.
I could not prize a love so light
That storms could change or seasons blight;
And if thy heart be lost to me,
However great the pang may be,
False love, I only wait to sever
The ties that bound us, and for ever."

"It might be better, for *thy* sake,
Even rudely thus those ties to break;"
Said Ethel, in a tone so low
It scarcely reached her lover's ear—
So full of that fixed, hopeless woe,
It chills the very heart to hear;
"It might be better thus; but, oh!
In anger we can never part;
I cannot leave thee, love, and know
I have no portion in thy heart.
Hear me; it is the only boon

That I have now the right to crave ;
We part before the yellow moon
Shall rise upon the ocean wave ;
But I have first a tale to tell—
Yes, then, but not till then—*Farewell.*

" It will be kinder to be brief,
For oft suspense is worse than grief ;
I will but lightly touch on years
When, in my sad and loveless home,
I prayed, but not with bitter tears,
For this, our meeting hour, to come.
Beloved ! I knew that I possessed
All that thy gifted soul could give,
And deemed that none were half so blessed,
Who shared the common life we live.
I only watched, with gentle sigh,
The flowers of summer droop and die.
I only hoped, as winter passed,
Each long, dark vigil were the last.
And there was one sweet hope that still
Gilded each hour's sad loneliness,
Like some bright watch-fire on a hill,
That shines into each dark recess
Of gloomy cave and shadowy steep,
When darkness broods upon the deep.
For, as I dwelt upon some trait
Of kindness in an earlier day,

I hoped there yet would come an hour
When, softened by my love and care,
My father's dream of rank and power
Would melt away before my prayer.
I feel, too well, that I might seem
To other minds a very child;
But, ah! it was a blissful dream—
'Twas happy to be so beguiled.
And when, at last, the phantom light
That seemed so tranquilly to burn,
And cheer the darkness of my night,
Departed, never to return,
I only wished still thus to rest
Deluded, not aroused to weep;
Or wrapt within that dreamless sleep
That none could ever more molest.

" It was a still and lovely eve,
And I was wandering on the beach
To watch the waters fall and heave,
As though they strove in vain to reach
The sky, that met them from above
With such a smile of golden love!
How brightly that bright hour is fixed
Upon my mind! I scarcely know
Why this should be—its close was mixed
With so much agonizing woe.
But I remember now so well

How, with the soft and gradual swell
Of song, across the listening waters,
The voices of our peasant daughters,
Blent with the fishermen's rude notes,
Would reach me from some wandering boats.
While thy dear image o'er me stole,
So free from bitterness like this,
There could not, in a human soul,
Dwell more of gratitude and bliss.

" So smooth, so level was the sand,
I had not heard a step draw near;
And, when I felt a grasping hand,
I started up with sudden fear.
It was my father's glance I met—
Ah ! heaven, why can I not forget !
I should have told thee, ere this day
I had refused the proffered love
Of him whose castle, tall and grey,
Thou mayst distinguish far above,
And looking, like a monarch, down
Upon the homes of yon fair town.
I knew it grieved my father—still
I little thought that it could fill
His heart with so much bitterness.
I saw his pallid lips compress
With scorn that shook his very frame,
Each time he breathed thy hated name.

I need not tell thee what he said—
'Tis better buried with the dead—
Save only, that unless I swore
That I would never see thee more,
That father's heaviest curse should be
The only dower I brought to thee.

"I tried to speak, but I forgot
All common forms of speech or prayer;
I tried to think, but I could not—
I only pictured thy despair.
The dim ideas that floated by
Seemed motes that caught yet mocked my eye.
For, at that fearful time, I felt
More strange bewilderment than pain—
Confused and stupefied, I knelt—
Speechless—imploring—but in vain!

"Thow knowest well—alas! too well—
How changed I am since last we met;
There is no need of words to tell
I might forswear thee—not forget.
Long, weary years await us now;
So weary, that I need not cast
A deeper shadow on thy brow
By telling thee of what is past.

"The autumn leaves were dry and sere,
The winds were howling o'er the mere,

When, in a vault's despairing gloom,
I stood beside my father's tomb;
And felt, within its walls had perished
The last fond hope my heart had cherished.
Those lips could never now revoke
The curse that they so sternly spoke.
I thought of all those proud domains
They then called mine—the fertile plains,
The meadow lands beside the sea—
What were they now to him or me?
Ah! rather, all that once was glad,
The fragrant heath, the wooded height,
To me became each day more sad,
More filled with sorrow in my sight.
I only knew my bosom burned
With shame, to think that love like thine,
A gift so noble, had been spurned
For such possessions as were mine.
But yet I cannot be thy bride;
For both of us is now despair
And anguish, even side by side;
A father's curse awaits us there.
Then urge me not; but if thy heart
Still loves me as I would be loved,
Hear not my bitter prayer unmoved—
Pity—forgive me, and—depart."

He calmed, with one angelic look,

The fearful tumult of her breast ;
He soothed the shattered frame that shook
With grief so hard to be repressed—
Then gently raised her drooping head,
And pressed her trembling hand, and said,
"Unmoved ! O never could I hear
Unmoved, a prayer from one so dear ;
Whatever after-suffering
The granting of that prayer might bring.
I go, then ; never more to seek
To see thy face, to hear thee speak ;
But I will still return to thee
In dreams, and wander on this beach,
To picture joy beyond our reach,
A joy that now may never be.
Look up, and let me gaze once more
Into thine eyes, love, as of yore.
Hast thou no parting look to give—
No fond embrace—that I may live
In after darkened years, and dwell
Upon the love of this farewell ? "

The weary watch of many years was o'er ;
The light within the chamber shone no more.

Canto IV.

Fair hour of eve! by angels given
To soothe the careworn sons of earth,
When sunset leaves its glowing heaven
To orbs of an inferior birth,
And Labour, looking to the west,
Sees that the wished-for hour has come,
And, faint and weary, seeks the rest
Found sweetest in a peasant's home ;
Thou purest balm to those that grieve
O'er human weaknesses and crimes,
Whose beauty woos the world to leave
Its busy thoughts for fitter times,
How often, at thy tranquil hour,
We feel the past arise again,
So vividly as to o'erpower
Each colder purpose of the brain,
And seem to live once more in days
The brightest that we may have known,
Made brighter by the magic rays
That Memory throws around her own !

And yet not always canst thou bring,—
O hour of holiness and rest !

The thoughts that have no secret sting,
The memories that are only blessed.
To him, who to thy peaceful sky
Uplifts so sad and worn a face,
Thou hast but brought the bitter sigh,
Thy joys have found no resting-place.
It is a young yet grey-haired man—
That face and form are finely set,
And yet, alas! what eye can scan
Their noble lines without regret?
Although we see the mien of one
Not strange to free and noble thought,
Both energy and strength are gone—
Or seem but fitful and o'erwrought.
The leaden cheek, the fevered brow,
Of dissipation speak too well,
And languidly is beating now·
The heart that once could warmly swell!
He seeks no more the glorious aims
Whose hopes had made his youth so bright,
And Friendship finds no nearer claims,
And Love has lost its purer light.
And yet, without an envious smart,
He sees, in happier homes than his,
The blessing of a trusting heart,
The sweetness of domestic bliss.
For never hath he worn the sneer
We see the disappointed wear,

Nor less hath flowed the ready tear
To soothe another's woe and care.
There have been times when brighter years
In all their former hues returned—
When Sorrow dried her bitter tears
In fires that on her altars burned ;
But, ah ! the Genii brooding there
No earthly hope could long allure,
His was the acme of despair,
The grief that scarcely sighed for cure !

Most beautiful and young the form
Reclining now at Ernest's feet ;
But, if that brow be strong and warm,
'Tis scarcely womanly or sweet.
Alas ! its anxious lines express
A fate but thinly veiled by pride,
Too dearly won was that caress—
Poor maiden ! she is not his bride.
We miss the timid, modest glance,
The charm of woman's countenance,
The downcast eyelids, that express,
Yet half conceal, their tenderness ;
But nothing of the helpless air
That marks her lover's mien is there—
Whatever pangs that breast have torn
They have been met with equal scorn.
To her the retrospect that brings

The placid brow—the soothing sigh—
Can calm no pent-up sufferings,
Nor bring the tear-drop to her eye.
Unbent—untouched—she thinks to meet
The fate that holds her sternly down;
The world that scorns her she can greet
With not less proud, disdainful frown.
For such an earthly Paradise
As that she forms around her now,
Who would not leave the purer skies
That light the moralist's cold brow?
Thou wildest dreamer! it is vain,
Thou canst not hush the voice within;
Thou canst not break the gnawing chain
That links together grief and sin;
Think not this vaunted outward show
Is like the peace that thou hast lost—
How little that warm heart could know
Of all its love and sin would cost!
Forsaken by thine own esteem,
Thy Paradise is but a dream;
It fades ere yet the frailest flowers
Have vanished from their summer bowers,
And, once departed from the earth,
Alas! it knows no second birth.

Music and laughter float around,
Fair forms and sunny brows are there,

The hall re-echoes to the sound
Of many a soft, seductive air :
Young voices that are rich and sweet,
And hearts that warmly, wildly, feel,
Bright eyes that flash whene'er they meet,
With joy they care not to conceal,
These are with Ernest—but they wake
No chord responsive in his breast ;
Whatever form their mirth may take
He cares not, so they let him rest !
Although the master of that hall,
He seems a strange and silent host,
His thoughts are far—his spirit lost,
Beyond their, or his own, recall.
They give the lyre into his hand,
They bid him sing a song of joy—
Some legend of a fairy-land,
Where love exists without alloy.
He takes it with a brow unchanged,
And, as he lifts his dreamy eye,
They mark his mind is still estranged,
His gaze intent on vacancy.
He sees no more the present scene,
Nor yet Marcella's changing mien,
Forgetful of the startled throng,
He wakes this sad and solemn song.

DREAMS.

"Dreams ! how they haunt the brain
With fantasies as beautiful as vain;
　　The long-lost dead arise
And bend on us their unforgotten eyes,
　　Until we start from sleep
To find them fading into air—and weep !

" Forms that so long have lain
In marble rest—in undisturbed repose,
　　Return to us again
With recollections of departed woes,
　　And bring the bitter tears
That wept the sorrows of our buried years.

" Eyes that the icy hand
Of DEATH hath long since set, unclose again—
　　And from a far-off land
The absent come, a pale and silent train,
　　Whose mild yet tender gaze
Recalls the fervid love of youth's fond days—

" Lips that his cruel seal
Hath sternly fixed, again look warm and bright,
　　Hearts that no more can feel,
Seem wrung with grief or trembling with delight.
　　Aye ! all that we can learn
Of human life may thus in dreams return !

" Yet sad it were, if all
We loved should pass for evermore away,
          Shrouded beneath the pall
Whose sômbre folds conceal their dread decay—
          'Twere better that once more
They thus should visit those they loved before.

          " Yea! bitter though it is,
When in these mystic dreams some gentle tone
          Recalls a faded bliss,
To waken from our joy and find it gone—
          Far greater were the pain
To know that love and memory were in vain!

          " So come, ye shadows pale,
From the dim regions where may be thy rest!
          Not with despairing wail,
Or sad hands clasped upon each shadowy breast,
Rather with memories of a happier time,
When youth was bright and sorrow seemed a crime."

          Hush ! ere the echoes of that lay
          Die in the spacious halls away,
          Another voice, of richer sound,
          Pours its full, glorious notes around.
          None present those clear accents heard
          But felt the singer's soul was stirred ;
          Though, haughty and disdainful still,

No tremor in her tones was caught,
But yet there was a mournful thrill,
And oft a vein of bitter thought :
Alas ! too plainly they expressed
The tortured passions of her breast.

" Day closed upon the plains of ancient Rome.
And they who wandered in the flitting light,
Communing with the Genii of the past,
Paused silently beneath the wakened stars.
And both were young ; and one a youth, whose brow
Was glorified by Hope—yet undeceived !
The other was a maiden, pale and grave,
Long used to Sorrow, and not strange to Thought.

" And timidly she touched, with faltering hand,
A lyre that she had loved from early youth,
Nor ever, till that hour, had tuned to lays
More soft than pæans to eternal Rome ;
But now her heart was changed, and knew no more
The wan enthusiast of forgotten tombs ;
Like one bewildered by a waking dream,
Her song was faint and tremulous with love.

" HE listened, but his heart was far away
In some fair region of the distant West ;
Where, by the borders of the sounding sea,
Dwelt one as beautiful as morning light,
Who loved him with the pure, unshaken love

So rare among the daughters of the earth,
And he was hastening homeward, o'er the wave,
To find a home upon her faithful breast.

"Alas! the Roman maiden had a heart
Warm as the hearts of old romance—too true
For peace or rest.   She followed him across
The deep Atlantic, and forgot her home!
They met again: the youth was then a changed
And sadder man; like others, he had learned
The fatal lesson of this human life—
For Hope had been deceived and Love was false.

"Thou weakest of mankind! who still recalls
And mourns o'er visions that have long proved false,
Who still permits a love forsworn to reign
The empress of the strongholds of thy heart—
How long shall all the glory of thy youth
Be dimmed by sickly fancies from the past?
How long shall summer bloom for thee in vain,
And music wake no echo in thy breast?

"Far in the loveliness of a fair land
I buried the free soul, that once was stirred
By feelings that can find no utterance here—
So let it rest, forgotten 'mid the flowers!
But thou! who art a man, yet shaming not
To weep the tears a woman can despise—
Degenerate son of earth, why slumber thus,
Forgetful of the mission of thy youth!"

Marcella ! never more shalt thou
Forget the low, the smothered sigh,
That cools the fever of thy brow,
And shames the mockery of thine eye !
But now the lights—the guests—are gone—
The weary hostess sits alone.
Quenched is that bosom's angry fire,
Her head droops sadly o'er her lyre.
And, musing thus, a gentle kind
Of tremor seemed to thrill her frame,
As though, upon her darkened mind,
The dawn of better feelings came.
With timid steps she seeks the room
Where Ernest oft retires to rest ;
That chamber now is left in gloom,
The lamp is out, the couch unpressed.
For in his once-loved studio, where
But rarely prying steps intrude,
He sits in drooping attitude,
Nor knows what watchful eyes are there.
And she is softly drawing near,
Her look is pensive now and sweet ;
She thinks to drop that glistening tear,
And seek forgiveness—at his feet.
Ah ! heaven, what portrait meets her gaze,
What young and lovely face is this?
What tells it of those fatal days
His memory cannot yet dismiss ?

How nobly—calmly—sits that air
Of wisdom on the brow of youth !
How tender the expression there !
How full of purity and truth !
And if too much of passion lies
For perfect rest in those deep eyes,
So much of earnest faith and trust
To regulate its depths is given,
That, if that fragile form be dust,
The spirit is inspired of Heaven.

Alas ! alas ! whate'er thy sin,
Poor maiden, none, without a sigh
Of sympathy, could look within,
And read thy heart's fierce agony,
As wildly thy scarce conscious hands
Tear thy long tresses from their bands !
Thou feelest that thy reign is o'er,
That thou hast drained thy cup of bliss—
The cup that shall be thine no more ;
But, oh ! 'tis bitterer than this
To know thy own no unjust fate ;
Thine own mad fingers wove thy chain,
Thine own mad act hath closed the gate
That ne'er will ope to thee again.
The world despised—that world will now
Receive no more thy branded brow !

He speaks to her with soothing tone—
This man whom she hath loved so much—
He lays his hand upon her own,
She only shudders at the touch;
His words fall coldly on her ear,
They bring her neither sigh nor tear;
She listens motionless, but seems
Like one who only hears in dreams.
" Thy heart was happier once; yes, thou
Wert happier on the mountain's brow,
While listening to the shepherd's notes,
Or tending to thy flocks of goats,
Than 'mid the hot and fevered din,
The glitter of our halls of sin.
Thou hast a mother there—return!
At least thy mother will not spurn
Her penitent and sinning child—
At least thy mother, who hath smiled
Upon thy babyhood, whose tears
And prayers have watched thy early years,
In fond remembrance of those days
Will never turn from thee her gaze!
Go then, poor maiden, go and rest
Once more on her forgiving breast—
Return—"

"Return; oh! yes, return!
To some it is a joyful word,

But in mine ear it seems to burn
As though a demon's voice I heard."
And, starting from her seeming trance,
She turned to him th' imploring glance
That might to tears of pity move,
But could not win a look of love.
" Nor home, nor country can I claim ;
Alas ! they would disown my name.
But thou, cold heart, what dost *thou* care ?
What, unto thee, is my despair ?
I would thou wert no longer dear !
I would I had the strength to tear
Thine image from my mind, and fling
Away that soul-less, faithless thing !
But, oh ! I own myself so weak,
I cannot even hear thee speak
Of aught that parts us—let me be
Thy servant, or whate'er thou wilt ;
But little choice is left for me,
The slave of love, and worse—of guilt."

" Marcella ! no ; 'tis best we part.
But not in anger be it said ;
For thou hast loved me, and thy heart
Hath pillowed oft my sleeping head.
I hoped that I might there forget
The sorrows of my early troth ;
But would that we had never met,

It had been better for us both !
It is but mockery thus to live—
Thou seest I have no heart to give.
Farewell for ever."

        " Then farewell !
That word, for thee, shall ring the knell
Of all that life might yet bestow
Of happiness and peace below !
I loved thee well, unfeeling man,
Yet I have knelt to thee in vain ;
Thou dost despise me ; but I can
Turn, like the trodden worm, again !
I go ; but even as I go,
The love of woman leaves thy hearth ;
It shall but bring thee tears and woe—
Not cheer again thy earthly path.
Farewell."

        She waits not his reply,
But turns to him her dull, fixed eye—
Her brow, from which all light is gone—
Her lips, now set like lips of stone—
Then draws her mantle round her face,
And leaves him with a measured pace.
He sits alone ; his brow is damp,
His hand is trembling, and the lamp,
That long a sickly light had cast,

Sank, dying, as Marcella passed.
It is not for the curious eye
To read that soul's dark mystery—
So leave him there : the hour is late,
The timid stars, that only wait
The breaking of another day,
Fade slowly in the dawn away.

Canto V.

Sweet Ethel! surely time hath cast
Few shadows o'er thee as he passed.
Thy form hath still its simple grace,
The bloom is yet upon thy cheeks,
And still the same soft, pensive face
Thy gentle, tender soul bespeaks!
Alas! the light within thine eye
Is like a watch-fire lit by Death—
The leaf that wears the richest dye
Falls soonest at the Winter's breath.
In vain that brightness would deceive,
In vain that young and girlish air;
But, oh! in reverence let us grieve,
For more of heaven than earth is there.

Down in the village, as the low
Of cattle fills the morning air,
She wanders, with a footstep slow,
As though she loves to loiter there.
Whatever tempests have beset
The simple pathway she hath trod,
They have been meekly, humbly met,
Her grief was only shown to God.

And hers is now th' untroubled mind
That suffering, nobly borne, will bring,
When earthly love becomes refined,
And memory scarcely knows a sting.
I once was shown some simple lines—
They say she wrote them at this time—
I give them here, but not as signs
Of either gift or power sublime,
But simply to denote the calm
That oft so pure a mind attains,
When Thought and Fancy bring but balm,
And only speak in peaceful strains.

THE VILLAGE CHURCH.

" The village church ! no proud, assuming tower,
No lofty spire, it raises to the sky ;
It hath no outward show of pomp and power,
Attracting haughtily the stranger's eye ;
But, often hidden in some shady nook,
Its lowly outline, as declining day
Gives to the earth the twilight's dreamy look,
Mingles with other shapes and fades away.

" The village church ! it boasts no arching aisle
That echoed once the lordly abbot's tread ;
The sun that glimmers in with tranquil smile
Shines on no monument of noble dead ;

Nor bears it trace of Puritanic crimes
Or virtues, to reward the curious search ;
The rude, defacing hand of early times
Molested not the humble village church.

"The village church ! its quiet shade it throws
Not on the tombstones of the rich and brave,
But rather on the scarcely marked repose
Of him who slumbers in a peasant's grave.
And in its lonely churchyard may arise
The earnest accents of a mourner's prayer,
Uninterrupted, to the clear, grey skies—
The only murmur on the summer air.

" The village church ! its bells are loud and clear,
Not silvery, as within a city's wall ;
But, mellowed by the distance, on the ear,
Like fairy melodies their changes fall.
The shepherd hears, far off, each swelling note,
The woodman listens in his wooded fells,
And pauses from his work ; for merry float
O'erhead the echoes of his native bells.

" The village church ! the owl by daylight sits
Amid the ivy, as it richly trails
O'er the grey walls, and wakes and dreams by fits ;
Nor stirs abroad until the daylight fails ;

For only few and straggling steps pass by
To scare it from its green and pleasant perch ;
The spot is sacred, and the very sky
Salutes with loving smile the Village Church."

We are forgetting, for a while,
How Ethel wanders in the morn,
Now leaning on some rustic stile,
Now wandering through the fields of corn.
And now she rests beneath a tree
Bent with the burden of the sweet
Ripe mulberries; but who is he
Who kneels so wildly at her feet ?

They meet who have not met for years !
And Ethel, whose enraptured glance
Breaks often through her gushing tears,
Looks down on Ernest's countenance.
Ah ! feebly, faintly, words express
The joy of meeting such as this ;
The rapture of the first caress,
The clasping hands, the clinging kiss.
And even if that joy be brief,
Like stars that vanish as they shine,
'Tis worth an age of tears and grief
To live in moments so divine !
Alas ! too soon that rapture fled,
And faintly, sadly, Ethel said,

" Mine own dear Ernest, can it be
Thy heart is still so true to me ?
It may be sweet to know it thus—
To read as clearly on thy face
As thou on mine, nor time, nor space
Nor circumstance had power o'er us.
I can but feel this joy, and yet,
Could I now speak in tones of blame,
'Twere wiser that we had not met,
To learn each other's hearts the same.
I fear, beloved, it will but add
Another sorrow to thy heart,
The life that is already sad
Will be but sadder when we part."

" Speak not of parting ! nay, I can
Be calm no longer—let me speak !
Why thus assume me more than man ?
I am but human—erring—weak.
I cannot longer lead this life,
This strange, divided life, of ours,
I live but on the sea of strife,
I am the slave of unseen powers.
We have been parted long, and yet
How lovely is thy brow—more fair
Than when we parted, for regret
Alone, and not remorse, is there.
How ruby are thy lips ! how bright

ETHELSTONE.

The glow upon thy cheek ! that eye
Emits such brilliant, fervid light,
It might have shamed an Indian sky.
Oh ! my belovèd, when I read
The life that in thy gaze is clear,
Well may my heart be wrung, and bleed
To think upon mine own career—
So reckless, and so stained with sin,
The bye-ways that my steps have known;
If e'er a holier life I win,
I shall not win that life alone !
Ah ! they who dare to separate,
And leave the loving to despair,
And load the buoyant with a weight
Beyond his youthful strength to bear,
Must have a dark account to pay
When human periods pass away.
Dear love, it was not right or wise
In thee to aid in such a wrong,
It ne'er is right to sacrifice
The loving to the proud and strong.
I dare to call thee much to blame
To take that cruel—unjust vow,
Forgetting I, too, had a claim—
But yet more wrong to keep it now.
Thou wert the anchor of my soul,
And, oh ! when fiercely torn away,
Where'er the restless waves might roll,

They bore me, a resistless prey.
Be thou that anchor once again—
Restore, reclaim me! I will be
What I have sought to be in vain,
When separate from love and thee.
Is there no fond, persuasive voice
For me within thy heart to pray?
Ah! Ethel, can it be thy choice
To cast thy lover's soul away!"

"Beloved, I feel that thou art right
In part—that I did wrong to swear
A vow that had the power to blight
Thy youth, and leave thee to despair.
I often feared it might be so;"
Said Ethel, tenderly and low.
"Yet, not the less I deem it wrong
To break that vow, thus held so long,
So solemnly—so sadly given—
And kept with so much faith to Heaven.
But, oh! I cannot keep this creed
And hear thy voice so wildly plead.
I cannot leave thy soul to sink
In darkness, or thy heart to break;
Even if it be the sin I think,
I will commit it—for thy sake.
I will be thine; whate'er betide,
My place is henceforth at thy side.

And if there yet be time to win
Such glory back as once was thine,
Such peace as once reposed within,
Dear Ernest, let that task be mine."

"O if there yet be time!" this phrase,
So touching in its meaning—words
So rarely heard in youthful days,
How must they wring his heart's deep chords!
No; nothing hath he heard, or hears,
Save this, "I will be thine."   O Grief!
Stern ruler o'er so many years,
Yield him this respite; it is brief.
And slowly, with a joy too deep
For utterance, up the grassy steep,
And through the scented meadow land,
Homeward they wander, hand in hand.

Fair broke the morn, the very flowers
Seemed smiling in their mossy dells;
And joyfully, through woodland bowers,
Rang out the merry marriage bells.
Lady of Ethelstone! that day
How many gay young girls were dressed
In white rosettes and white array,
To look their loveliest and best!
Thou wert so much beloved, that they,

Who scattered roses on thy path,
Turned oft aside to weep, and pray
That Heaven might bless thy home and hearth.
One only, muffled in her hood,
And scarcely noticed by the rest,
Despairingly, in silence, stood,
And clenched her hands upon her breast.
It was Marcella! but whate'er
The fell design that brought her there,
The awful grief that closed that day,
Turned her revengeful thoughts away.
The power that seemed to stand before
Her mad and desperate hand and crime,
It may be, at that moment, wore
A form so threatening and sublime,
It calmed and humbled her; she went
Back on her joyless way once more;
It might be henceforth to repent,
It might be otherwise; but o'er
Her fate for ever hangs a veil—
We guess, but do not know her tale.
None, who had known her in the flower
Of youth, beheld her from that hour.
But, ah! so many live and die,
Who take the path that she hath done,
We yield them but a passing sigh,
Remembrance rests with Heaven alone.
Man, busy with the little stir

Of his own greatness, lacks the time
To track the trembling steps that err,
On, down the dread abyss of crime.

The hour grew late, and soft and slow
Closed in the evening; one by one
The clouds, that caught its parting glow,
Went down the pathway of the sun.
Ah! never shall that sun arise
On earth, to glad again the eyes
That watch, with such an anxious gaze,
The gradual fading of its rays.
And is she—can she—be resigned?
No; but the sorrows of that mind
Heaven will forgive; yea, even forgive
Her momentary prayer to live.
The cold, damp shadow of the grave
Is closing round her even here;
But, oh! not for herself that brave
Strong heart shrinks back with sudden fear!
For o'er yon sable bier there bends
A figure shaken by despair;
Ah! how that sob her bosom rends—
It is her husband weeping there!
And, torn by this strong agony,
She turns her pale, despairing face,
To meet that husband's grateful eye—
To take—to give—the last embrace.

He knew not then—he could not guess—
The world of grief and love expressed
In the convulsive tenderness
With which she held him to her breast.
And knew that on his rapturous heart
Her own, ere long, would cease to beat;
That thus, scarce wedded, they must part,
To meet—ah! where and when to meet?

Through twilight's soft and silvery haze
Looks down the well-loved star of eve,
For ever, with the same meek rays,
Alike for those that joy or grieve!
The owl is hooting from the tree,
And Ethel's pale lips move in prayer;
And, sinking at her husband's knee,
She rests awhile in silence there.
But something like a sigh—a sound,
Faint, feeble, fluttering, meets his ear;
And Ernest lifts her from the ground,
Like one appalled with sudden fear,
And sees, O heaven! what sees he there?
His Ethel's beautiful, warm eye
Now fixing in the dull, cold stare
Of nothingness and vacancy.

And all is over now, the hurrying tread,
The busy hands that fain would wake the dead;

The sound of grief—the glare of lights—all gone—
They leave him, by his own command, alone.
Ah! why is it so much of sorrow clings
Round the fond idols that on earth we form;
Exalted, prized, above all human things,
Fair in the sunshine, nor yet changed in storm,
Yet torn, in one wild moment, from our side,
When Love seems victor—Circumstance defied?
Is it that we dare raise them even above
The holier smile of an Eternal Love?
Thou heart-bereaved! when in the grave they lay
The form so madly loved as more than clay,
They bury there thy hopes, thy joys, but oh!
Curse not the fate that leaves thee still below;
Plant thou the cypress o'er that grave—and wait:
God hears the Meek, and cheers the Desolate.

THE LOST STAR.

AN APPEAL TO FRANCE.

A LETTER TO ——.

IMPROMPTU LINES ON HEARING OF THE
HOPELESS ILLNESS OF ——.

THOUGHTS IN THE CHAMBER OF DEATH.

THE LOST STAR.

Farewell! farewell! my dream of thee is o'er,
And I may watch and weep for thee, but never
Look on thy pale, unearthly beauty more;
Thou'rt gone from this sad world of mine for ever.
Within our shadowed sky thy place is dark,
And there are few that vacant place to mark—
Few in whose mind thy light will dwell, as when
Thou wert beloved, admired, and sought by men.
The world revereth not departed things,
But, turning from the thoughts their memory brings,
Lost in some future vision, dares to tread
O'er the green mould, remembering not the dead!
True; but it may be folly thus to yearn
O'er dreams that may not to the heart return,
To touch the notes of song that thrill no more
With that deep sweetness they possessed of yore.
Oh! now that I no more can strike the lyre
With prophet's daring hand or poet's fire,
Now that my soul is faint, my hand unstrung,
And o'er the heart its own wild hopes have wrung,

There pass no images of love and light,
To gild the darkness of its heavy night,
'Twere better that its music were forgot
Than waken thus to quiver and to die,
All harsh and unmelodious; but I
Have prayed I might forget, and—I could not!

Why, in thy lofty beauty, hast thou passed
Without one lingering look, one pitying ray,
To be remembered, treasured as thy last,
When thy bright dwelling-place is far away?
Have I, then, watched thy gentle light so long,
And loved thee with a love too true and strong?
Not as with passion of an earthly stamp,
That, like the blue flame of a quivering lamp,
Through the deep stillness of the summer air,
While midnight skies are clear, burns bright and fair,
Then, when the change and the wild storms come on,
One last expiring flash, and it is gone!
No—I have loved thee with a love unshaken,
Through storm and sunshine—yet am thus forsaken!
Oh! I, who though a dweller on this earth,
Have turned from the light words of hollow mirth,
And marked the thoughtless brow—the wanton eye—
To feel they had but little sympathy
To touch my heart; must I, then, never know
The speaking gaze, the soft and thrilling tone
Whose secret spell binds heart to heart below?

Are these things shut from me—and me alone ?
Ah ! must I never see the dark eye melt
With that fond feeling kindred hearts have felt,
Though loving still with that deep, burning swell
Of thought and feeling words can never tell ?

I would have died—have suffered all—for thee
Had there been but one echo in thy heart;
Had there been but one kindly thought for me,
I could have borne to see thee e'en depart !
But there was none—thou wert so far removed
From the low, humble sphere wherein I dwell;
And I did wrong to love as I have loved,
My heavy grief I have deserved too well.
Alas ! the Hand that hath created thee
Hath made thee beautiful, but far from me !
It was not wise to love so bright a ray—
To seek from mine own trodden path to stray.
My recompense is now in bitter tears—
All that is left, a grief of many years—
The cruel knowledge that I did but rave
To think that pale and peaceful light of thine
For ever on mine earthly path would shine;
It will not even gleam upon my grave !

Once more, Farewell !   My dream of thee is o'er,
And I may watch and weep for thee, but never
Look on thy pale, unearthly beauty more;
Thou'rt gone from this sad world of mine for ever !

AN APPEAL TO FRANCE.

I WOULD not seek to argue with thee, France!
The sophist's triumph never lit my brow;
And if it had, but small would be the chance
Against one famed for subtilty as thou;
But to thy feelings, to thy heart, I would
Appeal, even in thy present angry mood;
For thou hast much within thee true and good,
Mixed with the recklessness of thy half-southern blood.

I would not argue of decree or law,
But to thy past experience appeal;
Thy right to right thyself dispute not, nor
Bid thee for monarchs more respect to feel;
For there may be oppression we know not.
I would not wish thee tamely to submit;
Thou may'st *mean* well, but hast thou then forgot
Thou canst not quench, at will, a flame so madly lit?

Hast thou no other method of redress
Than that fierce weapon now upraised by thee?
Must, then, the cry of terror and distress
Follow the steps that seek for liberty?

Alas! in these "enlightened" times, must still
The trumpet's peal sound o'er the startled earth,
Thy daughters' eyes with tears of anguish fill,
From fear to what dark woes its echoes may give birth?

Yes! "Mourir pour la patrie!" be thy cry,
Yes! battle—but against a foreign foe.
Lift not thy warlike arm so madly high,
Against *thyself* must now rebound that blow!
Go forth into the battle if thou wilt;
Thou hast brought out thy sword—gird on that sword—
But not by thee a brother's blood be spilt,
Or dare not let *thy country* be the rousing word!

I would remind thee of a time gone by,
When a dark curse had fallen on thy land,
And nations looked upon thee with a sigh,
Or pointed at thee with deriding hand.
I would recall to thee a fatal tale
By gory fingers on thy annals traced—
I would recall to thee a long, sad wail,
That rang then, shuddering, o'er thy country's ghastly
    waste!

Forget it not! that cry so madly wild
Against thee, unto God in judgment rose;
Forget it not! thy hearth was then defiled
By all the crimes that man's dark bosom knows.

Remember if—as in that hellish time—
Thou dost pretend oppression's bonds to free,
Yet loosen but the chains of rage and crime,
Great was the punishment and great again shall be !

[NOTE.—These lines were written one evening, on bearing the rumour
of a fresh Revolution in France—happily a false one.]

A LETTER TO ——.

THEY who have o'er thee watched, year after year,
They who have prophesied Life had in store
For thee a brilliant and a high career,
Now turn aside and silently deplore!
They who once loved to watch thy lofty brow,
Now shame to see the change that guilt hath wrought.
Why was thy faith so lightly shaken—thou
Forgetting all thy lips were early taught?
I knew thee once as one of nobler mind—
Thou wert not, once, ungentle or unkind,
Thou loved'st me then—dost thou remember how?
Those days were happy—art thou happier now?
Those summer evenings—do they haunt thee not?
Those pure amusements—are they quite forgot?
Thy youth's bright visions—have they all passed by,
Demanding no remembering hours?   And I—
Have I, too, loved thee with a love unshaken,
So long, so fondly, to be thus forsaken?
Could I have lifted, once, the heavy veil
That hides the future, and have learned thy fate,
Could I have read the dark and bitter tale,

Whose later knowledge leaves me desolate,
Have known that thou wouldst tarnish thus thy youth,
Forgetting all thy lips had learned of truth,
To be a scoffer, with unholy men,—
I had not loved thee as I loved thee then !

But go ! I have forgiven thee—my heart
Pities, but hates not, even the thing thou art.
I loved with too much truth to wish thee ill,
Too fondly not to sorrow for thee still.
Go ! but remember that though now thy name
I hear not uttered but with tears of shame,
And from mine heart thine image seek to wring,
Day after day, as but a worthless thing,
Remember still, if, in some distant days,
The world should grow distasteful to thy gaze,
Turn from its tinselled scenery once more,
To all that thou so fondly loved before—
A lesson bitter, but yet wise to learn—
Oh, fear thou not reproach from me—Return !
I will not welcome thee as many would,
Not with cold counsels of the sternly good
Will I receive thee, nor with saddest tears
Watch o'er the close of thy embittered years ;
But from the world to which thy chains were fast
Lift up thy heart to hope—to heaven—at last !
Soothing thy restless spirit to repose,
Till o'er us both the grave in peace shall close !

IMPROMPTU LINES ON HEARING OF THE HOPELESS ILLNESS OF ——.

They tell me thou art dying, while the sound is on the
    breeze
Of the hum of many beetles, of the wild birds in the
    trees;
While those that watch beside thee with heartbroken
    murmurs pray
That the hand of the Destroyer yet a greater Hand shall
    stay.

O! thou friend of many seasons, oh! thou faithful friend
    of years,
I cannot hear thy fate without the rush of bitter tears!
The calm walks of our girlhood are returning to my
    mind,
When spring's bright gladness faded, or the summer's
    sun declined,
When we strolled beneath "our fir trees," with soft moss
    beneath our feet,
And the smell of early roses and of new-made hay was
    sweet;

And when you went wandering onwards with a closer
    friend than I;
Ah! those days of early friendship whose dear memories
    cannot die!

Companion, wife, and mother, all in one brave heart
    combined,
Few had thy powers of soothing, or thy gentleness of
    mind;
No words of careless mockery *our* friendship ever marred,
Thy sympathy was certain—e'en reproof was never hard.
In illness you remembered me with all a sister's kindness,
And my faults you treated leniently, with more than
    sister's blindness.
We, who may follow, well may wish so pure a close as
    thine
To Life's long weary pilgrimage—'tis *we* who must
    repine;
While we tread the arduous path that thou so patiently
    hast trod,
And remain below to mourn thee, thou wilt be at peace
    with God!

[NOTE.—Mrs. —— and I had always been devoted and unwavering
friends, through circumstances of great family difficulty, and it may
interest some to know that she dictated an answer to these lines,
which were read to her shortly before her death; which answer I
preserve as the last memento of a faithful friendship, among my best
treasures, and from which I may quote one passage, dear for its thoughtful kindness: "Thanks for your beautiful lines, which —— read to me.
Your and your husband's friendship have always been the greatest
comfort to me."]

THOUGHTS IN THE CHAMBER OF DEATH.

Men pass it by—that solitary light
That shines from Death's sad chamber through the night,
Nor ask they why it glimmers there so late;
The grief within is hopeless, desolate !
In loneliness our vigil must we keep,
The stars look on, but marvel why we weep.
There is no sympathy in outward things
With the deep woe that oft the human bosom wrings.

So, as with sinking heart and heavy eye,
We sit and watch beside the untrimmed lamp,
And listen to the sufferer's deep-drawn sigh,
Or wipe from his cold brow Death's fearful damp,—
There cometh in a bright and sudden ray
Through the half-opened shutter, as of day,
Lighting the chamber with a vivid smile—
Draw softly back that curtain—morning breaks, the
    while !

It is a moonbeam ; sullenly and slow
The heavy clouds from night's fair planet roll,
And night is glorious, yet we feel as though
That glory were a weight upon the soul.
The stars shine out as brilliantly as when
In summer-time the clouds are all forgot,
Yet shrink we from their beauty, as from men
Who pass us by in joy and know our sorrow not !

There is a weary sadness in this life,
That all must feel, yet none with us can share ;
The heart that wars most boldly with its strife,
Trampling most proudly on its stern despair,
Yet sinks beneath that seeming lesser ill,
That cometh as a twilight o'er the heart ;
For something beautiful and holy, still
With its deep melancholy claims a kindred part.

Alas ! the consciousness of life's decay,
E'en when by beauty's side, fills us with awe,
And we would fain that knowledge fling away—
In some loved form forget its fatal law.
Reluctant—nay, refusing oft—to learn,
From the dull fading eyes of Death we turn,
For something unto which the heart may cling
In fearlessness to love, as an immortal thing !

Yea! we unto ourselves a world would make,
Unlike the one we live in! peopling it
With forms decay knows not, for whose sweet sake
To live, with whose fond feelings ours to knit;
Fearing no more that, when we love them most,
Beneath their fair young feet may yawn the tomb,
That when we call them ours, with love's sweet boast,
E'en then they may depart and leave the world in gloom!

Vain fancy! near the spot where Death is shrouded,
The wild flowers bloom and deck the mossy stone;
Their blue-bells, like a summer sky, unclouded—
" Within, but not without, Death! is thine own."
So sing we, while the summer days are ours—
Alas! those days depart, and we awake,
And find we did but dream; the fair, young flowers
Depart, and all but Death that silent mound forsake.

EVELINE:

A TALE OF THE VILLAGE.

"Turn Thee unto me, and have mercy upon me; for I am desolate and afflicted."—PSALM XXV.

"I looked for some to take pity, but there was none; and for comforters, but I found none."—PSALM LXIX.

EVELINE.

Canto I.

It was the closing of a day in spring,
The herdsman led his cattle to the stream,
The swallow caught upon its glancing wing
The tranquil glory of the last sunbeam.
Meanwhile, the wind, that o'er an English vale
Wafted the breath of the departing hours,
Told all it passed the same delicious tale
Of hidden violets and acacia flowers.
That vale was little known, and meet for him
Who loves to dwell beneath a placid sky;
Its simple rustic dwellings—calm and trim—
Had even made Ambition heave a sigh.
The lofty hills, that shut it from the world,
Were clothed with giant trees, of age unknown;
The quiet smoke that through their branches curled,
Arose from village cottages alone.
No haughty noble built his mansion there,
Nor pride, nor fashion marred its sanctitude;
'Twas too remote from City heat and glare,

For wealth's delusive pleasures to intrude.
The villager went forth upon his way,
As morning starlight faded on his path ;
Returning, at the closing of the day,
To seek contentedly his humble hearth.
No dazzling dreams his peace of mind destroyed,
For him the present day sufficed alone,
Its unbought pleasures calmly he enjoyed,
Nor prayed for life less toilsome than his own.

One spot within this beautiful retreat
Was yet more fair, more peaceful than the rest,
The flowery turf felt softer to the feet,
The ring-dove cooed securely from her nest.
And there—beneath the branches of a wood,
That formed a graceful background to the glade—
The low-thatched cottage of a peasant stood,
Embowered, like some fond secret, in the shade.
That evening, listening to the sighing leaves,
A maiden sat beneath its lowly eaves ;
And with her earnest eyes intently raised,
Through long green avenues of beech trees gazed,
To mark how far the mountain shades were thrown
Across the village that she called her own.
In truth she was a village child, though thought
Shone through her gaze no rustic life had taught.
'Tis rarely that we meet with eyes like those —
They spoke not of unrest or of repose—

Not wild and yet not quiet—but their glance
Inspired a feeling even of awe—as though
Through the soft bloom of that young countenance,
Spoke the stern prophecy of future woe.
Yet ever, as the rolling year passed by,
Had Eveline, with careless hand and light,
Gathered the flowers beneath a smiling sky,
Or watched for glow-worms through the summer night.
The sun that rose behind the eastern hill,
Each morn awoke her with its early rays,
To seek some solitary spot, and fill
Its listening depths with her clear hymn of praise.
The same bright sun had shone upon her path,
As hastening homewards in the evening hours,
She crossed the greenwood to her humble hearth,
Her fragile basket filled with fruits or flowers.
And yet at times a gentle sadness played
Around her beautiful and childlike mouth—
A something that no English birth betrayed,
A look of the soft languor of the South,
A pensiveness that scarce was grief, and yet
Too often showed itself in sighs and tears :
Those eyelids, too, with their long fringe of jet,
Drooped somewhat painfully for her young years.

'Tis said there was a gossip-loving dame,
Who, o'er her tea, used often to relate
How Eveline from foreign climates came ;

And how her parents met some fearful fate,
And left a little orphan girl below,
To weep o'er an inheritance of woe.
So she was sent across the sea, to find
A sweet, though simple, home—and friendly smile,
From one to whom her parents had been kind,
When once they visited the English isle.
Alas! this good old friend the livelong day
Would spend in chatting with some neighbouring crone,
So left her tender charge to steal away
Far—far into the woods, and muse alone.
Full oft in their warm shadows she beguiled
The weary hours by some too glowing thought,
Then once again resumed the playful child,
And garlands for her lambs, of woodbine wrought.
The very bird, that in the deep hedge-row
Built its neat nest with carefulness and pains,
So that no eye except its own might know ;
The goat that browsed along the grassy lanes,—
She called her friends ; and oft she could rejoice
In such companions, when no human voice
Found echo in the young and thoughtful mind
That secretly for love more kindred pined.
For though she loved the summer-time—the sweet
Green earth, and the blue sky that bent above—
The warm fond heart that in her bosom beat,
Still whispered her there was a deeper love
Than that which filled her dark eye with the tear

Of pity, for the dying flower or bird;
And passions strong as death, which have their sphere
Where the great voice of human life is heard.

As summer skies grew warmer, she forsook
All old and well-worn tracks—and wiled away
The long soft evenings by some lonely brook,
Where she could watch the water-birds at play;
And throw them crumbs betimes—then start to feel
That tears were slowly gathering in her eyes,
And wonder grief upon her heart should steal,
In such fair scenes, and under such fair skies!
Then, when the sorrow of the desolate
O'erpowered her with its weariness and weight,
The maiden, with a timid step, would seek
For comfort in the village homes around.
Alas! that delicate and lily cheek,
That voice so low and tender in its sound,
Found not its likeness or its echo there.
Though, with most sympathizing ear, she sat
And listened to the matron's tale of care,
Or joined the rustic maidens in their chat,
There was not one to hear *her* tale—the breast
On which her young and artless head might rest,
However gentle, was too unrefined
To feel or soothe the troubles of her mind.

So passed her life away, till o'er her head   .

Her seventeenth uneventful year had sped.
For winter came and went, and spring-time flung
Her spells again upon the earth, and hung
Festoons of blossoms on each verdant bough;
And where those flowers were freshest and most fair
The maiden sat, and one with youth's smooth brow,
Dark and yet beautiful—sat also there.
They met at first by chance—some fancy took
A tourist's footstep to a shady lane,
As Eveline sat musing by the brook—
We need not marvel that they met again.
The slender stream that murmured at their feet
Reflected now two faces—one was sweet,
The other noble, with a look of fire,
That seemed in his companion to inspire
Already that wild worship, which we see
Bend oft to human deity the knee.
There was a fascination and a spell
About him, that enslaved her but too well.
The self-possessed, insinuating air,
That marks a man to whom the world is known—
That eloquence of language, rich and rare,
That voice, persuasive, musical in tone—
And lastly, those deep eyes that flashed with light—
Were scarcely gifts her maiden heart could slight.
So as he spoke her deep eyes she would raise,
And gaze on him with childhood's artless gaze,
That fears no scrutiny, and knows no sin.

The while he watched that open face, therein
To read each new idea and passing thought,
That in their yet unsullied loveliness,
Though free as air, unstable and self-taught,
Were such as angels might have dared confess.
He read that unto him the power was given
Of forming her young mind—the power to make
A pure and tender spirit fit for heaven,
Or chained to sin and sorrow for his sake.
Alas ! her fate is common—the world hears
Of such too often to be moved to tears.
Our glance may scarcely linger as we pass,
Our footsteps pause not as we hasten by
The very mound of stones and untrimmed grass,
Beneath whose weight a broken heart may lie.

    Not yet he spoke of love, but rather led
Her fancy by the tales of old romance ;
And over all the glow of love he shed,
By tender accent and impassioned glance.
Or with an altered look and graver tone,
He told her of the far-famed Indian war ;
Spoke of the victories led by him alone,
Till Eveline looked up to him with awe.
Next changed the subject, with a ready wile,
To paint the beauties of the sea and land ;
So made her weep with him, or sigh, or smile,
Till heart and soul were both at his command.

And oft he gathered wild flowers of the field,
Or pulled such mosses as the forests yield,
And sat down at her feet, to show how fair,
How wonderful in form and hue they were.
Then, lastly, as the evening hours grew dim,
And cottage lights were gleaming from afar,
He wooed her to remain and watch with him,
While he would name to her each gentle star,
That when the shades of night fell dark and low,
Came forth into the cool and placid sky;
And as the leaves above them shook, even so
Shook Eveline beneath her lover's eye.

'Tis known not what the village matrons said,
It may be that the lovers used to meet
Where boughs hung closely round and overhead,
So none had penetrated their retreat.
'Tis certain that her lover's noble name
The maiden never breathed—the modest shame
That flushed a cheek so generally pale,
Re-closed her lips when trembling with the tale.
What need had she of counsellor or aid,
How could it be a sin that she was loved
By one who seemed a god on earth, and made
To glorify the world in which he moved?
Ah! they alone whose true love knew no strife,
Who trusted with a trust that could not fail,
Can dream how sunny must have been her life,

That one short period of her mournful tale.
We mark too often by our sighs and tears,
The changing seasons of our life's few years;
To her, Time had no changes, save in this,
That each day brought a fuller cup of bliss.
'Twas often said, that never English year
Had boasted skies more beautiful or clear.
The spring was full of blackthorn and of may—
The summer had a brilliant Southern look—
And flowers sprang up beside the village way,
And water-lilies blossomed in the brook,
Until the streams and woods were studded o'er
With glorious plants that none had seen before!
To them—the youthful lovers—each new day
Brought forth some pleasure dearer than the last,
And as each gorgeous evening stole away,
More like a dream of fairyland it passed.
Yet the Elysium of that summer air
Dwelt not to them within the flowers or skies,
The spell that breathed such strange enchantment there,
Spoke in the tender glances of their eyes.

The summer grew more sultry, and the flowers
Drooped their pale blossoms in the hot noontide,
And waited patiently for evening hours,
Ere, bathed by the cool dew-drops, they revived.
And languid as the flowers the maiden sat,
Beneath the graceful willows of the brook,

While o'er her face she drew her rustic hat,
To hide it from her lover's ardent look.
For lo! he speaks to her of love, and now
She turns away from him, but draws her breath
In thick and heavy sobs, while her young brow
One moment flushes, then is pale as death.
He spoke first of the world that lay around,
Like some vast dream, the spot in which she dwelt;
And told her therein Faith was never found,
That Love was but a phantom—seen—not felt.
He said that there the laws of man enthralled,
And urged to guilt the true, devoted soul;
Until his listener, trembling and appalled,
Sank at his feet and wept without control.
Then, in the tenderest tones of Love's own voice,
He drew, in specious lights, what Love might be,
Bound by no law save that of its own choice,
Warm as the sunbeams are, and not less free.
And murmured such a love as this would make
Her present home a paradise below,
Where he would live and die for her sweet sake,
So that her heart no human grief should know.
Something in accents tremulously sweet
She answered, whose low, thrilling words were sighed—
Scarce spoken—but we need not here repeat
All that he said, or all that she replied.
Enough!—by those persuasive tones o'ercome,
The inward voice that might have warned was dumb.

As in some fairy dream her mind was tossed,
She listened—hesitated—and was lost.

Time passed—the autumn months were on the wane,
Still her delirious love, with all its trust,
Ruled her too loving heart and dreamy brain,—
Not yet had she awakened—as all must.
So one calm evening, as the sun went down
Behind the great unfathomable wood,
Now rich with autumn's hues of red and brown,
As side by side the two young lovers stood,
'A musical though trembling voice was heard
To break upon that forest sanctitude,
More gently than the wood-notes of a bird,
When evening's light grows pallid and subdued.
"Beloved! I am too happy.   I have said
Even in my childhood that the world was fair,
When I have watched the blue heavens o'er my head,
And thought that I saw angels in the air.
And mine was then a lonely life—but *this*—
It is too much—I suffer from such bliss."

She lifted to her lover her pale face—
Earnest and pale it was, and even a trace
Of passionate and burning tears was there—
Her joy was greater than her heart could bear.
Then, as she met his answering gaze, it shook
Her very frame—that long and loving look—

Blending his ardent soul in hers, as though
It never more could part therefrom below.

 " And yet, dear life, one sad and tender fear
Breathes on my spirit even now, and here.
There is a doom from which no love can save—
It may be—long before *thy* hour of rest—
That form may lie within the spoiling grave
Which now thou claspest closely to thy breast.
Ah me ! it would be happier far to die
Together—thus—beneath this glorious sky,
Than so to leave thee—weeping and alone—
For who could comfort thee if I were gone ! "

 " Mine Eveline, thy thoughts are much too sad.
Dear one ! while youth is on thy brow be glad !
Sit down upon this mossy bank, that we
May watch the rising of the autumn moon ;
How strangely dear hast thou become·to me !
These hours of evening ever pass too soon.
Hush ! is it not the nightingale ? that song
Hath never sounded sweeter than to-night—
Each note that on the breeze is borne along,
Is like the voice of some unseen delight.
Oh ! let us sit and dream away the hour ;
The thoughts it brings us are beyond our reach
In the broad daylight, and they still o'erpower—
We do but mar them by our human speech.

I only ask—I only pray to dwell
Through life beside thee, gazing on thy brow;
To clasp thee—thus—and feel thy bosom swell
For ever with the same warm love as now."

    Her moment's grief was o'er, her heart was calm,
No doubts disturbed the gentle head that lay
Confidingly and fondly on his arm :—
So passed that long-remembered eve away.

Canto II.

Night, dull and starless, fell upon the world.
The earth lay motionless, the air was chill
And heavy with the wintry mists that curled,
In huge fantastic shapes, o'er wood and hill.
The village homes looked tenantless and dark—
The hour was early—yet their lights were out ;
The very watch-dogs held their usual bark,
For neither voice nor footstep was about.
The same strange lifeless silence—far and near—
Seemed brooding o'er the forest and the plain ;
The only sound that ever met the ear
Was, now and then, the gentle plash of rain,
That trickled slowly from the cottage eaves,
And formed upon the path its baby floods,
Then fell with sharper sound upon the leaves,
The fallen leaves, of the now barren woods.

That cheerless night, beside a dying fire,
A mourner sat—in negligent attire ;
Not in a widow's robes her form was clad—
Her look was rather wild than simply sad.
It was not death she mourned—a grief like that
With less of sternness on her face had sat.

No ray of hope lit up her heavy brow,
But languidly the eyelids rose and fell
O'er her dim sunken eyes—expressing now
That self-abasement words can never tell.
And oh ! as seen in that unsteady light,
No human pen could have portrayed a form
More spectral, or a face more deadly white,
While yet the pulses of the heart were warm.
A letter lay beside her—freshly writ,
The ink whereof appeared but barely dry ;
No tears had fallen there and blotted it,
No outward sign of anguish met the eye ;
Yet scrutiny more careful might have told
How much her frame was shaken as she wrote ;
Its crooked characters betrayed what cold
And trembling fingers had inscribed the note.

EVELINE'S LETTER.

" Once more I write to thee—alas ! once more
I pray for pity vainly asked before.
My heart is weary of its violence—
I now am calm and even resigned, and hence
I trace these lines, that in my altered mood
Their words may touch thee and be understood.
Thine image is beside me still, and nought
Can drive it thence, though bright and pure no more ;

Yet I will own to thee that I have thought
I judged too kindly of thy heart before.
It was not well of thee to leave me thus—
Nor by my shame and frightful anguish moved ;
Oh that the cold grave had divided us,
And not thy colder heart, my still beloved !
And yet I write not to reproach—nay, I
Have often thought it sweeter far to die
Than live to loathe thy memory and thy name :
'Tis I—not thou—that have been most to blame.
But abject in my misery, I implore
That thou wilt write to me one little line—
One word of gentleness—I ask no more—
'Twere useless to demand what once was mine,
Thy heart's warm love—I know that this is lost,
I—that once deemed it of myself a part.
Ah! words can never tell thee what it cost
To tear that fond delusion from my heart.
But this is retribution well deserved—
Against which it were sinful to rebel ;
Nay, rather retribution I had nerved
My heart to bear with patiently and well.
If I alone might be the sacrifice,
I would not murmur at the kind decree,
But unrepining veil my guilty eyes,
And go where none again should hear of me.
I do remember I once made a vow
To suffer well and murmur not, but now

I cannot wrestle longer with despair—
Oh God! *not I alone* this shame must bear."

The rest was scarcely legible, defaced
By blotches here, and there so feebly traced.
And yet no word of kindness in reply
Even to that sad appealing letter came.
He had forsaken—left her there to die,
Or bear, as best she could, her grief and shame.
'Tis possible he gave a false address,
At least our charity may hope thus much
That fearing lest the tale of her distress
Too inconveniently his heart might touch,
He was content in ignorance to rest—
So banished her sweet image from his breast!

Reluctantly and slowly from the earth
Now disappeared the dazzling robe of snow,
Whose late, unusual fall had checked the birth
Of all the flowers that March and April know.
That spring indeed was marvellously cold,
The new-born lambkins died within the fold.
Yet something like a cheerful sunlight smiled
Upon a face and head most sad and sweet,
That bent in prayer above an infant child,
Now slumbering in a cradle at her feet.
The languor of long sickness was expressed
In eyes that looked yet unresigned to fate,

A sense of lassitude that was not rest,
But rather overpowered her with its weight.
A stupor too was on her brow, as though
Her mind had wrestled with its frightful woe,
And from that conflict—terrible and rude,
Came forth—not lost—but utterly subdued.
Nay—yet not utterly—for when her glance
Rested upon her infant's countenance,
A something of her former self returned—
Her dull eye lost its fixed and vacant gaze,
A soul once more in its expression burned,
Whose tenderness was that of happier days.
But oh! too often after this there came
A strange reaction o'er that shattered frame,
That shook with the fierce combat waged within,
Until you wondered if the better part
Of that once pure and gentle mind would win,
Or leave her but a wrecked and hardened heart.

It was upon the morn of which we spoke,
Ere yet her infant from its slumber woke,
That in a tremulous and solemn tone,
So unlike the sweet bird-notes once her own,
She sang a song, or rather hymn, whose first
Calm words had done but little to prepare
A listener for the overpowering burst
Of mad, despairing grief that closed her prayer.
Yet blame her not—a heart so tender must,

When wronged where it has placed its holiest trust,
From all its human joys and hopes shut out,
Have its dark season of despair and doubt;
Ere the sad eyes that tears and passion blind,
Their only safe and home-bound path shall find.

    " I thank Thee, O my God,
That Thou hast breathed upon my heart again,
And turned away the reckless steps that trod
The downward path from whence return is vain.

    " It was but now I prayed
That Thou wouldst end my sorrow and my sin ;
Despair my heart so wild and hardened made,
I dreaded life, and saw no hope therein.

    " My head was bowed with shame,
I dared not lift from earth my heavy eyes ;
I even feared to call upon Thy name,
Lest Thou Thy guilty suppliant shouldst despise.

    " Oh ! pity and forgive
The heart that knew Thee not except through fear,
And hear the voice that now implores to live,
That it may yet perform its mission here.

    " My Father, if Thou wilt
Chastise me heavily—Thy will be done.
But ah ! let not my error and my guilt
Fall on the fair head of my little one.

" I ask Thee but for this—
Not selfishly before Thee now I kneel—
Imploring not my faded youth or bliss,
Or praying Thee my broken heart to heal.

" No ! but with burning tears
And supplicating hands entreating Thee
That I may guard mine infant's future years,
And save her from the fate that mine must be.

" My God ! my God ! I hear
Thy awful voice from the vast heavens reply—
It falls like thunder on my mortal ear ;
Thou dost refuse my prayer ; then let me die.

" Thou sayst I am unfit—
Dishonoured—stained and lost—for such a task ;
I know Thee wise, yet can I not submit;
'Tis mercy and not justice that I ask."

She clasped her hands upon her throbbing breast,
Lest her deep sobs should break her infant's rest ;
Then hastened wildly from the spot and flung
Her tender form upon the cottage floor.
Oh ! it was sad for one so fair and young
To lie and pray that she might rise no more !
It was not till a weary time had passed,
That something like a purer, holier vein

Of feeling brought a gush of tears at last,
To calm her heart and soothe her fevered brain.
And hushing in her arms her waking child,
That melancholy voice was heard once more,
A song more sweet and gentle and less wild,
Upon the peaceful morning air to pour.

    " Lullaby, Lullaby,
        Dear one—rest !
Pillow thy head on my yearning breast,
For never, oh ! never, shall sleep like this
Revisit thine eyes in after years,
The fond warm touch of thy mother's kiss,
Will have changed, on thy tender cheek, to tears.

    " Lullaby, Lullaby,
        Soft and deep
Falleth the shade of thy infant sleep.
Like a veil that a summer evening throws
On the tranquil brow of the parting day,
So deepens the calm of thy pure repose,
Till the light of thy face hath passed away.

    " Lullaby, Lullaby,
        Ne'er below
Shall thy mother again such slumber know,
Or the holiness of a peace like thine

Return to her worn and weary brain.
Thy dreams are the dreams of Eden—mine
Are now but the echoes of waking pain.

      " Lullaby, Lullaby,
         Yet no more
From the mercy of Heaven my lips implore,
Than to guard from thy sweet young life the blight
On the guilty brow of thy mother cast ;
'Tis the prayer that I breathe by day, by night—
'Tis the prayer that in death will be fondest—last !"

    Beneath a cypress in the churchyard green,
One eve was raised a white and simple stone ;
There, as the sun shone calmly on the scene,
A mourner knelt—forsaken and alone.
Oh ! marvel not her brow was pale and sad,—
Beneath that fresh and myrtle-planted mould
Was laid the last—the only friend she had—
A friend whose dying words were harsh and cold.
And yet that stern and " virtuous reproof "
Was not for sinning lips like hers to blame ;
She, who so long had dwelt beneath the roof
Of that once kind and gentle-hearted dame,
Had brought but dark dishonour and distress
Within its simple tenement, of late—
Ah ! it was well deserved, yet not the less
Heart-breaking, to be left thus desolate.

It was the severing of the only link
That bound her to the outer world, and she,
When evening's purple sun began to sink,
No longer knew where aid or hope might be.
She could not seek for sympathy among
The homes where she was welcomed once with pride;
The old would shake their heads at her, the young
Shrink with disgust or pity from her side.
Such were the maddening thoughts that now passed o'er
The mind that struggled with their course no more.
Her brain became bewildered, and possessed
Of but one longing—the desire for rest.

There was within the woods a mimic lake,
Whose depth was hidden by green moss and weeds,
Down o'er its edges fell the briar and brake,
Tangling their branches in obnoxious reeds.
There, with infatuation strange and wild,
She often came, and brought her infant child,
To gaze, as with a fascinated eye,
Upon its most unfathomable part,
And find it each day harder to deny
The urgent pleadings of her guilty heart.
'Twould be so sweet her aching eyes to close
Upon a world that she had loved too well;
To know again the charms of a repose
Which dreams could not affright, or tears dispel;
And sweeter still to know that none could sever

Her infant from her; folded to her breast
They would be then together, and for ever,
At least in peace—if wept not, and unblest.

The moon was rising far behind a wood,
That looked gigantic in its partial light,
The hour that by an open casement stood
A pale and wasted figure clothed in white.
Her hands were clasped—the gaze of her dark eye
Was fixed upon her childhood's scenes, that lay
Beneath the midnight calmness of that sky,
And scarcely looked less lovely than by day.
Something like holiness was breathing there,
That would have moved another mind to prayer;
And often through the unclosed lattice came
That strange—sweet perfume—never called by name,
That sometimes steals among our earthly bowers,
As though it had been shed by angel wings.
Howe'er this be, we know that there are hours
When earth is teeming with unearthly things,—
And this was one of them; but she whose look
Was thereon bent as with the gaze of death,
Felt not its influence, nor moved, nor shook;
Some ghastly purpose froze her very breath.
Hush! hush! she moves—a deep and holy charm
Lies in the wailing of that infant child;
She raises it upon her nerveless arm,
Though gazing still with troubled looks and wild,

Till on a pillow softer than its own
It rests its head, and stays its little moan.
Thank Heaven! this baby confidence, within
The breast that was a mother's still, awoke
A keener sense of her intended sin
Than if the voice of an Archangel spoke.
She clasped it to her bosom with a cry,
That, like her troubles, found no listening ear,
Yet met, perchance, a sympathy on high,
Which human charity refuses here.

Morn glimmered—but its first grey hours were spent
In timid prayers for pardon and for aid,
That from a mind most penitent were sent,
To One to whom none such have vainly prayed.
For now some hope seemed on her mind to dawn,
That filled her darkened eye again with light—
The calmness of some holy purpose, born
Even in the fearful travail of that night.
Then broke the morn, as one, tear-worn and pale,
Yet tranquillized by some now fixed intent,
Took the green footpath leading from the vale—
Bearing her sleeping infant as she went.
No step was yet abroad—the frost lay still
Upon the unpressed violets, and the rays
Of sunrise just appeared above the hill,
As Eveline turned back her parting gaze.
Ne'er had it seemed more lovely in her sight,

As, feeling that it was her last farewell,
She shaded from her face the sun's red light,
That she might see the home she loved so well.
Though earth could scarcely .boast a fairer spot,
Not this, but memories that were therein shrined,
Gave unto it a charm it else had not,
And made it a lost Eden to her mind.
She had been once the pride, too, of that place,
Both for her winning ways and sweet young face,
And for her girlhood's innocence and bloom—
Now buried, like her love, in one dark tomb.
She went forth as an outcast on her way,
No one befriending her, though some might pray
That she might find—what they would have denied—
A place wherein her broken heart to hide.
Alas! for us, who, judging of the sin,
Deny the pardon that *we* hope to win;
Who, hearing not the victim's piteous tale,
Turn from the prayer of her imploring eye,
And coldly shut her from our social pale,
To find without no friend or home, and die!

Canto III.

One, with the seal of sorrow on her face,
Clasping a sickly infant to her breast,
Through a great city went with weary pace,
As crimson daylight faded in the west.
That brilliant glow reflected from above
But now, on lofty tower and monument,
Had vanished gently as the smile of love,
So slowly and reluctantly it went.
And timidly the moon, that had so long
Awaited the departure of the day,
Gave forth her light—that hourly grew more strong,
Till all the city glistened in its ray.
While, almost imperceptibly, the hum
Of life in the metropolis died out,
So left it unto prayer and sleep, though some
Who had no homes to seek, were still about.
Even these at last retired with weary feet,
To choose some covered court wherein to lie,
And left the lonely watchman on his beat,
To count the stars that lit the narrow sky.
Then she, who had been latest of the late,
Regarding not that she was all alone,

Went slowly through a mansion's open gate,
And sat down on its noble steps of stone—
Silent and chilly.　None disturbed her there,
But left her to her bitter thoughts, or prayer.

Aye! none disturbed her there—for there were few
Among that city's myriads, who knew
No spot, however rude, wherein to rest
The head that vice or poverty oppressed.
Yet nothing like complaint or anguish dwelt
In eyes that wept o'er selfish griefs no more;
Disgrace—neglect—were now no longer felt,
The struggle with her heart's despair was o'er.
And she had won!　Submissive to her fate
Her look—though not rejoicing—was serene;
Though lonely—cold—forsaken—desolate—
Her heart was calmer than it long had been.
Not all the ravages by sorrow made,
Had marred a certain beauty in that face;
A light that yet no sickness seemed to fade—
A sweetness no unkindness could efface.
And purified and chastened from her sin,
She dared look forward now with hope, beyond
A world so fair without—so foul within—
From which her soul was breaking its last bond.
Once only—when her trembling hand undid
The shawl that wrapt her babe with scanty fold,
Tears dimmed her eyes and fringed each drooping lid,

Then fell as though they would not be controlled.
And long and fondly on its face she gazed,
Where Death had but too plainly set his seal—
But uttered no complaint, although she raised
Her eyes to heaven as with a last appeal.

The summer of that year had left again
The warm green earth another season old,
As through the broad street and the narrow lane,
Both day and night that hapless wanderer strolled.
And yet to her that summer brought no sign—
For what in that great world could meet her gaze,
Except the sky became less clear and fine,
Or early lamplight spoke of shortened days?
Alas! her mission yet was unfulfilled,
The lost came not—though day succeeding day
She scanned each passing face, one moment thrilled
With hope—then turning—sickening—away.
Yet long and fondly to that hope she clung,—
Love's last—most strong—possession in the mind,
She once so passionate, and still so young,
Grieved much ere this one dream could be resigned.
Then when its cruel and bitter trial was o'er,
She raised her eyes to God—earth-bound no more.

No one molested her—they passed her by
Most frequently, with cold or vacant eye.
None spoke to her in accents coarse or rude;

The little babe that to her bosom clung—
Her look—her step—so quiet and subdued,
Guarded from insult or licentious tongue.
Some few that passed her even again would turn,
As by a sudden impulse moved, to give
The pittance that she had not strength to earn ;
'Twas little—scarce enough whereon to live.
In truth her cheek—so hollow and so pale,
Told but too well starvation's horrid tale.
Yet with her thin and bony hand she took
The well-meant offering with a grateful look.
It was enough to hush her infant's cry—
The rest must follow soon—and with a sigh
That even a martyr could not have repressed,
She clasped her loved one closer to her breast.

*   *   *   *

*   *   *   *

*   *   *   *

Far o'er the meadows sounds the pleasant low
Of cattle, and the goatherd's rugged song ;
The peasant leaves his work with footsteps slow
And weary—musing as he strolls along.
The shepherd lingers in the fields awhile,
Returning not upon his homeward way
Till he has prophesied, from sunset's smile,
The cloud or brightness of the coming day.
The fine and plenteous harvest of that year
Is gathered from the earth—the golden grain

Lies treasured in the barns, that scatter near
The villages and hamlets of the plain.
And far away as human eye can reach,
Through the green pastures flows a gentle stream,
Now shadowed by some solitary beech,
Now dancing gaily in the bright sunbeam—
While over all the wide and rich expanse
Of hill and meadow-grass, and wooded lands,
Uplifting its grey, time-worn countenance,
The castle of an English noble stands!

The fair young heiress of these vast domains
Is tempted by the softness of the hour,
And wanders with her lover o'er the plains,
Till lost within a distant, autumn bower.
Thy life hath known no troubles, and thy years
As yet have been unmarred by care or tears—
No grief was ever known thy breast to swell
With early bitterness, young Isabel!
And yet, this beautiful and tranquil eve
There is a sadness in thy lustrous eye—
Thy snowy bosom seems to fall and heave,
As if disturbed by an unwonted sigh.
Alas! upon her lover's brow a cloud
Is falling like the darkness of the night:
His lips are deadly pale—his head is bowed,
His deep eye has a strange and troubled light.
Too often—even in the festive hall,

That blighting shadow had been seen to fall,
Though none of his companions seemed to know
The secret of that dark, mysterious woe.
But she, who walks so sadly by his side,
Years his affianced—soon to be his bride,
Had never found it difficult till now
To chase that heavy sternness from his brow.
Alas ! to-night that cold abstracted air
Scarce seems to recognize that she is there !
'Twas strange that sweet young face should still return,
To haunt him with its fixed, reproachful gaze—
That glance, which seemed his very soul to burn
With the remembrance of departed days.
Yes—it was strange, but often would a tone
Of more than ordinary sweetness thrill
His bosom, and recall again that one
Clear bird-like voice that had been sweeter still.
No other fancy to his heart had clung
So pertinaciously as this—although
Many whom he had wronged had been as young,
With star-like eyes, and bosoms white as snow.
She had a beauty which no other had,
A soul of tenderness, most deep and rare.
Oh that he could forget her, for her sad
Pale face seemed gazing on him everywhere !

．

    He started, for the voice of Isabel
Upon his guilty conscience sternly fell.

The air had been so breathless that a bird
Was startled by the strange, unwonted sound,
Disturbing thus a leaf that next was heard
To join its withered brethren on the ground.

"Oh! deem me not unworthy of thy trust,"
The lady said, in tones that somewhat shook.
" Tell me thy secret sorrow, love, why must
Thy brow so oft be clouded by that look ?
My every feeling I confide to thee,—
I do conceal no impulse of my heart;
It is not well a woe like thine should be,
In which I have no portion—take no part.
Give me thy confidence!   Nay—wherefore shake
Thy head as though in anger or disdain ?
I ask not selfishly, but for thy sake—
I grieve for thee, and fain would ease thy pain.
Am I not thine ? can aught now sever us ?
Thy trust and confidence—or mine—destroy ?
Say—if this be—what grief consumes thee thus,
Why is it greater than thy love or joy ?"

He turned from her too curious eyes the brow,
That, pale before, grew even paler now.
" I have been dreaming," he replied—"no more—
It was the dark remembrance of a woe—
A stern affliction—suffered long before
I met thee ;"—then in hollow tones and low

He added : " For thy sake I will dismiss
Henceforth these moody habits of my brain,
And thou—if thou art wise—will grant me this,
To probe not thus my inmost thoughts again."

 This bitter answer roused the lady's pride—
Her eyes flashed both with anger and defiance ;
'Twas strange to be so haughtily denied,
Even now—when she might well expect compliance !
More white than marble grew that proud young face,
As some few words—both taunting and constrained—
She answered him, and then with queen-like pace
Walked onwards till the broad high-road was gained.
That road went winding through a lordly wood,
Whose ancient oaks for centuries had stood,
And o'er the worn pedestrian's weary head
Their gnarled old branches hospitably spread.
There—rising from its most remote recess,
Was heard the gentle cooing of a dove.
That scene of rich, autumnal loveliness
But needed this—the voice of peace and love !
In the green distance herds of deer were seen ;
Some basking idly on a sunny bank,
Some bounding lightly o'er the mossy green,
While others paused beside a stream and drank.
At times, the timid hares would venture out
Into the sunshine—or a pheasant soar
From some impervious shades, and wheel about,

Then drop into their quiet depths once more.
It is a lovely spot, and well doth he
Who, all regardless of yet early hours,
Chooses that yon fair bank his couch shall be,
So rests his head among the autumn flowers.
Ah me ! it is a woman's long dark hair
That mingles with the leaves and quaking-grass ;
Those white and wasted limbs are partly bare,
The winds caress them gently as they pass.
She sleeps—poor lonely wanderer—doth she sleep ?
There seems no motion there of heaving breath—
That slumber is too perfect—is too deep—
It is not slumber—it is surely death !
" Oh ! hasten, dearest, ere it be too late,
Raise her, and bear her to the castle gate."

No words have power to picture what *he* felt,
Whose horror-stricken heart and guilty eyes—
As by that scarcely breathing form he knelt—
Failed not the lost—the wronged—to recognize.
Clasping an infant to her breast she lay,
Whose cold brow told of death, but not decay.
When—where—that hapless infant died—or how,
There is no record left to tell us now.
It may be, when its life was almost o'er,
The mother's thoughts returned to home once more.
One wish may have been strong within her soul—
The wish to lay it in its native vale ;

K

At least, it seems, her footsteps sought that goal,
From early morn till day began to fail.
Alas! how frightfully afar it lay!
The road was long and lonely, and but few
Perchance had succoured her upon her way,
And day brought showers—with evening fell the dew.
Who knoweth what she suffered, when the eyes
Whose failing light would soon be quenched for ever,
Fixed their last look upon the western skies,
That lit a home—loved—lost—forgotten never!

Alas for him! who, gazing on that form,
Felt thus revive the tenderness intense
Which, when the summer days were long and warm,
Had once inspired his fatal eloquence.
'Twere well the tear of pity even to shed
Upon that brow impure and guilty head.
He gazed as stupefied—nor moved—nor spoke,
As memory in his maddened brain awoke
Her girlish innocence—her perfect trust—
The love that he had trampled in the dust.
Yea, though so altered by one year of woe,
With tattered garment and dishevelled hair
Veiling alone her wasted breasts of snow—
He felt her dearer—thought her far more fair—
Than all the daughters of the earth beside.
Forgetting all ambition and all pride,
He raised her—called her each endearing name

That memory could recall or love could frame.
Even this was useless—she could hear not now
The voice that once her very being stirred.
And Isabel looked on, but with a brow
Rigid as death, and uttering not a word.

   *   *   *   *

   *   *   *   *

Another hour of that strange eve steals by,
Bearing its burden to eternity.
And by an open casement now they lay
Her feeble form—within a spacious room:
'Tis strange—the peaceful closing of her day—
A life so sad, a death that brings no gloom.
She lives—but yet is dreaming—her dim eye
Seems vacantly to watch the twilight's veil
Usurp the place of sunset's golden dye,
Through which, as yet, the stars look dull and pale.
The earth is fading with a sleepy look,
The hollow cawing of some drowsy rook
Comes hoarsely from some elms, that, tall and green,
Grow down upon the edge of a ravine.
And far away, a long and lofty chain
Of hills that bound the meadow and the plain,
With that deep softness only twilight lends,
Its outline with the sky above it blends.
While slowly brightening in that sky's clear space,
The stars smile down upon the watcher's face.

Hush! the last notes of wood-birds, sweet and clear,
That fill the grove with an autumnal strain,
Are wafted faintly—softly—to her ear—
Music that she may never hear again.
They pause, as evening's last expiring flush
Grows paler, and then fades upon the sight;
So leaves the earth reposing in the hush,
The breathless hush of a most perfect night.
'Twere sweet to die in such an hour as this,
To melt away into a dream of bliss!
And she was dying—for the hand of Death
Upon her marble brow was sternly pressed—
There came at times a painful gasp for breath,
Her misty eye seemed languishing for rest.
The heart beat fitfully—paused—beat again—
Shapes grew unshaped to her disordered brain;
A sudden breeze that from some distant bower
Brought the sweet perfume of the jasmine flower,
Then raised her hair as with an unseen hand,
To her seemed whispering of a brighter land—
The curtains, as their rich folds slightly moved,
The murmuring voices of the lost and loved.

A form bent o'er her—'twas her lover's form,
A hand upon her brow felt kind and warm.
Alas! her failing eye no more could trace
The pale and grief-changed features of his face.
But when his ne'er-forgotten voice she heard,

Hoarse—tremulous—yet tender as of yore—
It seemed as though a long-forgotten chord
Of life responded to its sound once more.
Yet though she heard him—knew him, and around
His neck her wasted arms she feebly wound,
She could remember not her recent woe ;
Oblivious of all grief, her thoughts returned—
As oft in dreams—to joys that long ago
So brightly—fondly—in her heart had burned !

EVELINE'S VISION.

'Tis summer once again, and where the boughs
Of forest trees droop almost to their feet,
Two youthful lovers sit—exchanging vows—
Their trembling hands are clasped, their fond eyes meet.
'Tis past the hour of sunset, and behind
The western hills yon cloud of purple fades—
And gently springeth up a low soft wind,
That woos the green leaves in the forest shades.
In the far east, a line of silver hue
Extends behind the mountain heights, and now
The moon is up, and lights a distant view
Of rock and valley with her broad white brow.
A little longer, and that chastened ray
Is stealing in among the beech-wood stems,
Kissing the dewy flowers upon its way,
Until they glisten in its light like gems.

Next lights the lovers' faces as they sit
Forgetful of the hour, and watching it !
While breaking on the solitude around
A distant song at intervals is heard,
It hath a strangely wild and joyous sound,
The clear, sweet singing of that native bird !
We call it only earth who thereon gaze,
With pensive thought and meditative air—
It is the moon—and we receive its rays
As sent to cheer our paths of grief and care.
To them it is not earth, but Paradise !
A dwelling meet for perfect love and trust,
Warm—deep—as that now melting in their eyes,
The love of angels—not of human dust.
Words had been uttered on that summer eve,
Fond—earnest—passionate, and such as leave
A memory that can never more depart :
They echo now within that dreamer's heart.
She speaks ! her words, though faint, are strangely clear,
And fall like thunder on her lover's ear !

" And yet, dear life, one sad and tender fear
Breathes on my spirit even now, and here.
There is a doom from which no love can save—
It may be—long before *thy* hour of rest—
That form may lie within the spoiling grave
Which now thou claspest closely to thy breast.
Ah me ! it would be happier far to die

Together—thus—beneath this glorious sky,
Than so to leave thee—weeping and alone—
For who could comfort thee if I were gone!"

She paused and seemed confused, some trembling gleams
Of dawning reason struggled with her mind,
Though, with the sweet bewilderment of dreams,
Her past and present joys were still combined.

"'Tis strange! it must be night! I cannot see
Thy face—I cannot gaze upon thy brow,
And yet I know that thou art close to me—
I seemed to see thy loving eyes but now.
The sky is gone—I thought the stars were bright;
I feel a numbness and an icy chill
Steal o'er me, like the damp cold dews of night.
It matters not, for thou art near me still!
Thy trembling hand within mine own I press,
I feel thy kind and tender arm caress
And clasp me to thy heart—oh! it is sweet
To feel that heart so fondly—warmly beat.
'Beloved! I am too happy. I have said
Even in my childhood that the world was fair,
When I have watched the blue heavens o'er my head,
And thought that I saw angels in the air—
And mine was then a lonely life—but *this*—
It is too much—I suffer—from such—bliss.'"

Faintly and falteringly these accents fell,
Her soul was darkening with its long eclipse;
None wished that bright delusion to dispel.—
She died with these last words upon her lips.

THOUGHTFUL MOMENTS.

THE GRAVES OF THREE BROTHERS.

THE FIRST AND SECOND.

One sleeps beneath the wild Atlantic wave,
But records of his resting-place are none;
His desolate and undiscovered grave
Undecked by flowers, unmarked by gilded stone.

His brother lies beneath the northern pines,
Where rabbits brood and wild doves build their nests;
Yet not more calmly that cold brow reclines
Than his who sleeps beneath the Atlantic crests.

Neither from gloomy vault nor marbled urn,
Where love may slumber, sin lie unconfessed,
Can we dare pray our lost ones to return
To life's wild turmoil or to grief's unrest.

They have a happier fate than those who strive
In vain to break the iron prison bars.
Oh, melancholy thought! to pass our lives
So oft in craven peace or bitter wars!

There grief is silent, tears no more are shed,
Nor hearts sink low beneath their own sad weight ;
Oh, envy not the slumbers of the dead—
It is the living who are desolate !

Under eternal warfare of the sky,
Or under smiling suns or flower-strewn sod,
It matters little where our bones may lie,
So that our souls return from thence to God.

THE THIRD.

Neither beneath the ocean's crest,
Nor where the pine trees' shadows fall,
My third young brother takes his rest,
But by an abbey's noble wall.

His slender, wasted form they lay
'Mid long green grass and pale wild flowers,
Where sun-dials point the hour of day,
And warn us of our wasted hours.*

Full of a gentle, kindly wit,
He was the genial friend of all—
For none were e'er unkindly hit,
No malice from *his* lips could fall !

* There were two fine old sun-dials in the ancient churchyard of ——.

Where tall grass waves and daisies grow,
'Neath winter's storms or summer's skies,
He waits the day that no one knows,
When Heaven's own voice shall bid us rise.

What suns may rise—what suns may set—
Howe'er apart their graves may lie,
One faithful friend will ne'er forget
The brothers of a day gone by!

TO DR. ——.

THEY listen for his footsteps on the stairs—
   To them distinct through all the city's hum,
Hushing their painful sighs, heart-broken prayers,
   To count those footfalls as they nearer come !

And sadly, as he bends above the bed,
   They wait for words of comfort from his lips;
Death shuts the fatal wings so darkly spread,
   And Life smiles out behind her black eclipse.

His soothing hand relieves the racking pain,
   Wipes the cold death-damp from the haggard face,
Brings hope and peace to the o'er-troubled brain,
   And stays pale Death in his too-rapid pace.

No wonder that they bless him as he leaves
   The darkened bedroom and its fevered air ;
The saddened brow, the bitter heart that grieves,
   Are happier, better, for his presence there.

Ever serene and calm himself, he goes,
  Heedless of place and time, where duty calls ;
Be it to soothe the mightiest monarch's woes,
  Or suffering penury in prison walls.

He, too, hath suffered, though his brow is calm ;
  Grief, sickness, pain, are not to him unknown ;
But he, from whom so many seek their balm,
  Seeks from on High the solace for his own.

LINES TO MY LOVE.

Mine own true love! from the first hour I clasped
Thy firm and gentle hand, the magic touch
Was even as though my future life I grasped—
A life of hope, although I feared it much!

Thou wilt not leave me—if thou dost I die!
Thou canst not leave me—let the hours pass by,
And count them not for happiness nor sorrow,
Remembering only, there is yet To-morrow!

That strange To-morrow—oh! I fear it less
Than earthly days that darken and depress,
Without a silver lining to the cloud,
Or lifting of the head that grief hath bowed.

My heart is full of love—of tender pride,
Although my days are passed not by thy side;
For where thou goest I can rarely go,
Not mine the power to heal or soften woe!

I cannot thank thee, oh, thou best beloved—
To me the truest, purest among men—
Nor can I paint thee, with my heart so moved,
Either by eloquence of lips or pen.

But I will wait for thee, Life's latest hours—
Age shall not alter me, or Grief's weird powers ;
Knowing that from the first bright hour we met,
I lost the right to freedom—to forget !

No human power our hands' true clasp shall sever—
Love, while thou livest I am thine for ever.
Nay ! nor in future realms mine eyes can see
A life, a state, that is not passed with thee !

L

OLD-FASHIONED PRAISES BY A LOVER OF SUMMER.

Oʜ, summer flowers are fresh and fair,
And summer skies are bright, I ween,
To those that leave the City air,
To wander in the woodland scene !

For beautiful it is to be
By rippling stream and bending tree,
To leave the dull and crowded street
For leafy bough and blossom sweet,
To watch the graceful deer bound by,
With footstep light and sparkling eye,
The timid hare, with frightened look,
Steal from the shade of its own nook.
   Oh, summer flowers, etc.

For beautiful it is to see
The sun rise o'er the dusky lea,
To watch it pierce the tangled shade
Of coppice dark or briary glade,

Glistening in each bright drop of dew
That hangs upon the harebell blue—
Pouring its cheerful light o'er all,
Unchecked by tower or city wall.
      Oh, summer flowers, etc.

For sweet it is at close of day
To stroll through woods with twilight grey,
Or when the moon is looking down
Through graceful ash, or beech tree brown,
To hear the dove coo in the glen,
The wildcock cry from marshy fen,
The pheasant, from its evening rest,
The moor-fowl from their rushy nest.

      For summer flowers are fresh and fair,
And summer skies are bright, I ween,
To those that leave the City air,
To wander in the woodland scene.

TREASURED MEMORIES.

Oн, ye past days, so anxious yet so dear,
Full of a countless list of tender stories—
With shifting lights of hope, of joy, of fear,
I would not change ye for a world of glories !

Our little ones !—across the chequered past
I see their tiny figures gaily flit,
Fair human memories that the longest last—
Gay with the pretty laugh of childish wit !

I care but little what the dull world seems,
It costs no pang its trivial ties to sever,
So that my early loves come back in dreams—
Bright, sunlit joys that will be joys for ever.

No envy, with its sharp, envenomed stings,
No hateful spite can this sweet past destroy—
For Memory hath a world of gracious things,
The vilest tongue is powerless to destroy !

They cannot hush the gentle, tender voices,
With all their merry laughter—infant cries,
There is no human spell my heart rejoices,
Like the sweet spell of childhood's mystic eyes!

There may lie grander treasures at our feet,
And wealth or glory be within our call,
And friends may flatter—flattery is sweet!
But one dear, childish lisp outweighs them all—

One childish lisp—*Mamma*—no angel tone
Can thrill the heart as that one tone can thrill,
That little word—that one—is all mine own,
Its first, soft accents are remembered still!

And oh! I pity with a thousand pities,
Those who in such sweet music have no part,
Not for the treasures of Ind's fabled cities
Would I yield up these treasures of my heart!

September 12, 1880.

DESPAIRING WORDS.

I CANNOT hear where thou art dwelling now,
'Tis seldom that I even hear thy name—
Grief, since I met thee, may have seared thy brow,
Or it may still be fair yet not the same !
But when recalling thy pale countenance,
And dreaming of thy deep and pensive eye,
'Tis as when first I met its thrilling glance,
Though years since then—long years have fleeted by.
Thy voice—it may be gentle now no more—
Thy vision now be dim—thy very heart
May be so changed from all I knew before,
I scarce could love the thing that now thou art !
Or it may be that yet a sterner seal
Than Grief's, upon thy brow has been impressed,
And all that once could breathe and move and feel,
Now shrouded lies in its last dreamless rest ;
And Hope's own flickering star, whose cheering ray
Still lingered, when all else had passed away—
Dark homes of sorrow to illumine yet—
That last lone star of love and life hath set !

I watched it as it faded—night by night,
Hour after hour I watched its waning light,
And sighed to think the fitful gleam it gave
But glimmered, as a lamp within the grave,
To light the very dead with its wild glare
And show the depth of desolation there!
'Tis gone! and I am lonelier than before.
Joy hath no promise—Life no pleasure more,
Except that even thy very name be lost,
And buried with the suffering it has cost.
Thou hadst been but too fondly cherished—thou
Wert—all to me—but must be—nothing—now!

I never watched the deepening of twilight,
I never looked out on the sky at night,
To calm the anguish of mine aching brow,
But something even then—I knew not how
Or why it came—some sympathetic tone
Came back, as though an echo of thine own,
And brought me that wild swell of loving thought,
No tones but *thy* deep tones, have ever brought.

Oh! yet must I forget thee—was it wrong
To cherish thee, as I have done so long?
And must I turn from all that I have loved,
Or look upon it coldly and unmoved—
Feeling the desolation and the chill
Within—without—and yet concealing still!

I *must* forget thee, even although my heart
Breaks with the chains that it would rend apart,
I must forget thee still—aye, even forget
That hour—that hapless hour, when first we met !

I write not now as I have done before,
With one yet lingering hope to meet thee more.
No ! that wild dream is past—I buried all
Before my hand could trace this hurried scrawl.
Farewell—farewell—and never over thee,
May come the shadow that o'ershadows me.
A light is gone that nothing can restore,
The dream of day, the midnight watch is o'er !

IMPROMPTU ADDRESS TO CALUMNY.

O Calumny! thou cruel and poisonous snake,
That crawls from filthy swamp, or nettled brake—
O Calumny! upon whose hateful trail
The fruit falls rotted and the flowers grow pale—

None can escape thy snares—the meanest—least—
Who crawl life's thoroughfares—the holiest priest
Who prays within his cell—secure—alone—
Nor even a monarch on the proudest throne!

None can escape thee! not the noblest fame,
The humblest footsteps or the loftiest name.
And heads revered must meet thy dastard blow,
Nor brow escape that shall be pure as snow!

The mother, bending o'er her dying son,
The knight whose laurels had been hardly won,
The maiden and her lover—even the child
Thy foul and falsest slanders have defiled!

Who hath not known thee ? who, however pure,
From thy degrading shadow is secure ?
Who hath not been with noble anger stirred
When first thy vile and loathsome voice he heard ?

Insidious, crawling viper ! on thy track
There is no marching forwards, or yet back.
More wary than the fox and far more vile,
For Reynard bites, but Slander wears a smile !

Thou meanest worm ! who would compassion feel,
When placing on thy head his hardest heel ?
None than thyself more shameless words have spoken,
None than thyself more sinless hearts have broken.

There is no spot where Poverty is sure,
No hearth where truth and honour are secure—
No home where Calumny hath not its berth—
Heaven is exempt, but never man—or Earth !

POEMS BY THE "SAD SEA WAVES."

NEAR THE HOARSE WATERS OF THE DEEP.

Near the hoarse waters of the deep
There is a grey and crumbling stone,
Memorial of the solemn sleep
Of one who lived and died alone.
And when the moon is on the wave,
When idle strangers haunt it not,
A step is by that lonely grave,
A voice is in that silent spot!

I would not stranger hearts should know—
I would not stranger eyes should see,
The heavy agony of woe
That I, so long, have borne for thee.
So fondly though our hearts were knit
None ever read it on thy brow,
For thou hast lived, concealing it—
Then none shall ever know it now!

I heard from the Red Indian's land,
That thou wert life and love's no more—
I did not strike him with mine hand,
Who first that fatal tidings bore—

But listened—till the worst I heard,
Then turned away without a word,
Nor wept thee with a single tear,
Though thou hadst been so deeply dear !

Alas ! it is not words can tell
How heavily the heart may swell—
For there is a dark depth of woe
For which the tears can rarely flow.
And tears will sometimes fill the eye
And flow, and yet we scarce know why,
While grief may be too fixed and dark,
For sigh to speak, or sob to mark.

Why was I not beside thee, when
The throes of sickness shook thy frame—
Thou know'st I had no fear of men,
I loved thee not with love so tame.
I never feared but for thy sake
That they might look on and condemn,
And if my heart should ever break,
It will not break through dread of them !

Not, love—that, uselessly, thy name
Should ever lightly uttered be,
In tones of pity or of blame—
Although that blame were linked with me.

But oh ! in love so deep as ours,
Had I but watched thy life's decline,
I might have soothed its parting hours—
So grief, alone, had not been thine !

It may be anguish to have gazed
Upon the dark eyes of the loved,
To our own glance once fondly raised,
And now so vacant and unmoved—
But deeper anguish to have known
That they had suffered—died—*alone,*
And we had not beside them knelt,
To soothe the sorrow they had felt !

'Twas well to bury thee, beside
The quiet moaning of the tide—
To bury thee where all is bright
And beautiful, within our sight—
For wild flowers of the sea-beach grow
Around thy tomb, and knowing not
The wasted form concealed below,
Cluster in joy around the spot !

For thou wert lovely, and should be
Where loveliness around may dwell—
I would not they had buried thee
Within a cloister's vaulted cell,

With bones not kindred—it was meet
To bury thee where all is sweet,
And all around thy grave is rife
That thou most deeply loved in life!

Sleep calmly where thou art—I will
Watch on through life's long pilgrimage,
Thy last dear wishes to fulfil—
And none shall ever read the page
Of Life that thou didst from them hide,
So slumber on—for none shall chide—
The very stars will vigil keep
Above a form so kindred—Sleep!

For thou wert even as one of them
That in another sphere had birth,
Whose ray, though from so bright a gem,
Could pierce not the dark spots of earth.
And men looked up to thee with praise,
So constant was thy smile—because
Though tracing not their darker ways,
Thou wert no mocker of their laws!

But when thou fellest, as they fall,
Into the sullen depths below,
And darkness settled over all
That earth's dull eyes were wont to know—

And looking through the empty air,
Men saw that thou hadst left no trace
Of what thou wert when dwelling there,
They marked no longer that lost place !

Sleep !   I will watch beside thee, while
Mine eye may meet the moonbeam's smile.
Sleep !   I am near thee—till no more
Mine ear may catch the ocean's roar.
Then, though my grave be not with thine,
It will no hour of sorrow be
When that deep grief no more is mine—
To live a life unshared by thee !

M

THE FISHERMAN.

(Lines for music.)

Oh ! a lonely life the fisherman leads,
By the shores of the mighty ocean,
His music the sigh of its broken reeds,
Or the moan of its ceaseless motion.

He watches at eve the sun's red globe
Sink down in the glowing water,
Till the earth is veiled in the dusky robe
That the twilight hours have brought her !

Then he steers o'er the sea his fearless boat,
Though the shades of night are falling,
And he hears the sea-fowl's evening note
From the rock to the island calling.

Oh ! a lonely life the fisherman leads,
By the shores of the mighty ocean,
His music the sigh of its broken reeds,
Or the moan of its ceaseless motion.

Yet the Finland hunter dwells afar
In the North, without repining,
And blesses the light of each brilliant star,
On his frozen pathway shining !

The chase of the deer, or the grisly bear,
The long dark days beguiling,
Is dearer to him than a clime more fair,
Or a sun from a blue sky smiling.

And the Arab, who lives a life so free,
Where the desert sun is glowing,
Is happier there than he e'er could be,
Where our own cool winds are blowing.

So well may the fisherman love his cot,
Where the fire is brightly burning,
As he merrily seeks the cheery spot,
From his evening work returning.

Yet a lonely life the fisherman leads,
By the shores of the mighty ocean,
His music the sigh of its broken reeds,
Or the moan of its ceaseless motion.

ENGLAND'S DAUGHTER.

FRETTING the waves of the Atlantic sea,
Full many a weary day thy barque must be;
But one fond heart is with thee on the water—
Forget her not! thy country's lonely daughter!
>   Remember! when thy head
>   Thou layest on thy pillow,
>   When long the sunset's red
>   Hath faded on the billow,
>   That where thy footsteps used,
>   Hour after hour to stray,
>   And where thy heart hath mused,
>   At closing of the day,
>   One, mournfully may stand,
>   Watching each setting star
>   That seeks a southern land—
>   Weeping for those afar!

Fretting the waves of the Atlantic sea,
Full many a weary day thy barque must be;

But one fond heart is with thee on the water—
Forget her not! thy country's lonely daughter!

> The glorious Southern eye,
> Whose warmth is like the sky
> That lights a southern spot—
> Have England's daughters not!
> Their eyes are blue, and thou
> With darker ones may meet,
> With broader, nobler brow,
> With tones more rich and sweet.
> But never can there be
> A heart more fond and true,
> Than that which beats for thee
> Beyond the waters blue!

Fretting the waves of the Atlantic sea,
Full many a weary month thy barque must be;
But one fond heart is with thee on the water—
Forget her not! thy country's lonely daughter!

THE FISHERMAN'S BRIDE.

THE harvest moon is on the wane,
    The mist lies on the lea, love,
When will the hours return again
    That bring thee back to me, love?

The deer seek shelter in the glen,
The moorhen in the sedgy lake,
The wildfowl haunt the marshy fen,
The hare is hiding in the brake.
October flowers are fading fast,
The cold winds strip the yellow trees,
For autumn days are nearly passed—
Ah—never were they sad as these!
The skies, but now of richest blue,
Are changing to the winter's hue—
And midnight fogs will render vain
    The lamp I burn for thee, love.
When will the hours return again
    That bring thee back to me, love?

'Tis sad, *alone*, as evening wears,
To hear the waves dash on the shore,

Or watch, through hot and blinding tears,
The setting sunlight catch the oar !
Or listen, as the hours drag on,
The tolling of some distant bell
Across the waves, whose mellowed tone
Swells sadly as the waters swell.
'Tis sad to mark, day after day,
Without thy presence pass away—
Then after all its hours of pain
The close of night to see, love.
When will the hours return again
That bring thee home to me, love ?

O ! winter nights are long and dark,
Through which my vigil oft I keep,
To catch the first glimpse of thy barque,
When it shall bound across the deep !
Too oft the petrel's warning note,
The sea-gull, with yet wilder scream,
Forboding evil to thy boat,
Awake me from some mournful dream.
Alas ! mine is a troubled sleep,
And yet to waken is to weep,
Or listen to the stormy rain
That plashes on the sea, love.
When will the hours return again
That bring thee back to me, love ?

MURMURS BY THE "SAD SEA WAVES."

BY THE WHITE CLIFFS.

MURMURS BY THE "SAD SEA WAVES."

MURMUR I.

WHEN sunset glitters o'er the moaning waves,
Oft by the shore, in sad and sober moods
I muse, upon the thousand mournful graves,
Where Hope lies dead and Love in silence broods.

Silent I sit upon the lonely beach,
To hear the ocean sobbing on the shore.
O love ! O joy ! ye are beyond my reach—
Love is a dream—Ambition cheers no more.

O ! for an hour when the chill heart might rise
Above the drear thoughts of this common earth—
In vain—in vain ! sad Echo still replies,
Youth hath passed on—Love hath no second birth.

O ! for an hour when the young feet were swift
To tread the flower-bright plain—to climb the hill ;
Ah, Pity ! let thy sad-hued curtain lift,
And eyes look bright and hearts beat fondly still.

Too late ! despairing word—will nothing raise
The heavy pall that low and lower falls,
Bring back the glowing hopes of youth's bright days,
Dispel the gloom that more and more appals ?

Earth is forsaken—save in some fond dream
Youth comes with bounding step and song of joy—
Fancies that some dark hours will still redeem—
Hours of delight no Day-fiend can destroy !

Under the waters of the boundless sea
Gems for an unborn age may brightly shine,
Gems that *our* eyes will vainly seek to see—
Not for *thy* vision, brother ! nor for mine.

Life ! thou art dreary in some moods of mind,
Full of pale thoughts of hopelessness and grief,
Thy silver rusts, thy gold is unrefined,
Age brings no wisdom—care hath no relief.

The sea is silent and the sun hath set—
There is no answering brightness from the sky ;
The dying breezes sigh— *Youth will forget,*
As falls the leaf so Love and Hope must die.

MURMUR II.

O LIFE! O love! if aught should chance to sever
The links that bind our souls with ties so sweet,
Then would my fond heart cease to beat, for ever—
Cold as this granite whereon rest my feet.

O life! O love! if one should e'er depart,
Leaving the other by the moaning sea,
Death would reign, only, o'er the lonely heart,
The bond that binds us is—Eternity.

O life! O love! together we have trod
The paths of life, from earliest youthful years,
For ever more companions, sent by God,
Joy hath not severed us—nor yet shall tears!

O life! O love! whate'er shall yet betide
In this conflicting life we lead below,
Still ever keep ye faithful, side by side,
Through morning tempests to the sunset's glow!

O life ! O love ! together to the last !
Till the fair goal of Life in Heaven we reach—
Neither appalled by fury of the blast,
Nor by cruel rocks that strew the stony beach.

Murmur III.

"NO MORE—NO MORE!"

AGAIN she lingers by the darkening main,
Recalling sadly days of past delight—
Her eyes are wandering o'er the seas in vain,
No sail, no vessel glads her weary sight.

"No more—no more!" these words ring in her ears—
"Thy sighs are useless—stay those futile tears."
No more, no more—yet Hope will still believe,
In liege with Youth—with Pleasure—to deceive!
"No more!"—oh! dreary words! and scarcely Age
Can read, with eyes undimmed, Life's fatal page.

A ship goes forth—to meet its lonely fate—
No more she sees—the hour grows dark and late.
A skilful mariner may guide the helm,
Yet winds will rise, and billows overwhelm!

No more, no more! fair Spring can ne'er return,
Nor the tired heart with love and pleasure burn.

The green blades of the grass are dry and brown—
The pearly blossoms fade—the fruit falls down,
Dies ripened in the turf below our feet—
Ah! truth is bitter, only dreams are sweet!

No more, no more! it is the mermaid's song—
Gaily the light wave bears its notes along,
Until they rest in silence on the main—
Hope dies despairing—youth and love are vain.

BY THE WHITE CLIFFS.

O ! LITTLE hands and little feet !
I see them through the blinding tears—
O ! little voices—soft and sweet,
I hear them through the roll of years.
The tiny white and trembling hands,
That tell of sickness and of pain—
Filled with the treasures of the sands,
How memory brings them back again !

I see them wandering, side by side—
Those treasured loves of early days—
They come again at eventide,
With all their pretty childish ways—
And sweet it is, awhile, to dwell
Apart from life's too busy hum,
Wrapt in the sad and tender spell
Of sorrows past—of joys to come.

Thou pine-girt place—how calm thou art !
The moon that shimmers through thy trees,

Seems of thy woods a very part,
When parted by the wild sea breeze.
Not even the boatman's carol rude
Thy sleeping echoes bear along—
Thou art the very solitude
For lovers' sighs and poet's song.

White cliffs that breast the ocean wave,
Fringed with dark shades of birch and pine—
Bright stars that light the pirates' cave,
And through their gloomy branches shine—
Flag of the yacht, or idler's sail,
That gently flaps the dying gale—
Across the darkness ye return,
Like visions—mournful but not stern!

Away! for busy life is near,
Whose constant murmur thrills mine ear;
It is the world—the world of strife—
It is the voice of eager life.
Give not to grief, to vain regret,
The moments that are granted yet;
There still is work that may be done,
There still are victories to be won!

Bournemouth, September, 1880.

A FEW SONGS OF LIGHTER HOURS.

THE SPITEFUL BEE.

(A supposed Fable of Gay's.)

A BEE one day, in bitter mood,
Resolved to fight the whole bee brood !
No sooner said than done, she flew
At once amidst the busy crew.
And in a moment stung them all,
The Queen, the drone—the big, the small.
And, happy, as she cleans her wings,
Of Troy and "joys of war" she sings.
Then proudly, later in the day,
"Saul might his boasted thousands slay,
But I with millions line the floor,
Piled up in heaps that block the door !

" Where is the She so brave as I ?
A She, who half so fiercely stings

The weak, the old that cannot fly,
The rash, or ' feeble, silly' things !
Lay up their food for rainy days !
I hate such hypocritic ways !
'Tis greed, wise mankind thinks with me
And scorns, at heart, the busy bee.
He brightens the sad ways of life,
But *I* would have things full of strife,
I love to hear the sharp reproaches,
The cries ! at bites of vile cockroaches.
Ye tears !   I love to see ye flow—
Joy I detest—*I* feed on woe.
So merrily around I fly,
To see the feeble droop and die !"

October, 1880.

THE WAY WE LIVE NOW.

WITH APOLOGIES TO MR. TROLLOPE.

(Supposed to be contributed by one Hodges,
Hertfordshire boörn!)

"A duke will ride in a second-class carriage, and a duchess come
down to breakfast in a linsey gown."—*Proclamation of a modern novelist.*

"I HITS Stodges maäny hard blows,
For un desarves um, that I knows—
But if Stodges hits back agin,
I sez, sez I, 'tis a shaäme and a zin !
    For that Missus Raikes, *she* sez ut, you know,
    And it mun be true, mon, if *she* sez zo !

"For who bees Stodges ?—a *hig*norant vool,
He doänt goo to charch and he doänt goo to school,
He aint got no larning, nor courage nuther,
And t' missus more hignorant nor the t'other !
    For that Missus Raikes, *she* sez it, you know,
    And it mun be true, mon, if *she* sez zo !

"For Stodges—he b'longs t' the good old times,
When folly and hignorance wurnt no crimes—
He doänt write no letters and t' books never reads,
But he drives t' oold plough and he zoes t' tare zeeds.
　　For that Missus Raikes, *she* sez ut, you know,
　　And it mun be true, mon, if *she* sez zo.

"The hoäme that he's gotten he caänt maäntain,
And his wifen's rare zilly, voolish and vain ;
He caänt e'en gie un a round good blow—
She thinks it rare clevvur nothun to know.
　　For that Missus Raikes, *she* sez ut, you know,
　　And it mun be true, mon, if *she* sez zo !

"And his chillun wull grow up all the zaäme,
Folly and zilliness *their* pooty gaäme—
What not to dew, mon, and what not to zay,
'Tis all that they duz, mon, the whole, live day !
　　For that Missus Raikes, *she* sez ut, you know,
　　And it mun be true, mon, if *she* sez zo !

"Noa ! they dunno what in t' warld to doo—
Nar they dunno where in t' warld to goo—
And they zits or they strööls, droo th' vields all day,
Sometoimes o' this un—then that un way !
　　For that Missus Raikes, *she* sez ut, you know,
　　And it mun be true, mon, if *she* sez zo !

" When *they've* gotten money, oh ! doänt they dress vine ?
Nuthin' to remind un o' pigsties and swine—
And in grand old halls goo merrily around,
All to pianny or to viddles' merry zound.
      For that Missus Raikes, *she* sez ut, you know,
      And it mun be true, mon, if *she* sez zo.

" And doänt they live also on nice food nuther ?
Venison and jellies—one a patch on t' other—
There's nuthin' too vine for their stomachs, I'm thinking,
And nuthin' too prime for their throats for drinking.
      For that Missus Raikes, *she* sez ut, you know,
      And it mun be true, mon, if *she* sez zo.

" And when un's in town, too, 'tis rare good vun
To loäke at the shops and the things in un,
And buy the vine dresses, mon, that you zees there,
'Tis better, least, than going, mon, *you* knows where !
      For that Missus Raikes, *she* sez ut, you know,
      And it mun be true, mon, if *she* sez zo.

" And even in travellun', if the zeats be haärd,
There's the last penny nooz, or the last c'rect caärd—
And if um's squeezg'd close, why, it doänt much matter,
For um all wears ' linsey,' and it caänt get flatter !
      For that Missus Raikes, *she* sez ut, you know,
      And it mun be true, mon, if *she* sez zo.

"For this is what duchesses wear, I'm told,
So it caänt hurt in crushing, if I may maäke bold—
And they ought'n much t' care, for it ain't much cost,
And it doänt much show, when its crumpled and crossed.
　　For that Missus Raikes, *she* sez ut, you know,
　　And it mun be true, mon, if *she* sez zo.

"Since our missus' grey dresses are all made t' hum,
There ain't no bills vor at Christmas to cum,
There woänt be no ribbons or fal-lals to pay for,
And there woänt be no hoops, hurrah, to make way for.
　　For that Missus Raikes, *she* sez ut, you know,
　　Zo it mun be true, mon, if she sez zo!"

"'Tis a werry good töime for the pigs and the asses,'
'Tis a rare good toime for the crowds and the masses,
With not no linsey gowns, but all velvet and silk uns,
O! a rare good toime for the reel Charley Dylke uns!
　　For that Missus Raikes, *she* sez ut, you know,
　　And it mun be true, mon, if *she* sez zo!

"For zum they be fat uns and zum they be thin,
And zum they sticks out and zum they caves in;
Zum looks loike our baäcon and zum poplar trees,
And they doänt care for purtyness, that I zees!
　　For that Missus Raikes, *she* sez ut, you know,
　　And it mun be true, mon, if *she* sez zo!

" Duz *hurn* ride in zecond class, or third class mebbe,
And thinks that's the way she proves she's a ledde—
And calls for a barrer that drives un on ends,
When she goos down to —— sheer to zee t' oold friends!
    For that Missus Raikes, *she* sez ut, you know,
    And it mun be true, mon, if *she* sez zo !

" Dew they *arl* go bumping in they second classes—
These vine young loärds and their vine young lasses ?
Duz they wear no zatin and other vine dodges ?
Then—*if that be their vineness—why—I'd rayther be*
    Hodges !"

MOAN OF THE DISCONTENTED!

MIDNIGHT'S veil o'er earth is spreading,
All is wrapt in gloom and shade,
Faint the light the moon is shedding,
Cold the wind in wood and glade.
But than midnight darker still,
The shadow on my spirit cast—
More biting than the north wind's chill,
Is disappointment's withering blast.

O trifler! when thy step is bounding
O'er some grave's deserted flowers,
Or, rather, when thy harp is sounding
Notes of woe in sorrow's hours—
Think of him whose heart is broken,
Dweller in a living tomb,
O'er whom the words of doom are spoken,
Hopes destroying ere they bloom!

Every one that I have cherished
From my dreary heart is banished,
All within of joy hath perished,
All without of light hath vanished !
Feelings wounded—feelings blighted,
Never from some trouble free,
'Mid the gloom of woe benighted
What on earth is left for me !

O ! it was Youth's fairy fingers
Wove the fatal spells that bound me,
He alone could bid them linger,
Evermore in brightness round me.
But the words of Fate were spoken,
All of joy I deemed my own,
Faded—wasted, or was broken—
Happiness for ever flown !

Chide me not—if, broken-hearted
Scared by Sorrow's heavy blow,
Scenes of joy—of hopes departed,
Haunt me still where'er I go !
O— O— O— O——
  *   *   *   *

[NOTE.—He was discontented even with his own complaint, by this
time, and so broke off abruptly.]

A YOUNG GIRL AMONG THE CHESTNUT TREES.

[This was, in fact, but one tree, of which twin stems, when about a foot from the ground, divided into four magnificent ones, each a tree in itself. It grew in the grounds adjoining the old manor-house of S—— Bury. And a wooden house was built in the tree.]

I DO remember well a wooden house,
Built 'mid the four stems of twin chestnut trees,
A mansion fit for the domestic mouse,
But scarcely made for giant, if you please!

There would I sit and ponder, if this world
Would prove as happy as I deemed it then—
While dew fell softly on the green leaves curled,
And rabbits sported in the moonlit glen.

There would I wonder if my love would come
To fetch me, from some lovely, sunlit land,
And bear me, smiling, to some happy home,
Heart pressed to heart and fond hand clasping hand.

No human clatter there disturbed my rest,
Only the titmouse, tapping on the bark,
Only the wood-dove, cooing on its nest—
Only the starlight, gleaming through the dark !

One foot on topmost bough and one below—
Like a descent from Paradise to Hades—
A nice descent for little boys we know,
But scarce so nice for timid girls or ladies !

But ah ! how sweet it was to rock about,
And hear the pattering of the summer rain,
The wild birds singing and the cowherds' shout,
And know all search for me would be in vain !

To hide in covert, like the timid roe,
Nor stir abroad until the red sunset,
These are the pleasures of long, long ago,
Remembered still with something of—regret !

IMPROMPTU LINES ON "MY UNCLE."

I HAD an uncle in former days,
A gentleman known for eccentric ways;
A grey, old banker and one, it seems,
With all the money that "banking" means.
But he lived in an unpretending street,
In a shabby house, for extremes *will* meet,
With a shabby carriage, and servants as bad,
All called him *stingy*, but no one—*mad !*

I dined with him once and I thought to eat
A dinner of soup, of fish and meat,
Some pudding to follow; perhaps, beside,
Some fruit from a garden that seemed his pride,
So full of cherries and green, young peas !
Alas for me ! we had none of these.
But you'll not believe it, you hardly can,
Unless you had known the sort of man—
The miserly rich ! His dinner was not
Of fish, flesh, or fowl ; not even hot,

But only a joint of fat, salt pig—
'Twas a *cheek*, I think, it was rather big
For only two—as for pudding or spice,
Or custard—ah me, there was nothing so nice !

" Mine uncle " quitted the world one day,
One winter's morn, in the oddest way.
His men were cleaning a muddy pond,
Once used for fish, in the field beyond ;
And the work was hard, or the men were idle,
And he, who could never his temper bridle,
At once declared, with an angry shout,
They didn't know what they were about,
And *he* would show them the way to do it ;
And so he did, but he lived to rue it,
Or rather *died*—from the lesson taught,
So fatal the chill that the teacher caught !
He left me money—not much—in his will,
I thanked him then and I thank him still !
I knew that money had oft its abuse,
So I put out mine to a right good use,
That brought me pleasure and profit as well,
But that's a secret I need not tell !

———————

THE SPURIOUS CRITICS.

(A second supposed Fable of Gay's.)

GOOD SIRS, when next you vent your spite
See your sarcasm is more bright !
Go home, and polish up your wit,
It needs some polish, all admit.
Your words have not the accents even
Of truth, that first, pure gift of Heaven.
You spoil even what you think you're praising,
Sure " Oireland " boasted your " upraising,"
Or backwoods in the " Coloneese "
But scarce old England, if you please !
We scorn the meagreness, the air
Of want of candour we see there,
Perchance ye bless some other shore,
And England boasts your race no more.

   O critics of a day gone by,
Of searching wit, of fearless eye,
Ghosts of Macaulay, Croker, Hume,
To wear your cloak some still assume,

But are as like the ancient clan
As Apes, who dare assume the Man !
'Tis but a passing phase, we trust,
Cowards there may be—will be—*must !*
Bright are the critic-rays, but rare,
And pass like meteors through the air.
And those that oft assume the place
Are poor pretenders in the race,
Are such a " mockery of the letter "
The sooner they are gone the better.
Not from a sculptor's hand are they,
Or formed of but his coarser clay.
'Tis true that when their rays are fine,
Few meteors more admired can shine,
But when but feeble beams they cast,
Sickly, pretentious of the past,
They are but shadows, at the best,
They are a mockery and a pest.

　　O critics of a nobler school,
Whose words could fire, whose pens could rule,
Whose ink was bright, whose strokes were keen,
Where have your wandering footsteps been !
In other histories are ye named,
Have other lands your service claimed ?
" Come back to Erin " was a cry
We all remember, years gone by—
Come back to *England,* critics dear,

Be sure a home awaits you here !
Where honest hands and glances sweet
Will ever honest service greet,
And welcome back to vacant places,
One of the " Literary Graces "—
The critics—that we knew of yore,
Bold, witty, fearless, brave—once more !

October, 1880.

HAPPY THOUGHTS;

" I BELIEVE what they have told me," said a caterpillar
    once,
And some few who heard the saying thought the insect
    was a dunce.
But there's many like that caterpillar, certainly I fear,
Who believe whatever's told them—credit everything
    they hear.

"O! it *must* be true "—they say, with gaping mouth and
    starting eyes,
"I am sure that 'So-and-so' would never tell me such
    bare lies—
I often thought it might be, for I always saw about her
A *something* I can *hardly say*, that could but make me
    doubt her.

"O yes! it must be true I'm sure, for I remember now
We met her once at Smithson's, when she scarce returned
    my bow—

She always was so stuck up and seemed scarce to care to
    know us,
But truly she shall pay for the contempt she seemed to
    show us.

"O yes! she gave herself such airs, her family was old,
And 'came before' the Conqueror, at least so we were
    told—
And never had their money from a business or a trade,
As if it mattered, so we got it, *how* the tin was made!

"O yes! she was so stuck up—said *good breeding* was
    the thing,
And did not care for wealth, or what proud grandeur it
    might bring,
She did not care for 'Sunday dress,' for which we
    snubbed her often,
And nothing her dislike to our 'gentility' could soften.

"For she came of a good old stock—she loved it more
    than money,
And more than dress or finery, which seemed to us so
    funny—
Was prouder of her family than even we of show,
And if there is a stupid thing that is the thing—I know!

"O! it is so ridiculous—that gentle, high-bred air,
'Tis everything what *we* are—nothing what our fathers
were—
But we who make the money can afford to treat with
scorn
The airs of all *such* people—the well-bred and the well-
born!"

October, 1880.

PADDY'S INVITATION.

*(Impromptu lines on suddenly hearing that Mr. ——
was going on a visit to Ireland.)*

Oh! Johnny, brave Johnny, ould England's own Johnny,
Come to the land that is peaty and bonny;
Come to the scenes that yer thoughts most deloight in,
Your heart all for pace and your hand fit for foightin'.
O! come o'er the wathers to Erin's green isle,
To a sodger's warm welcome, a purty girl's smile!

Give up the Sassenach's wicked ould schule,
We'll tatche you, sorr, how to conquer or rule;
We'll tatche you better nor they would have taught us,
We'll buy your favour as they would have bought us.
O! come o'er the wathers to Erin's green isle,
To a sodger's warm welcome, a purty girl's smile!

We'll tatche you Wisdom, Sobriety, Pace;
Till all the warrs in this wild woorld shall sace;

Till England's ould sheep wid our lion lies down,
And Paddy is crowned wid a conqueror's crown!
O! come o'er the wathers to Erin's green isle,
To a sodger's warm welcome, a purty girl's smile!

Och! come o'er the wathers thin, Johnny, me boy,
We'll welcome ye gladly, we'll meet ye wid joy;
We'll beat thim ould Southrons—O! *we'll* show ye how—
And if ye're no sodger we'll tatche it ye, now!
So come o'er the wathers to Erin's green isle,
To a sodger's warm welcome, a purty girl's smile!

1879.

FRAGMENTS OF AN OLD LEGEND.

FRAGMENTS OF AN OLD LEGEND.

INTRODUCTION.

FAR from the glowing clime of Italy,
Placed in the colder regions of the West,
There is an isle, in the Atlantic Sea—
The eagle builds upon its mountain crest—
The wild fowls breed upon its marshy moor—
Its reedy plains, that knew not life before.
Yet hath it, mixed with these, bright, peaceful dells—
Woods for the birds and bees and flower-bells,
Too beautiful to paint when summer's smile
Gilds with its gladdening beam that western isle!

Sweet Innisfallen! in thy ruder clime,
Although the colours of thy changeful sky,
Even in the brightest hours of summer-time
Know not, or rarely, Italy's deep dye—
Though thou hast not the rich, the gorgeous flowers,
That scent the south wind in Italia's bowers,
Nor the sweet melody that floats o'er all

In her voluptuous clime, at evenfall—
Yet, poetry is in the echoing roar
Of thy wild waves, known to no other shore.
Even in this distant age a spell is flung
O'er the weird plains where OSSIAN lays were sung !
And on the marshy waste and heathy hill,
The poet's spirit seems to linger still,
To call up phantoms in the midnight storms—
That shroud, in driving mist, their ghastly forms—
Pale shadows of the long-forgotten slain,
Haunting the rude mounds of some battle-plain,
That come, when evening's light is growing pale,
To pour o'er the unhonoured dead, their wail.

Canto I.

Long since—washed by old ocean's tides—
Bounded by rocks on other sides,
And visited by summer rains,
Stretched one of those wild battle-plains
O'er whose bleak wastes a spell is cast,
By weird old legends of the past !
The tangled briar-bush overran
The mouldering bones of fallen man—
And stones and rocks werc roughly piled
In cairns, o'ergrown with mosses green,
Yet, when the sunlight o'er it smiled,
Though rude, it was no dreary scene !
The wildfowl, nestling half concealed
By rushes—grass, and brushwood low,
Came out to feel the sun's warm glow,
The wilder sea-birds o'er them wheeled—
The petrel—with its wings of white,
That glanced and quivered in the light ;
And each sweet blossom that had found
A shelter on the marshy ground,
Lifted to heaven its slender head,
As if to bless the light it shed !

Built firmly on a craggy rock,
The centre of that wide extent,
Stood the old tower of Ballynock,
As though it were some monument
Raised by the spectres of the slain,
To guard each now neglected mound ;
For, monarch of that lonely plain,
High o'er the swampy flat it frowned—
And from its height, might be descried
The towers of Hugh O'Neil, that stood,
In all their old ancestral pride,
On noble rock—mid shaggy wood.
While opposite, far in the west,
There was the sweetest village nest,
Beyond which hills stretched far away,
Pine-girt or heathy, green or grey,
Till, fading from the gazer's eye,
Their outline mingled with the sky.

It was o'erlooking this wild scene,
At close of one of those bright days
When all looks peaceful, calm and green—
A maiden sat, whose pensive gaze,
From Ballynock's old casement, grey
With time, had watched the sunset pass,
Until the tints of evening lay
On mossy stone and bending grass.
A smile was lighting her blue eyes

And parted lips, that otherwise
Seemed, like those deep orbs, to express
Even in that face, so soft and fair,
That look of painful earnestness,
That tells the tale of youthful care !

    An orphan at an early age,
Hers were not childhood's happy years ;
And Morna soon had stained the page
Of life, with many bitter tears.
Graceful in form as fair in face,
Though daughter of no noble race,
There was that charm in her bright eyes,
Tearful and blue as her own skies—
That even made, by Morna's side,
High-born O'Neil forget his pride !
He would have given his haughty name
Fair Morna's snowy hand to claim !
And Hugh was young—of handsome mien,
With eyes that, beautiful and keen,
Revealed no lukewarm soul within—
Yet Morna's hand was hard to win—
Her heart had long been given to one
Who only by his love had won !
For his estates were barren plains,
That bounded Hugh O'Neil's domains—
His home was on a lonely rock—
His castle halls—rude Ballynock !

But Morna's soul was full of love
For all of beautiful on earth ;
The changeful sky that bent above—
The flowers that owed to it their birth !
And Morna, from a very child,
Had loved to hear the legends wild
Of Ballynock's rude plains—to tread
Upon the soil where heroes bled !
She learned to know each mossy stone,
Each broken rock with grass o'ergrown,
Each lakelet, where the wildfowl bred,
And wheeled with screams, above her head—
To hear the moaning of the waves,
Washing the fabled Sea-Kings' caves ;
And, wandering by the wild seashore
With Edgar, Morna asked no more !
Until, on one bright summer day,
A year had rolled its course away,
And war came,—and the youthful chief
With Hugh O'Neil to battle went,
And Morna's hours in lonely grief,
And prayers for his return were spent.
Alas ! he came not back again,
She watched and wept for him in vain ;
O'Neil returned alone, to tell
How in the battle Edgar fell.

Two years had passed since then, and though

Time softens e'en the keenest woe,
Yet Morna's was a loving heart,
And often still the tears would start
When some sweet sound—some sunny eve
Recalled the lost and loved to mind;
Although not idly did she grieve,
But gentle, pensive and resigned.
She shrank from melody and mirth,
And in the humbler homes of earth
Felt happy, when her hand could ease
The pangs of suffering and disease.
And other causes brought the smile
To Morna's careworn cheek awhile—
Though of the one beloved bereft,
Morna had still a brother left,
To watch for whose return she sat
And looked out from her casement grey,
Though hooting owl and flitting bat
Reminded her of parting day.

Dermid had been a fearless boy,
And legends of the wildest kind
Would make his young brow glow with joy,
And echo in his daring mind.
His eye would flash with generous fire,
To hear of deeds of noble worth,
He had besides, a wild desire
To visit stranger scenes of earth—

With free and joyous eyes to gaze
On foreign woods and rocks and bays!
But o'er that bold heart was, withal,
That glow of warm, romantic feeling,
That loves to watch, at evenfall,
The sober shades of autumn, stealing
O'er quiet plain and beech-wood dingle, .
The star of evening, wan and single,
Steal out through sunset's lurid gold,
And sadly light the plain and wold.
The moon that shone through broken clouds,
The fogs of even, as they drove
Like phantoms, in their ghastly shrouds,
O'er the dark vales would Dermid love!
And lingering like some pensive lover,
Upon the sands of the seashore,
He watched the sea-birds o'er him hover,
Or listened to the surges' roar.
Yet, checking the strong wish to be,
Where the green waves of that fierce sea
Upon some stranger shore might curl,
He lingered still by Morna's side,
And ne'er had quitted that fair girl,
Till, happy as young Edgar's bride
He bade her farewell in her home—
And went through newer scenes to roam.
*　　　　*　　　　*　　　*†
The night came on—one brilliant star

† A passage is here lost—evidently referring to Dermid's return.

Gleamed on the ancient field of war,
The mountain mists arose—but ere
The moonbeams quivered o'er the mere,
The watched-for came ! and as she heard
The accent kind—the first fond word
That she had heard from him for years,
Fair Morna's dark eyes filled with tears.

" And will you dwell for ever here
And never leave me, Dermid dear—
And shall we watch again together
The foaming sea in stormy weather—
And gather sea-shells or field flowers,
As we have done in earlier hours ? "

" Dear Morna, yes ! I have returned
From those wild scenes for which I yearned—
My heart is weary and oppressed,
I long for peace, dear, and for rest.
I wearied of the gorgeous dyes
Of foreign scenes—of foreign skies ;
There's rest in this wild solitude,
Where sounds are not, or sweet or rude—
Where e'en the sad forget to sigh,
'Tis here that I would live—and die ! "

Ere from his native land he roved
Dermid by many chiefs was loved,
For courteous manners—kindly heart—
And so from many a distant part

They came, to welcome back once more,
The wanderer to his own loved shore.
Even he, the haughty Hugh O'Neil,
Judged best his hatred to conceal,
Though Dermid had been Edgar's friend—
And this, he deemed had chiefly led
Fair Morna that young chief to wed.
'Twas hard that scornful heart to bend,
'Twas harder even to disguise
The hatred gleaming in his eyes!
But Morna still was loved, although
Her cheek had lost its first fresh glow,
And now was somewhat lined and faded,
How much of beauty still was there;
And by their pensive lashes shaded
How lovely still her dark eyes were!
And she grew lovelier, as the smile
That suited her fair face so well,
Returned again, to throw awhile
O'er all, its loving, tender spell.
Alas! it was a transient light,
A sunbeam quenched in stormy night!
But little then poor Morna knew
The heavy cloud of grief, that threw
Such shadows o'er her life's young scene,
With only transient light between,
Ere long, on her devoted path,
Would pour its last and darkest wrath!

Two miles from Ballynock and in
O'Neil's dominions was a cave,
And those who passed it heard the din,
And echo of the hidden wave.
Though near upon the water's verge,
The constant breaking of the surge
Defended all approaches, save
From those that dared that surge to brave.
Here sometimes met a reckless crew,
From what wild shore they came none knew!
They met by night and often laid
Their lawless hands upon the flocks
Of some poor villagers, that strayed,
At nightfall, o'er the neighbouring rocks.
And wild the revelry—'twas said,
Within that cave was sometimes heard—
The villagers, whose very bread
Depended each upon his herd
Of goats, complained to Hugh O'Neil—
Who promised, with apparent zeal,
To seize or to disperse the foe.
But strange to say none seemed to know
When danger threatened their domain—
The foe still managed to elude
Their search, yet still returned again
From some unheard-of solitude!
This led the villagers to say
Strange things of Hugh O'Neil himself—

Why lived he in a style so gay,
Whence came his grandeur and his wealth ?
Though high the race from whence he came,
He owed them little but the name !

But Dermid, ever bold of hand,
·Resolved to seize the robber band,
Ere he for many months had been
Inhabitant of this wild scene.
He manned his boats one stormy night,
Just as the pale and crescent moon
Withdrew from heaven her pallid light—
But Dermid's followers came too soon
To storm the lion in his lair—
Three only of the band were there.
These ruffians soon they safely bound,
But for their comrades watched in vain—
'Tis certain they were never found
Within that cavern-haunt again.
What chance detained them they heard not—
'Twas doubtless, in some safer spot
An oath of fierce revenge they swore,
Much for their comrades' fate, but more
For the rich booty they had lost—
The robes of silk—the gems of cost,
Which Dermid's band had dared to seize—
Wrongs vengeance only could appease !

It had been one of those hot days
When earth seems withered, by the rays
Of sunlight, and the flowers most sweet
Grow scentless in the burning heat.
The sky, till noontide, had been clear,
But, as the evening hours drew near,
Black, lowering clouds began to meet—
Like warriors gathering, seemed to greet—
Behind the mountains of the west,
Just ere the sun had sunk to rest,
And from behind the broken pile
Of mists, gave out his parting smile ;
Till craggy stone and rock and steep
That bordered here the moaning deep
Blushed gently and then fiery red—
And o'er the waves its glory shed—
Till, slowly, with one parting look,
It faded from the dazzled eye—
Leaving the scenes that it forsook,
The lightning, radiance to supply !
Now showing forms of rugged rocks—
Defining their majestic blocks—
Then passing—glancing down below,
It bathed the plains in softer glow.
Lastly, it quivered o'er the wave,
Where grey-stone rock and marble reef,
Gleamed in the vivid light it gave,
So beautiful and yet so brief !

The evening had been strangely warm,
Long after that red sun had set—
And watching the slow-gathering storm,
Dermid and Morna lingered yet.
Both silently, as if it brought
Some train of melancholy thought
To mind—some scenes of former years—
And Morna's dark eyes filled with tears.

"Brother!" at last she softly said,
"Time, these last years has sadly sped!
Though not upon my brow alone,
The veil of sorrow has been thrown!
I well remember when we parted—
'Twas near these wild rocks of the sea,
And thou wert merry and light-hearted
As though Life held no griefs for thee!
But where is that bright spirit now,
The roving thoughts that none could tame?
So altered is that daring brow
I scarcely know it for the same.
Nay, tell me not that illness traced
Those circles, ne'er to be effaced—
Some deeper grief thy heart oppressed,
To make it languish thus for rest.
I cannot look upon thy face,
Nor see each sad, indented trace,
That tells a tale of bitter strife,
Instead of warm and joyous life!

There was a time when o'er thy heart
Could come no shade of grief and woe
But I, dear Dermid, there had part—
O! would that it might still be so!"

  "Dear sister, ask not that of me—
I could not even speak to thee
Of her that I have loved and lost,
And all the anguish that it cost.
Forget, dear, that my cheek is pale—
'Twould madden me to tell—*that* tale!"

  "Forgive me, it was cruel to ask
Thy lips then, to perform such task."
And Morna's dark and wistful eyes
Turned sadly to the sombre skies.
A few stars glimmered in the east,
And, as the thunder-clouds unfurled,
Seemed struggling through their piles, at least
To throw some light upon the world!
Then as she gazed a meteor's gleam
Like lightning, lit a distant chain
Of hills—a momentary gleam—
Then left all dim and chill again!
The eyrie stillness of the eve—
Those storm-clouds with their threatening form,
Warned Morna to retire and leave
The dark earth to the coming storm!

Canto II.

Night closed o'er Ballynock's old castle grey,
The fury of the storm had passed away—
Through sullen clouds the moon serenely rode,
Gleaming one moment like a spectre through
The grey stone casements of that stern abode—
Then suddenly her ghastly light withdrew !
The muttering of the thunder, low and hoarse,
Still marked the tempest's slow, receding course.

Though past her usual hour of rest
Fair Morna's couch was still unpressed.
'Twas not to watch the lightning's flash
Grow paler, or to mark the sound
Of billows, as they strove to dash
In anger, o'er their rocky bounds.—
She neither saw that grim midnight
Was gathering o'er her silent halls,
Nor that her lamp's expiring light
Was flickering o'er the tap'stried walls.
A sudden light that from afar
Gleamed through the darkness, like a star
That startles at the gloomy sky,

Just then caught Morna's tearful eye,
Who paused to wonder what sad wight
Was wandering out that stormy night—
And then returned to her sad train
Of melancholy thought again.
How long she sat she never knew—
Her lamp, low in the socket, threw
A ghastly light around, that came
By starts from its expiring flame,
When suddenly, distinct and clear,
A fearful cry struck on her ear!
Then came a pause—it seemed so long,
So frightfully—so strangely still!
The heart that first beat—wild and strong
Grew pulseless suddenly—and chill.
Her brain seemed darkened and then reeled,
Her blood felt icy and congealed—
One answering shriek—and o'er her sight
Had crept the shades of darkest night!

  'Twas well that consciousness had ceased—
Some hours of bitterness at least
Was spared that gentle, tender heart.
Meanwhile her household, with a start,
Had gathered in the hall, to share
Their master's danger—but they were
Unarmed, unable to withstand
The pirates' wild and reckless band.

Yet came a struggle—fierce but short—
Resistance but too dearly bought!

And woe befell all household gems !
Though there were no proud diadems
For queenly brows—no ingots rare—
Or diamond stars for raven hair,
No bands of gold to bind the tress,
Or deck the brow, to which was lent
Too much of nature's loveliness
To need aught other ornament—
Yet those she had, to her were worth
Far more than richer spoils of earth—
Her father's portrait—set in gold,
Though only simply, plainly set—
Her mother's crucifix—these told,
To one who loved not to forget—
Though environed by storm and strife—
The sweetest lessons of her life.
And there was more than one rich pearl,
Her lover's hand had placed above
Her snowy brow—when, yet a girl
She blushed at the first gifts of love !
These and some other gems, her care
Had treasured in a chamber lone,
The far, blue hills were seen from there,
And Morna called that room her own.
'Twas in the west wing of the hall,

That looked out on a western sky,
The sun lit up its tap'stried wall,
Before it faded from the eye !
And gentle Morna loved to sit
In summer evenings—watching it,
With Memory's fond and tender look,
To mark the shades, as they declined—
Where every little gem, or book,
Recalled her lover to her mind.
Here came the pirates—to whose eyes
Seemed much of priceless booty there—
And more than one rich, costly prize
Soon glittered in their torches' glare.
For Edgar, when he brought his bride
His lonely home to bless and share
Had decked it, with a lover's pride,
With much both beautiful and rare.
Vases of snowy marble, rich
With carving, from their stands were taken,
And yet more priceless ones, from which
Some wild, field flowers were rudely shaken,
That Morna had, the day before,
Found in some rich spot of the moor.
Here paused they—for they feared from none
Discovery, till their work was done.

　Mixed with their torches' fiery flame,
A ray of yellow moonlight broke

The veil of threatening clouds, and came
Through Gothic frames of ancient oak.
It shone not thus, on other nights,
On ruffian forms and glaring lights.
That moon, so silvery and cold,
Threw, then, the casement-shadows o'er
The tap'stry's weird and heavy fold,
Or on the inlaid, plaquered floor,
Now, as if sickened, it withdrew
Its pure and peaceful light once more,
Behind a cloud of blackest hue,
And night grew gloomy as before.
But first, upon the waters dark
It glanced, and lit the pirates' barque,
Then seemed to strive, with trembling beam,
Into a lonely room to gleam—
As one, who there, in darkness lay
In silence bled his life away!

Some time had passed—when, favoured by
The murky shadows of the sky,
From Ballynock's old postern gate
Two figures stole, with quickening pace—
They seemed to bear some precious weight,
And fear discovery or chase !
So hurriedly their footsteps traced
The rugged pathways of the waste—
Till they had reached the smooth sea-sand—

Far from the pirate vessel's stand.
There, in a little creek or bay,
A shallow boat at anchor lay—
This they unmoored, in trembling haste,
Their burden in it gently placed—
Sprang in and pushed it from the shore—
Then, while one swiftly plied the oar,
The other—who, by one long tress
Escaped in haste or carelessness
Beneath a shadowy hat and large,
Seemed of the gentler sex,—unwound
A mantle, her mysterious charge
That wrapt securely—closely round,
And damp as though with Death's cold dew,
Disclosed young Dermid's brow to view!
Then, with a firm and skilful touch,
She bound the wounds, that now had bled
So long, neglectedly and much—
A little more, and life had fled!
While a third figure that, till now,
Sat silent at the vessel's prow,
In mumbling tones began to tell
Her beads, or breathe some weighty spell!

It needed all that watcher's care—
So little now of life was there,
To bring it to that brow again!
Her efforts long could only gain

Some faint and interrupted sighs,
A quivering opening of the eyes,
That seemed already dim and glazed—
And once the arm was feebly raised
That hung down wounded by the side—
Yet still unceasingly she tried,
Though once she glanced, when passing by,
At Hugh O'Neil's dark towers, round which,
Half hidden in obscurity,
And bordered with the beech-wood rich—
Many a green romantic steep
Rose boldly, from fair Erin's deep!
Then looked back anxiously, but all
Was dark in Ballynock's grim wall,
For even the pirates' torches bright,
Lit not the darkness of the night.

Music was heard and wine was poured
That night at Hugh O'Neil's proud board—
His lofty halls rang back again
With laughter and with minstrel's strain.
And jewels flashed in raven hair,
For young and graceful forms were there.
Yet still the chief looked sadly on,
With brow and lips, stern-set and wan—
Though sometimes he would join the jest,
With hollow laugh, or sudden start—
While yet that brow and lip compressed,
Showed sterner thoughts were in his heart.

The night has passed—the banquet o'er,
The sound of wassail heard no more—
The hall was chill—deserted—bare—
Yet Hugh O'Neil still lingered there !
And on his forehead—cold and damp
Gleamed the dull light of one pale lamp.

" Thou'rt surely ill," a soft voice said
And broke the silence, almost dread,
That in dim space now held its reign—
And roused the chieftain from his train
Of moody thought—" thou'rt surely ill—
Thy brow, my son, is strangely chill !
Why didst thou, in the festive throng,
Join neither in the jest nor song,
But turn from minstrel's merry lay—
Thou ! once the gayest of the gay !
Nay ! smile not thus—too well I know
The smile of mirth from that of woe.
Alas ! that very smile betrays
It is no trifling cause that weighs
So heavily upon thy mind. . . . "
Thus spoke the mother of O'Neil,
In those soft accents—meek and kind,
Few hear and yet refuse to feel.

The blush of anger, or of shame,
To Hugh O'Neil's proud temples came—

" I love not questions " he replied—
Then moodily he turned aside,
And sought a Gothic casement, placed
Within a dark recess, that faced
The marshy flat and lonely rock,
Known by the name of Ballynock.
'Twas strange ! just then a vivid light
Brought those grim, distant halls to sight ;
A brilliant glare—a bursting flame,
From tower—from turret, leaping came—
And as the chieftain wildly gazed
Fiercely it rose and fiercely blazed !

O'Neil rushed madly from the hall—
His mother heard his frenzied call—
" Ho ! Morris—Rory—bring my steed,
And follow me with instant speed—— "
And then there came the trampling sound
Of horse's hoofs on flinty ground,
And Hugh, who rode at furious rate,
Soon left behind the castle gate.

O'Neil took not the circling road,
But straight across the plain he rode.
The wind was sullen, shrill and cold
And blowing o'er the open wold.
It had a weary, bitter tone,
'Twas almost like a spirit's moan,

It rose not ever loud or high,
But with a melancholy sigh
O'er reedy flats and fragments, rent
From rocks, like ghostly Banshee went!
The partridge started from its rest,
The moorfowl left its rushy nest,
And raised its shrill, complaining cry,
As Hugh O'Neil dashed madly by.
The curlew joined its mournful wail
With the faint piping of the quail.
And far around each note was heard,
Across that flat and lonely waste—
As each bewildered fluttered bird
Flew from its grassy home in haste!

He reached at last the burning hall,
Just as, like some funereal pall,
A column huge, of densest smoke,
From lofty roof—from lattice broke.
Then passed away—while sullen glare
Of leaping flames was fiercely shed
Upon the hot and heavy air!
And yet—he thought, with sudden fear,
No voice—no cry fell on his ear—
He listened for some piercing call—
The roaring of the flames was all!
A chill ran through his curdling blood,
Cold drops of perspiration stood

Upon his brow—and yet it seemed
As though some exultation gleamed
Within those eyes' fierce brightness, ere
Quenched by some sudden doubt, or fear!

The eastern wing was half-decayed,
Where flames their fiercest march had made;
But Morna and her household dwelt
Within the western—this reposed
Unscathed as yet, but Hugh, who felt
There was no time to lose, unclosed
A postern door, within the wall,
And vaulted roof and noble hall
Soon echoed back his headlong tramp.
'Tis true, he had no guide, or lamp,
Nor needed them, the air was bright
With glowing flames, a blood-red light
Came from each casement that he passed,
And through the courts their shadows cast—
While mingled with the roaring flame
Another sound rose, sadly clear,
The wail of lamentation came
Distinctly to the chieftain's ear!

Meantime the household of O'Neil
Had spared not spur, or goading steel,
But following him at utmost speed,
Each just had reined his foaming steed

As, issuing from a postern door,
A form dishevelled, pale yet fair,
Into the open space he bore—
And laid her down in cooler air.
Then, as the flames grew fast and faster,
The search grew wilder for " the Master "—
A search still vain, until they found
A track of recent blood, and traced
Its course without the castle's bound,
Then lost it in the marshy waste.

And now from distant hamlets came
The rustics—both the young and old,
Attracted by the lurid flame,
That lit afar the marshy wold.
Was there among them who wept not
For Morna ? one who there forgot
For *whom* her hapless brother brought
Such fearful vengeance on his head ?
Not one ! who had not gladly fought
And cheerfully his life-blood shed
For Dermid—but that fatal hour
Pursuit, alone, was in their power.
This promptly they commenced—a boat
Was quickly manned and put afloat,
Although they knew the chance was slight
Of chasing pirates such a night !
The rest remained and bravely toiled

To quench the flames, though often foiled,
And only paused when once they threw
A dark, suspicious glance at Hugh!

"Mount thou my steed," the chieftain said,
His quick and ready page obeyed,
"And see a boat be instant manned
With bravest heart and boldest hand.
For I will at the first pale streak
Of morn, the pirate vessel seek."

Then Hugh returned to Morna's side,
Whose weeping maidens long had tried
To bring back life and warmth again
To their young mistress, but in vain.
It was a long, yet happy swoon,
In truth, the waking came too soon!
There is no bitterness so deep
Like that of waking, as from sleep,
To find some evil hand hath been
To blast our life's most cherished scene;
To feel the sad heart so oppressed,
Its dearest longing is for rest—
Though it might come with the dull gloom
And voiceless silence of the tomb!
So Morna thought, as life returned,
And her foreboding heart had learned
Her brother's loss—the pirates' flight—

While burning towers that threw a light
Even to Dunhaven's distant crest
And pine-wood forests, told the rest !

The clouds were parted—soft and grey
Came the first breaking of the day.
Alas ! that sunrise never more
Will throw its peaceful shadows o'er
That home she once had known so fair—
That long had been so loved a place—
And with a gesture of despair,
Poor Morna hid her tear-stained face—
While, breaking on her bitter grief
Thus gently spoke the mountain chief.

" Lady," he said—" my home so near,
Why linger we in sorrow here ?
My mother there awaits thee—I
Will chase the pirates o'er the sea—
The gleam of morn is in the sky,
I may not linger—even with thee."
He took her trembling hand and raised
Her shivering figure from the ground—
But Morna turned and long she gazed
Silent and speechless—as spell-bound.
Without a murmur or a sigh
She stood awhile—with tearless eye,
Mute, motionless as sculptor's clay—
Then hid her face and turned away.

Canto III.

It was the noontide of a bright, warm day,
The air was scented with the summer flowers,
The long grass rustled with the breeze's play,
The wood-birds filled with song their leafy bowers.
The bees were winging, with a drowsy tone
From the blue harebell to the sweet-briar rose—
O'er earth and sky, o'er sea and rock were thrown,
An air of loneliness and calm repose.
The wood-pigeons were cooing in the shade—
The deer were basking in the sun's warm smile—
The rivulets went murmuring through the glade,
The fish-hawk watched the running streams the while!
Or dived into the clear, pellucid flood,
Then rising shook around the diamond spray,
As to some branch of broad, decaying wood
It flew, to feast in quiet on its prey.

    Deep in one of those sunny dells,
    Whose banks are clothed with flower-bells,
    Where human steps were known to pass
    But rarely o'er its haunted grass—
    Where human voices echoed not—
    There yet remained a ruined cot.

It suited well that greenwood scene,
Its broken roof with moss was green—
And birds, or winds, had sown the seeds
Of hardy plants or creeping weeds,
In crevices of broken wall,
Or where the woodwork seemed decayed,
Of lovely ferns, or foxglove tall,
To crown the ruins Time had made !
Though scarcely boasting chair, or bed,
Yet was this hut inhabited.
A woman, withered, old and wan,
Was basking in the glowing sun,
That shone in through the open door—
And seemed as though she muttered o'er
Some magic charm, or potent prayer,
As her shrunk hand arranged with care
Herbs, gathered in the dead of night,
Or culled beneath the pale moonlight—
When fairies wake their harps' soft strain,
Or darker spirits hold their reign.
One who, if we might Fame believe,
By magic process, could with ease
The couch of bitter pain relieve—
Cure fatal wounds, or dire disease !
Another inmate, too, was there,
With youthful brow and raven hair,
Who once was beautiful—her face
Still something had of beauty's grace.

But now that brow was marked—her eye
Was restless, feverlit and dry.
A sullen, dull despair, a stern
Unwavering resolution, seemed
Within those hollow orbs to burn—
And sometimes even fiercely gleamed
The hard look of revenge, within
Its lightning brightness—then awhile
It changed into a scornful smile—
The smile of mockery and of sin.

She bent above a wretched bed,
Where, wasted by long sickness lay
One, o'er whose clammy brow had spread
The very hue of soulless clay,
And seemed to watch with half-drawn sigh
And painful quivering of the eye,
The light of intellect again
Return to Dermid's wandering brain.
The first glance of the conscious eyes
Was one of wild, unmixed surprise—
Then, as he raised his languid head,
In faint and faltering tones he said—
" My sister "—" She is safe "—" Then how
Is it that I am here, and not
With her, and who and what art thou—
Why am I in this ruined cot ? "

" Nay—hush thee—thou art far too pale,
Too weak, to hear so long a tale."

Poor Dermid sank back slowly—closed
His eyes—she deemed that he reposed,
And watched in silence, but ere long
He spoke again—in tones more strong.

" Nay, tell me all, for o'er my mind
Suspicions dark, but scarce defined,
Have crowded, and are crowding still—
Like some foreboding shade of ill.
Fear not, my gentle nurse, but speak
The strength of life hath come again—"
A flush came o'er his sunken cheek
As slowly he arose, with pain.
" For all my recollections seem
The misty memories of a dream—
A frantic struggle—then a cry,
That thrilled my frame with agony,
My sister's voice ! then faces grim
And cruel as fiends seemed bending o'er
My own—then all grew dark and dim,
And faded, and I knew no more.
Thy voice is stranger to mine ear,
Who art thou, and what brings me here ? "

" I tell but what relates to thee—

It matters not who *I* may be—
·Ask not details—enough, I heard
Thou wert condemned to die, by those
Whose deadly rage thou hadst incurred—
The pirates' savage band—and I
Resolved to snatch thee from their knife!
I see that thou art wondering, why
A stranger's hand should save thy life—
'Twas for thy gentle sister's sake—
I knew her tender heart would break—
And joy for me would be in vain
If thou, so fondly loved, wert slain.
My mother's eyes in death she closed,
And blessed the spot where she reposed."

Some mournful, overpowering feeling
Seemed swelling in her heart, she bowed
Her head, and with her hand concealing
Her face, wept bitterly—aloud.
And yet, ere long, in firmer strain
And calmer voice, resumed again.

" Alas ! there seemed no help, and I—
I felt—I feared—that thou must die,
Unless I should betray thy foes,
And bring down ruin, both on those
That hated thee and one whose hand
Was in, but yet abhorred the plot.

For there is one in that dark band,
Who, though my heart may love him not,
With generous pity gave me all
I have of peace and comfort here—
And I would not that *he* should fall—
Though for myself I know not fear !
One hope there is, but faint indeed,
Yet cherished as a last resource,
As drowning men will grasp the reed,
And think to stem the current's force ;
But time is passing—To be brief,
The night of one dark expedition,
O'More was sent out by his chief—
I need not tell on what commission.
Enough—one dark and stormy night
We met, and we concealed our barque
Where there was neither shore nor light—
Within a sheltered creek and dark—
We knew that, e'er their work was o'er
Of pillage—hours might pass away—
And, entering by a secret door,
We robbed the murderers of their prey !
For well I knew if aught of life
Was left thee—by their vengeful knife—
That Ulrique's magic spells once more
Life, sense and vigour could restore !
There's little more—save I have learned
Thy sister's towers thy foes have burned.

She—as O'Neil the merit claims
Of having saved her from the flames—
Will now his honoured guest remain."

" And yet I know the lines of pain
That mark thy stern and knitted brow
Tell me thy tale unfinished now ! "

" 'Tis true ! but if those lips of thine
Repeat the tale that now I tell,
Ruin must fall on me and mine—
Then hear—but use thy knowledge well.

" Beware, beware of Hugh O'Neil,
The chieftain of that pirate band—
Howe'er he may his hate conceal,
Thy murder by his lips was planned !
He hates thee, with a hate as fell
As ever human breast could swell.
And knows that Morna ne'er will give
Her hand to him while thou shalt live.
And many months ago, he swore
That he would wait and woo no more—
That Morna should, whate'er betide
Ere long become his own—his bride.
Nay, shake not wildly thus thy arm,
Hear me, young madman—and be calm !
Be calm—there is no danger yet—

He deems thy sun of life hath set ;
He deems thy head is lying low,
And waits, until the heavy blow
That now is pressing on her heart
May be removed—at least in part.
From his foul grasp or from the grave,
Remember—thou alone canst save !

" Dost thou remember, weeks ago
The Lady Una sent to pray
Thy sister would awhile forego
Her dreary residence—to stay
Within that lady's brighter one ?
Canst thou not guess *why* this was done ?
But that, as Morna shrank from glee
And mirth, she stayed, instead, with thee.
It was to veil, thus, from her sight,
The horrors of that fatal night !
Not that the Lady Una knew
Her son's dark union with the crew
Of pirates—gentle, meek and kind,
She bends to his imperious mind,
Suspects not in the loved one ill,
Nor e'er disputes his haughty will.

" Dark is the soul of stern O'Neil,
His lip is smooth—his brow is steel,
And starts not at the boldest deed,

R

Whate'er may be the hearts that bleed,
He little knows what hand shall wreak
His ruin "—the triumphant glow
Of vengeance coloured her pale cheek,
As thus she spoke, and then the throe
Of anguish shook her wasted frame,
Yielding to burning tears of shame,—
" I see thou pitiest me—in vain
Thy lips would urge me break the chain,
That binds me still to those I hate—
'Tis vain to say, 'Tis not too late !
Thou little know'st how fastened in
Its links, become the slaves of sin !
And I am hopeless—helpless now—
But stay—for fever burns thy brow,
Rest, rest thy wearied brain, and I——"

She paused and waiting not reply
Rose hastily—her mantle wide
Drew round her form and left his side.

*   *   *   *

The flowers their tender leaves had curled,
And slumbered in their woodland bowers;
The spell of rest crept o'er the world,
The sweet rest of the evening hours.
The shepherd left his sleeping fold,
The sun had set upon the lea,
The mists of evening swept the wold,

And night came on.   Why lingers he,
The proud O'Neil, and still looks down
From heights on which the pine-woods frown,
To bleaker hills, where lately stood,
Fringed by a line of gloomy wood,
The time-worn towers of Ballynock,
Once record of far prouder days ?
There now is but a barren rock,
To mock the traveller's wistful gaze !

   " She must be mine "—he darkly said,
" Edgar and Dermid both are dead !
'Tis little I have now to fear—
She must be mine—the bitter tear
E'en now is dried—the brow is wan,
But grief's first heavy shock is gone—
All past remembrances, or all
Connected with her castle's fall,
Now it no longer meets the eye
Will soften, as the months go by "—

   Even as he triumphed came the sound
Of footsteps on the stony ground !
The chieftain turned, but stood transfixed,
For fear and horror both were mixed
In the wild glances of the eye,
The frame that shook with agony.
'Twas Dermid ! by that bearing proud—

Though like a spectre in its shroud,
Yet with the bright eye none could tame,
'Twas Dermid, changed and yet the same!
Emaciated, wan and pale,
He looked as though the ghastly tale
Of Death were written on his brow—
" O ! why, pale spectre of the dead,
Dost thou return to haunt me now ?"
The conscience-stricken chieftain said.
" So much of misery and of ill
As thou hast caused me while in life—
Wilt thou return to haunt me still—
And plunge my soul in darker strife ? "

" Chief of O'Neil—thou dost but rave,
I am no spectre from the grave—
No doubt "—said Dermid with a sneer,
" The brave O'Neil is glad to hear
I have escaped the pirate band,
To mar the crimes their chieftain planned."

The cheek that first with fear had paled
With deeper shame that instant burned—
Hugh knew his self-command had failed---
Yet proudly, fiercely he returned
The scornful and contemptuous glance
That shot from Dermid's countenance.
Then turned away his conscious eyes,

And muttered something of surprise
And pleasure—what he scarcely knew—
Ruin—discovery seemed impending—
His fears each moment wilder grew
For Conscience her sure aid was lending—
And stung by grief and pale with hate
He followed through the castle gate.

  *   *   *   *

Morna was lying on a couch, her eyes
Seemed watching calmly twilight's sombre dyes
Steal slowly, pensively across the bay,
Deepening with the declining hours of day :
Her head was resting on her snowy arm—
But Dermid started at that perfect calm,
And lifted tenderly the drooping head,
And pressed the nerveless hand,—but life had fled !

  *   *   *   *

Some weeks had passed, and when his strength returned,
The deeply injured brother only burned
To meet his foe upon the battle-plain.
They met and rumour said O'Neil was slain.
Though legends differ on this point, some say
He died within a convent far away.
One thing at least is certain—never more
Were seen his footsteps on his native shore.

OCCASIONAL PIECES.

THE MOTHER'S FAREWELL.

I HAVE watched over thee for many years—
Thou hast had all my hopes and all my fears.
Heaven only knows how anxious was the task
Of guiding thy young footsteps—but I ask
But one reward—refuse me not that one—
Return to me as now thou art, my son!

Thou leavest me—I shall not see thee more,
Till years of tearful absence have passed o'er.
Thou leavest me—to cross the Indian seas,
To brave the dangers of the Sutlej wild—
But oh! it is not perils such as these
I fear the most for thee—mine only child!

Thou goest forth into a world of strife—
Thy barque will bear thee to a pleasant coast—
But be not tempted by the worldling's life,
Or envious of the pleasures he may boast.
Return not to me with the brow of shame—
Wring not my heart with thy dishonoured name!

Forget thou not the lessons I have taught—
Remember, oh, my son ! that pleasures bought
By sacrifice of duty, ever leave
Upon the heart and brain their dark impress--
Thy better part, despite thyself, will grieve—
Thou mayst conceal it, yet not mourn the less !

Be kind, forgiving—be thou firm in right—
Pity the weak—exult thou not in might—
Go, then, my son—my fond and fervent prayer
Will follow, o'er the paths of the deep sea,
In joy, in sorrow—here and everywhere—
Thy mother's heart will still remember thee.

I have watched over thee for many years—
Thou hast had all my hopes and all my fears.
Heaven only knows how anxious was the task
Of guiding thy young footsteps—but I ask
But one reward—refuse me not that one—
RETURN TO ME AS NOW THOU ART, MY SON.

THE STUDENT'S GARRET.

Gleaming upon the moonlight scene,
With sickly and uncertain light,
The student's lonely lamp was seen,
Through the long, weary hours of night.
Yet, o'er that lone and thoughtful one
There bent a night so calm and fair
Its loveliness might well have won
His spirit from all thoughts of care !
Grey halls and towers, time-worn and rent,
And columns, shadowy and dim,
And many a pallid monument
That age had rendered stern and grim—
Yet beautified by moonlight, thrown
Upon their crumbling forms of stone—
Stood up, mysterious, silent, proud,
Each like some spectre in its shroud !
O God ! of all the tearless hours,
The quiet rest that Thou hast given,
To cheer this chequered life of ours,

Until its earthly links are riven—
Thou hast no gift that e'er can bring
Such peace to weary heart and brain,
Or change its look of suffering
To one as pure and calm again,
As moonlight on the summer deep,
Like Thy one gift of dreamless sleep!
Yet still, as moonlight passed away
And starlight faded from the sky,
The student, by his lonely ray
Sat reading, with unwearied eye!
And stars and moon looked gently down
With pitying, kind and loving glance,
Through the soft locks of palest brown,
That framed that thoughtful countenance.
Alas! though hope and strength might now
Shine on that young, determined brow,
The spirit yet may be o'ercast,
Th' avenging shadow fall at last!

Years since that brilliant moonlight night had flown,
And daylight's last and melancholy smile,
Through casement frames of grey and crumbling stone,
Lit a cathedral's dim and solemn aisle.
So sadly, too, and mournfully, upon
Pillar and arch and architrave it shone,
It almost seemed as though its light had caught
A tinge of human care, of grief and thought,

From the deep silence of the cloisters grey,
Grim homes of gloomy brooding and decay,
Where, all oblivious of past hopes and crimes,
The love, ambition, hate, of other times,
Each in his last and dreamless home enclosed,
The dead—the pale, unheeding dead—reposed !

O'er the dark woods a knell's deep voice was borne
And the brown leaves of autumn seemed to mourn,
And the cold flower-leaves in the copsewood curled
And shivered, as the sullen tones went by—
O God ! 'tis sad to gaze upon the world,
And watch its brightest things decay and die,
To know a deep, blue sky is o'er us bending,
And sunlight on the fair green earth is shed,
E'en while a hoarse and solemn voice is sending,
Through the calm air its wailing for the dead !

The dew fell heavily, as sunset's smile
Passed from each gravestone and its grassy mound,
And round the proud cathedral's dusky pile,
The wind was whistling with a dreary sound—
And through the vaults of death and cloisters damp
It came and went, unfelt, unheard by all,
E'en where, beneath the heavy sable pall,
Lay the young student of the midnight lamp.
O ! if that eye could raise its heavy lid,
To look back on the loved spot of its birth,

And if that heart could feel, as once it did,
A fellow-pilgrim of our weary earth—
Even if its share of human suffering
Deeply in its short sojourn it had felt,
Still with one yearning feeling it would cling
To those sad, toiling homes where it had dwelt—
And sigh to leave the lightless tomb, to cheer
The ceaseless grief of those remaining here—
Until they, too, the weary path had trod,
That leads us to our resting-place—and God.

LINES TO ——.

I SOMETIMES feel, love, when the moon is out,
And shining down on us with its calm light,
And bats in the grey twilight flit about,
And trees grow shadowy in the deepening night—
As if in those delicious, solemn hours,
The world were far too glorious to be ours;
As if a thought of bitterness and pain,
Could never dwell within my heart again!

FATHER! the world that Thou hast given us,
Seems far too fair and pure for grief or sin;
'Tis beautiful to watch it slumbering thus—
To watch star after star come stealing in,
Or the first streak of moonlight on the sky,
And listen for the curlew's shrilly cry,
And hear the leaves shake, with a faint, soft sound,
As if they feared to break the silence round—
To watch the owl fly round the ivied wall,
And know that Thou art watching over all!
One star is rising now, though dim and pale,
Its light is glimmering faintly o'er our vale—

Dear love ! above the roar and the dull sound,
That murmurs from thy far-off city dwelling,
How calmly it may shine upon thee, telling
Of that fair home to which we both are bound !

Go on in thy bright path, beloved—my heart
Is ever with thee in thy onward way,
So far away from me as now thou art,
Thy spirit seems with me, each passing day.
Thou art my guardian angel, and each thought,
Each holy lesson that thy life hath taught,
Is with me in all hours of joy and grief ;
And in the evening when the day grows dim,
And the wind trembles, from flower leaf to leaf,
And night with its deep shadows, lies before us,
And the heart turns from worldly thoughts to Him,
Whose kind, forgiving eye is ever o'er us,
Thy words seem spoken by each leaf and flower,
Thy spirit breathing in each passing hour.

Farewell, beloved ! the stars have passed away—
May joy and sunshine follow on thy way.
And oh ! while thy heart, dear, is with me still,
Thy love—that shields me in each hour of ill,
I *know*—no moment even of grief can be,
But it will bind me more to God—to thee

THE DYING GIRL.

Farewell—farewell.
Thou'rt dying with the spring of life before thee—
Thou'rt dying, while the primrose and bluebell
Are blooming, and the fair sky bending o'er thee—

Thou'rt dying while thy braided tress is dark,
Without one white line of decay to speak—
Ere thy smooth brow betrays one wrinkled mark,
Or one line mars the beauty of thy cheek !

A little time—in the sepulchral shroud
And winding sheet, unfeeling hands have wound thee,
And thy pale, thoughtful brow, so gently proud,
Rests calmly as the senseless dead around thee.

A little time, and thy bright intellect
May lend itself to earthly things no more—
The powers of thy lofty mind be wrecked,
And the deep musings of thy heart be o'er.

S

Thou'rt dying, though thy dear eye's sunny blue
Is sparkling with a softly brilliant light,
And on thy youthful cheek there is a hue
That seems for death too deeply rich and bright!

Yet thou wilt die in girlhood's sunny hours,
With the fair spring-time of thy life before thee,
Thou'rt dying while the primrose and spring flowers
Are blooming, and the blue sky bending o'er thee.

And spring will pass—pass without thee to mourn
Its dying flowers, as thou hast done before—
And summer fade and spring again return
And yet again, but never bring thee more!

And yet we dare not mourn that this must be,
For now thy gentle spirit will have passed
Before one evil breath hath withered thee—
Without one shadow on thy beauty cast.

It might have been if years had been thy lot
Thy heart had not been always calm as now—
Or sorrows' blight—disease's sadder blot
Had stained thy beautiful and placid brow.

His will be done, then, Who first placed thee here,—
To us is known not things of future days,
And we must worship still in awe and fear,
For Human minds can fathom not His ways.

LOVE! THERE ARE DAYS.

Love! there are days when I still live again
Through all our past of mixed delight and pain,
Days when the future shone so bright and clear
O'er the gilt clouds of the departing year,
When Hope smiled out through evening's closing portal,
When Grief stayed not and Love appeared immortal!

How dear to me hath been thy brow serene,
What power sustaining thou hast ever been!
Thy noble heart was ever strong to bear,
Scorning all tremors of my weak despair.
Scarce had I lived without thy tender touch,
That gave such comfort—that upheld so much!

No weak and useless aims thy hours employed,
Not thine the noisy fame that some enjoyed,
Yet hundreds praised thee—hundred lips have taught
The truths *thy* words of hope and faith inspired,
The joy thy words of comfort ever brought—
The noble efforts thy brave words have fired.

Helping the buoyant youth upon his way,
Soothing the sad fears of a parting day,
Few heroes e'er deserved more praise than thou
For deeds of unpretending greatness done,
No nobler laurels e'er can crown a brow
Than thou, with thy long patient toil hast won!

THE HOME OF MY CHILDHOOD.

Home of my childhood, green and placid spot,
Meet dwelling-place for those that sigh for peace,
Shunned by ambition and where wars raged not,
Beloved and wept for until life shall cease——

    There tumult and unrest
    Slept in my youthful breast,
I knew not life, save ever to rejoice,
    For through that peaceful glade,
    My childhood's fancies strayed,
Nor listened to Ambition's dark, insidious voice.

    No feverish pulse was stirred,
    No trumpet's blare was heard,
No echoes of despair, of battle and of strife;
    The cooing of the dove,
    The voice of peace and love,
These simple notes of calm, of pleasure were my life.

Through summer's brilliant day
The children, at their play,
Full oft made glad the sweet and peaceful air—
The sounds of simple joys
No fierce, wild note destroys—
Day brought no hopeless grief and evening no despair.

DREAMS OF THE PAST.

O ! VISIONS of times gone by,
Ye come with a tear, or sigh,
With a weary brow and a sad and shadowy form,
With a half-reproachful gaze,
And a murmur of better days,
When a youth's bright hopes were high and a poet's
fancy warm.

O ! visions of joys no more,
Of pleasures that long are o'er,
Thy glance is cold and thy footsteps dull and slow ;
And ye speak with a mournful tone,
A sound that is half a moan,
As ye tell of the happy days that are now so long ago.

Ye speak of decay and death,
With a faint and faltering breath,
Of delights that are long since dimmed, of a broken heart,
Ye tell how our young hopes fail,
How the brow grows weary and pale,
As the visions of love and the hopes of youth depart.
Yet still would I fondly pray,

For one hour of a by-gone day,
When love was constant and youth's bright hopes were
　　　high,
When our fears of change were brief,
And we knew no thought of grief,
So lived for love and for joys that cannot die!

————————

THE MOTHER AND HER THREE DAUGHTERS.

O'ER the dark waters of the stormy bay,
With straining eyes and pallid, parting lips,
She sees the fluttering pennants fade away,
Of one of Albion's noble, home-built ships.

She sees, with sad, prophetic eyes, the flash
Of lightning, as it gilds the crowded deck,
She hears the deafening thunder—the fierce dash
Of seething waters through the groaning wreck.

Trembling she turns away her inward gaze,
From all sad visions of her far-off child,
And seeks near home for calmer, brighter days,
For hopes more peaceful and for skies less wild.

There bends a face that she can ne'er forget,
Pure as the snowdrop, sweet as " Violet," *
Whose ear lists ever to another's moan,
Forgetful of all echoes of her own.

* Violet was her Christian name.

A brow of pallor, oft of bitter pain,
Yet one whose heart is in another's woes,
With lips that bless or praise, but ne'er complain ;
With angel-footsteps through the world she goes.

Another by an English hearth she sees,
A face all glowing with a mother's joy,
Watching the pretty gambols on her knees,
The rippling laughter, of her noble boy.

She hath, as yet, a calm, untroubled lot,
Unbittered by despair, unstained by tears ;
And yet we dare not, on earth's changeful spot,
Foretell the sunshine of our unborn years.

THE BROTHER SPIRITS OF DEATH.

(An old Poem.)

"I always fancy that Death should be represented by two brothers, one an angel, the other a demon, who travel separately about earth; the first on an errand of mercy, the last to inflict misery!"—BYRON.

'TIS the fairest hour of our lovely earth,
    When the bright sun is descending,
And a soft grey light in her bowers of mirth
    With the sunset's gold is blending;
When the heat and the toil of day are o'er,
And the voice of the world is heard no more;
But fairer that hour when shared with thee,
Then come to the greenwood, love, with me!

Come to the forest's massive shade,
Come to the banks of the mossy glade,
Where nought but the rustling moan is heard
Of the autumn leaves, by the faint wind stirred,
And the heart is awed by the want of sound,
By the solemn hush of the gloom around.

Come ! there are few that wander now,
    For the world is calm and still,
And the bird is slumbering on the bough,
    And the wild deer on the hill.
But hush ! there are two that linger yet,
Watching the rich and red sunset—
And the brows of both are young and fair,
Unwithered, as yet, by the touch of care ;
And the sound of their laugh is soft and sweet,
And bright is the smile when their dark eyes meet.

But the maiden has paused where the flowers are fair,
While he twines a wreath in her flowing hair.
O ! ask not what are the words they breathed,
And ask not why are their fond arms wreathed—
Thou mayst read the tale in the dark, soft eye,
Whose glance half seeks, half shuns reply—
Thou mayst guess, what words can ne'er express,
In the timid—half withdrawn caress,
And deem that happiness still may dwell
    Where once from her empire hurled,
And many a heart with rapture swell,
    Unknown to the busy world.
But a change hath come o'er the clear, blue sky,
The Demon of Death is hurrying by !

    *   *   *   *

    *   *   *   *

Now come with me—'tis that hour of night

When the earth is lit by the pale moonlight—
When the stars steal forth in the twilight sky,
And the hollow wind forgets to sigh.
Lo! under yon yew tree's dismal gloom
Thou see'st a lonely, fresh-made tomb—
. 'Tis the grave of her with the fair young brow
Whom thou saw'st in the woods—it seems but now.
But the fairest flower is borne away
From the earth to the tomb in an hour, or day!

O! little thought thou—when thou saw'st her there,
Braiding the flowers in her glossy hair,
The Demon of Death, with his poisonous breath,
  Was pressing her glowing lips,
And the flower was doomed, ere it scarce had bloomed,
  For a long and dark eclipse.

But he—whom I saw by that maiden's side—
Doth *he* live, to mourn for his hapless bride?

He lives—but his spirit passed afar—
And he may not sleep where the wild flowers creep,
In the grave where his hopes, all mouldering, are.
But dwells on the earth, unloved—alone—
Some say that his mind is now o'erthrown—
Some say that his young and noble brow,
Is furrowed by grief and suffering now.
They say that his heart is cold and changed,

That, ever, from others he keeps estranged—
That his auburn hair is thin and white,
And the form is bent that was once upright,
And they tell me the light will ne'er again
Return to his seared and shattered brain—
For the stamp of a fearful power is there,
The stamp of a fixed and dark despair!

    *   *   *   *

'Twas night and the winds blew cold and shrill,
And a tempest raged in wood and hill,
And the torrent swelled in the rocky glade,
   And ruin was spreading wide,
As a wretched wife knelt down and prayed
   By her dying husband's side.
And the thunder roared through her dwelling rude,
And the lightning flashed—in the interlude—
And shone on the languid head that lay
   On her thin and wasted arm,
And the face was fair as the sculptor's clay,
   But oh! it was scarce more warm.
And the eyelids drooped o'er the eye's wan light
   As though they never could rise again;
And the pale lips seemed compressed and tight,
   Yet quivered, at times, in pain.
And she who over that figure bent,
Whose heart to each throb of his was lent,
How bore *she* up in that gloomy hour
That tries the soul to its utmost power?
O! though full many a haggard trace

Could sorrow claim in that pallid face,
Though want had stolen the rosy hue,
From that deathlike cheek and those lips of blue,
And wrinkled her cheek with many a mark
And whitened the hair—once soft and dark,
It never could quell the spirit high
That dwelt in the dark, expressive eye,
That spoke of a mind both firm and strong,
And said she could suffer much, and long!
She scarcely heeded the thunder's roar,
Or the wind that howled through the broken door,
She trembled not at the raging storm,
But sadly bent o er her husband's form,
And soothed his brow with her gentle touch,
And moistened his lips with her falling tears—
And felt, though she long had suffered much
That moment outweighed the grief of years.
" They say that grief is more lightly borne
When we have one *with us* to mourn,"
She said, in a low and faltering tone,
As she kissed the brow that was now like stone,
" But oh ! I would rather pine alone
In a place where none might hear me moan,
And know thou wert far away, and free
And happy, as one on earth may be,
Than see thee, love, in thy youth die *thus*—
And the dark grave yawn for both of us."

   *   *   *   *

   *   *   *   *

The scene was changed, and the tempest's blast
With the cold and dreary night had passed,
And morning came, and the blue sky smiled
On a cottage lone, in a moorland wild.
But oh! within was a calm more deep
  Than the calm of that outward scene,
For there was a breathless, dreamless sleep,
  Where sorrow but now had been!
And there was rest for the broken heart,
  And rest for the eyes that wept;
A rest that could never more depart
  From the eyes of those that slept.
The brow was eased of its load of care,
  And the sad heart beat no more;
For the Angel of Death was dwelling there,
  And the sufferer's woes were o'er.

MORE HAPPY THOUGHTS.

OLD ladies like their scandal and old ladies like their tea,
But which is it they love the best, I think I hear you
    say—
O scandal by a hundred times ! or so it seems to me,
For that they can have served to them at all times in the
    day !

O scandal is delightful ! for it makes the hours pass by
Without a break upon the way, so rapidly they fly ;
It soothes and comforts one so much, wherever one may
    be,
To think our friends so foolish, that so much more wise
    are we !

O scandal is delightful ! the most tasty of all food—
For it makes one feel so comfortable, O ! *so* wise and
    good—
For *we* don't do as others do—are not such fools as they,
And can we say a wiser thing, or one more pleasant, pray ?

T

Yes ! tea comes in the morning, or the evening of the day,
But scandal ever fills the mighty goblet on the tray—
Our tea we swallow down but in small cupfuls at a time,
*But scandal is served up to us in bumpers, when it's
     prime !*

November, 1880.

A BOUNDLESS EMPIRE; OR, LA CALOMNIE— THE MIGHTY EMPRESS.

I HAVE been a mighty traveller, I have seen unnumbered
    lands,
And my swift, unwearied glance has swept the wildest
    desert sands.
I have scaled the loftiest heights by human vision never
    seen—
And through the darkest valleys have my curious foot-
    steps been.

I have been a mighty traveller—I have breathed Sahara's
    air,
I have strayed through densest forests, where the homes
    are few but fair—
And when I saw a casement that seemed far too bright
    and clean
I have breathed upon it heavily, then passed away
    unseen !

I have been a mighty traveller and my steps were full of
  joy,
When with Paris and frail Helen I was gay in ancient
  Troy,
To Telemachus, alone, I ever failed to deal a blow,
While Minerva was beside him to protect the boy from
  woe.

I have dwelt within the palace, I have lingered in the cot,
There is no sacred refuge or retreat that knows *me* not!
I have whispered words of misery to the happy and the
  young,
I have wakened ghastly music when the harpstrings were
  unstrung.

No one can ever conquer me, my power is over all,
And even the mightiest empires I have shaken to their
  fall—
Nay! often have I held in bond the proudest heart and
  hand,
For even Death itself obeys *my* whisper or command.

If the path thy foes are travelling seems to thee too fair
  and bright,
If there is glowing brilliancy where thou wouldst have it
  night,
Invoke me in the sunshine or invoke me in the shade,
I am ever near—and solemnly I promise thee my aid.
  November, 1880.

A FEW SCRAPS WRITTEN BETWEEN THE AGES OF TEN AND SIXTEEN.

DYING WORDS.

My friend, the world is fading from my sight—
Unclose the casement—let the sun's warm smile
Yet once again my darkened vision light—
'Tis well, now hear me patiently awhile !
The hand thou claspest in thine own—that thin
White hand, a few years back was firm and strong.
O ! if to scorn existence be a sin,
'Tis one that will be charged on me ere long !
For I am prematurely old, and now
When other men are in their very prime,
Dying, I lift to heaven my haggard brow,
Imploring grace—forgiveness—for the crime
Of having wasted, in the heart's mad grief,
Each noble purpose of a human soul ;
Asking no counsel—seeking no relief—
My sorrow was indeed without control !
Death's voice is in mine ear, or I would fain
Live yet—repentant—but I must submit—
I pray not, even—for such prayer were vain—

For further time than daylight may permit.
This only, oh my God ! I dare to ask—
That Thou wilt grant me, while yet life shall last,
Such strength as may fulfil a farewell task,
Whose pangs may win some pardon for the past.
Thy days are young, my friend—the world is still
A mystery to thee—with its sin and strife—
Bear with my failing accents and I will
Teach thee one lesson of its dreary life.

I have been much a wanderer, both by land
And sea—and dwelt where Indian sunlight smiles—
Braved the sirocco of the Lybian sand,
And mused a summer in the Western Isles.
Still the remembrance of one English spot,
Like some lost Eden, ever haunted me—
I could have wished below no happier lot,
Than life, in that sweet vale beside the sea !
Full of true village pictures—calm and green—
Meet for the peasant or the poet life—
It wore no features of a sea-coast scene,
The screaming petrels knew it not—the strife
Of winds and waves but faintly met the ear,
Of him who wandered on the hills at eve,
To watch the storms of sultry skies draw near,
Or the white bosom of the ocean heave !
'Tis sadly altered now—so I am told—
Its noble woods have fallen, and the bold,

Far stretching hills lie desolate and bare,
Swept by the fierce winds of an open sky—
With only shelter for the timid hare,
Such as the heath and furzen may supply.
Fresh flowers and leaves with spring-time come no more,
The sheep feed unrestrained upon the waste—
The sportsman strides across the open moor,
Nor knows what holy ground his steps have traced!

When first I saw it spring was in its prime,
The gentle winds that fanned my youthful face,
Filled with the fragrance of that most sweet time,
Told of the violet's secret dwelling-place,
Eve fell as, in returning through the glade,
I came upon a rustic cot that stood
Deep in the shadow of a sylvan wood.
There dwelt a village child, whose glorious face
Shone like a meteor in that homely place.

Such eyes as hers mine own had never seen,
Nor yet a brow more peaceful—calm—serene,
Lips that could smile the softest smile of earth,
Yet brightly part with ringing, childlike mirth.
This happened years ago, but I have read
Since then the story of her sad career—
Alas! upon its pages have been shed
Full many a penitent and bitter tear!
She who had no companions, found relief,

When left in solitude and worn with prayer,
In making records of her joy and grief—
That piteous record have I still, but dare
Not look upon its trembling lines again ! *
Those broken characters would waken yet
Too much of human frenzy for the brain
Of one whose star of life is almost set.
Entomb them on my bosom, I implore—
I ask of thy long friendship only this,
That never eye of stranger ponder o'er
Its wild, fierce words of doubt, despair or bliss.
I tell, alas ! no new, romantic tales—
Yet common as they are all effort fails
To speak the thoughts of madness they recall—
The hopes—the fears—the struggle and—the fall !
So fare thee well—the time is flitting fast—
I die—not in the present—but the past !

* It is impossible not to have longed to read that mysterious record,
but it was honourably buried with the dead—its contents unknown.

THE MOTHER'S LAMENT.

They bore her from her father's hall,
  The beautiful! the young!
And o'er her form the sable pall
  In gloomy grandeur hung.

They bore her from each cherished scene,
  From ruin wild and grey,
From mountain brook, from forest green,
  They bore her far away—

And laid her in the silent tomb
  All feelingless and cold,
They laid her in the damp and gloom,
  And o'er her trod the mould.

And evening came—without a cloud
  The summer's.sun had set,
But twilight's soft and dusky shroud
  O'er earth was lingering yet.

And one pale star—one lonely star
    Came stealing to the sky,
And soft, calm light it shed afar,
    From its lone space on high.

And on the face of one it smiled,
    Who o'er a grave was weeping,
Alas! alas! her only child
    Beneath the sod was sleeping!

Her countenance was worn with woe,
    And mournfully she spoke,
Yet gentle was the voice and low,
    That on the silence broke.

" They've laid thee in the cold, damp grave, the last, long
        home of rest,
They've laid thee in the cold, damp grave, the sod is o'er
        thee pressed.
And I shall never see thee more, the voice I loved is
        stilled,
Thy warm and gentle heart, my child, the hand of Death
        hath chilled.

" Yes! I shall never see thee more, thy brilliant eye is
        shaded—
The soft, deep bloom upon thy cheeks for ever now has
        faded,

Thy hand is damp and powerless—thy dark and glossy
  hair,
All—*all* are shrouded in the tomb—in darkness spoiling
  there.

"O! I shall miss at break of morn, thy footsteps gay and
  light,
And I shall miss thy soothing hand and tender voice at
  night—
Yet—dearest, I will weep no more, for brighter far must
  be
The home that thou hast gone to seek, than that thou
  sharedst with me.

"Thou'rt sheltered now for ever from all earthly trial and
  woe,
The pangs of disappointment, love, thou never now canst
  know—
Of envy, or of love misplaced—affection unrequited—
That might have crushed thy spirit or its native fresh-
  ness blighted.

"Yes, dearest, I will weep no more, for we again shall
  meet,
Where I shall hear thy gentle voice—so musical and sweet,
Where sorrow is unknown and where affection is un-
  crossed,
There shall I meet thee once again—my beautiful! my
  lost!"

A THOUGHT.

Too much the human heart is given
To sigh for what it cannot get—
Except the prize that men call heaven,
And this some scorn and some forget !
Perchance it is when they despair
Of ever being welcome there !
Each sighs for something out of reach,
Some El Dorado just in view—
But if each soaring mind but knew
The troubles that belong to each,
The cottage girl would scarcely sigh
To leave her own calm, wooded dell,
The colours of a deep, blue sky
In rich and castled halls to dwell !
Or beggar prize the miser's hoard,
Or sailor envy landed lord.
To all are sorrows—though to some
With such o'erwhelming power they come
Health, energy and hope are wrecked

Nay—even, perchance, the intellect!
But oh—to *some* that purest grief
That turns from earth to One above,
And looks for mercy and relief
To Him " Who chastens but in love."

L'HISTOIRE SE RÉPÉTE.

THE little stream that rises from the hill
Swells to a mighty river at its base,
Bearing broad ships upon its bosom, still
We see the same marked features on its face.
A thousand years—the world is still the same,
Gloomy with tempests—sparkling in the sun—
Nature and ages differ but in name,
The next will finish what was last begun.
E'en Nature's face scarce shows a wrinkle more,
Though kingdoms change and centuries roll o'er !

PEACEFUL REFLECTIONS.

My own true friend, the day is slowly dawning,
Methought the dreary night had never passed !
That I should never live to see the morning,
Yet slowly, peacefully it breaks at last.
What will arise in these unfolded years,
Whose unknown scenes are yet before mine eyes—
Will they bring bitterness, regret and tears,
Or calm and peace upspring, as sorrow dies ?
God only knows ! in patience we must wait,
Sorrow comes early—joy is ofttimes late.
And trustful ever must we wait the close
Of winter's storms—the dawn of Heaven's repose.

MOORISH BURIAL CHANT.

We lay her in her last, still home, the damp and dreary
    grave,
Though she is fairer than the flowers that o'er her sadly
    wave.
We lay her in the darkness there—ye call her back in
    vain—
Mourn for her, oh! mourn for her—she cannot come
    again!

We looked on her but yesterday, when light was in her
    eye,
We looked on her but yesterday and said—" She cannot
    die!"
So full of glowing life she seemed—alas! how altered
    now—
For Death hath borne her far away—oh! stranger—ask
    ye how!

It was as spring's first leaf, that breaketh when the
    winds sweep o'er it—
And fling it on the wintry ground, yet leave the branch
    that bore it.
It was as droops a lonely rose-bud, gathered scarce in
    bloom,
Yea—silently as falls a star, Death bore her to the tomb!

Mourn for her, sad lover—lo, thy cherished hope has fled—
Mourn for her, sad father, mourn—thy only child is dead!
O! vainly do ye call her back—ye have not now the
    power,
To join the broken heart again—to raise the trampled
    flower.

Pour forth the parting song and fling the last buds on the
    bier,
Ah, lover—father—gaze once more—thy cherished hope
    lies here!
We lay her now beneath the earth—ye call her back
    in vain—
Then mourn for her, oh! mourn for her—she cannot come
    again!

QUESTION.

Hast thou forgotten that green, shady slope
Where once we sat and talked of love—alone,
When thy soft eyes were full of light and hope,
And mine were almost joyous as thine own?
Hast thou forgotten that dark, spreading tree,
Beneath whose shade I told fond tales to thee?

MELANCHOLY ANSWER.

It would be better far *could* we forget
That we had ever loved—had ever met.
Yet—there is joy still in recalling back
Each gleam of sunshine on that early track—
Ere yet we knew the hopeless withering
Of early fancy—it is sweet to bring
From memory's mournful land the many hours
Of joy—the dreamy thoughts that once were ours.
'Tis all now left us of that peaceful past—
And I *am* happy—while those memories last.

To dream again of thy young, open brow—
Alas! I feel I scarcely know it now!
To meet again each loving, trusting glance
That *then* beamed brightly from thy countenance.
All that is left me—yes! but this is joy
That neither time nor sorrow can destroy!

A REFLECTION.

Ah! little can we know what grief and crime
May wait for us when we would hasten time.
And when the long and weary days have passed,
How often on its fleeted hours we cast
Such glances of repentance or *despair*
'Tis more than even the stoical can bear.
O! could we but recall them—be again
All that we were—is then our prayer in vain!

CONCLUDING VERSES.

LINES TO ——.

Far more of heaven than earth, my own, shines in thy
    calm and placid eyes,
Though thou hast yet the warmest love for all our earthly
    loves and ties ;
And yet there is a placid look, even in the hours of
    bitterest pain,
And few a peace so pure as thine can ever in this world
    attain.
Thy gentleness, thy calm submission, more of heavenly
    grace have taught
Than all the wisest sermons teach, or all by sore ex-
    perience brought.
The peace of Heaven is in thine eyes—so beautifully soft
    and clear,
And even the accents of thy voice seem almost heavenly
    to mine ear.
God is with thee, my darling, I can read it on thy gentle
    brow—
O ! if I ever trusted Heaven I know my trust is in Him
    now.

Thy pure and sinless life has been a noble lesson to us all,
Let those who think their footsteps firm take wiser heed
    for fear they fall!
For they may boast their sinless lives yet there are few
    can live like thou,
While racking pain thy frame disturbs, *but not the
    Patience on thy brow.*

November, 1880.

TO WOMAN.

Woman! from whom his first lisped prayer he learns,
To whom in all his early woes he turns,
In whose fond arms, upon whose faithful breast
His cares are soothed—his troubles laid at rest—
Who smiles with him in joy, grieves in his woes,
And save when shared with him no pleasure knows,
Heaven hath ordained her his one constant love,
Both here on earth and in the world above!

MORNING.

Now voices pour forth on the busy air,
Now riseth up the voice of earnest prayer,
Now in the city stream the multitudes
Into the court, the alley and the streets !
While from the depth of forest solitudes
The breezes greet us with their woodland sweets.
O morning ! beautiful thou art, the while
Thou pourest o'er the earth thy first glad smile.

EVENING.

So art thou lovely, evening ! if less bright
Than morning and less peaceful than the night.
Fair—and yet so unlike the while—for one
Brings the gay gladness of the laughing sun,
Thou the deep softness and the calm repose,
The tender silence of thy waning hours,
That rest from all its busy, worldly woes,
That makes earth seem too peaceful to be ours !

THE VEIL OF NIGHT.

(*Written in the City.*)

Night in the city walls !
Deserted are the street and thoroughfare,
The lights are gleaming in the festive halls,
The lamps light idly the untrodden square.
The deep hum of the mighty multitude,
The roll of carriage wheels, are now subdued ;
Only the bell from the cathedral tower
Is heard, to hoarsely toll the passing hour !

The moon is high in heaven,
The stars are with her, and their mingled light,
To tower and dome and monument are given,
Looking far nobler in the sombre night
Than in broad noontide ; while a filmy cloud
Across the atmosphere at times may fly,
But cannot hide, with its pale, misty shroud,
The deep blue beauty of that midnight sky !

O woe! that night so fair
Should ever hide the pale brow of despair,
The sunken cheeks, the hot, repentant tears,
That tell a tale of sad, or misspent, years—
That it should listen to the guilty rave
Of those who, standing by the yawning grave
Wringing their wasted hands, foresee their fate—
And fain would fly, but know it then too late!

O woe! that night so calm
Should bring with it the wild, imploring prayer
Of hearts to which it can impart no balm,
Of spirits broken by the weight of care—
That when its shadow veils the midnight skies,
To him whose brow by guilt is overcast,
The ghastly fantoms of the wronged arise,
Demanding retribution for the past!

And woe—that night so pure,
Should not o'er scenes as pure its vigil keep—
That its deep, heavy shadows should allure
To reckless orgies, not to holy sleep.
That ever o'er the calm, unheeding earth,
Should steal its planet's penetrating ray,
To witness the unholy scenes of mirth
Man dares not frequent in the eye of day.

O man !—too little wise,
And yet so boastful of his mind and sense—
That he should watch the midnight stars arise,
What time his secret revels to commence—
Knowing the retribution time must bring,
The years of grief, of hopeless suffering
That wait for him—till weary of his woes
The dark grave o'er his whitened head shall close !

THE END.

PRINTED BY WILLIAM CLOWES AND SONS, LIMITED, LONDON AND BECCLES.

favourite with womankind at large. She is as generous to the men as to the women, and shows . . . that there is a preponderance of good over evil even in characters that are far from faultless. . . . We have a series of shorter essays, besides 'Tea Table Talk,'—musings, memories and criticisms, . . . all of which are boldly treated, affording as much pleasure as surprise to the reader."—*British Mail*, November 2, 1880.

"The essayist's object is to controvert something that has been said to the disparagement of women by one of their own sex, the authoress of 'John Halifax, Gentleman,' who, in a spirit of censoriousness, has asserted that 'women are feeble, useless, and half-educated, and taught to believe that ignorance is amusing, and helplessness attractive.' . . . Of course we should be, as the author's title has it, 'versus' the woman who has said it."—*Daily News*, November 2, 1880.

"One of the most curious books that the reader is likely to find."—*Morning Advertiser*.

"One of the very oddest, if not the wisest essays we have ever read."—*Saturday Review*.

"'Versus a Woman, Pro Women' is designed as a defence of women. It abounds in criticisms of the writings of lady novelists . . . and there is an amount of originality about them that will afford amusement."—*Daily Chronicle*.

"The chief part of this pungently written volume is taken up with a defence of women and to some extent of the sterner sex. . . . Mrs. Dobell finds in the recent novel entitled 'Young Mrs. Jardine,' by the authoress of 'John Halifax,' the following passages: 'The man who has will to choose, courage to win, and faithfulness to keep is almost unknown to modern chivalry ; as rare, alas ! as the woman who deserves to be so adored,' and 'Women are feeble, useless, half-educated ; taught to believe that ignorance is amusing and helplessness attractive.' It can hardly be wondered that a woman should be found to gird on her pen against such libels. . . . Mrs. Dobell is quite justified in much that she says against the pessimist views of women so often taken by the authoress in question, and women generally will thank her for her vigorous defence of her sex, while the array she brings forward of women who have distinguished themselves of late in both public and private life is in itself sufficient to show that the sex can claim the possession of the highest virtues and excellences of humanity. . . . The authoress of 'Young Mrs. Jardine' has laid herself open to many of the severe strictures Mrs. Dobell has inflicted on her. . . . The miscellaneous articles, such as those on 'Kleptomania,' 'False Judgments,' 'Novels,' and 'Servantgallism,' are of a very readable character ; that on 'Servantgallism' is especially to be commended, as touching on one of the great domestic grievances of modern life."—*Standard*, October 20.

A LIST OF

C. KEGAN PAUL AND CO.'S
PUBLICATIONS.

10.80.

A LIST OF
C. KEGAN PAUL AND CO.'S
PUBLICATIONS.

ADAMS (F. O.), F.R.G.S.
The History of Japan. From the Earliest Period to the Present Time. New Edition, revised. 2 volumes. With Maps and Plans. Demy 8vo. Cloth, price 21*s.* each.

ADAMS (W. D.).
Lyrics of Love, from Shakespeare to Tennyson. Selected and arranged by. Fcap. 8vo. Cloth extra, gilt edges, price 3*s.* 6*d.*

Also, a Cheap Edition. Fcap. 8vo. Cloth, price 2*s.* 6*d.*

ADAMSON H. T.), B.D.
The Truth as it is in Jesus. Crown 8vo. Cloth, price 8*s.* 6*d.*

A. K. H. B.
From a Quiet Place. A New Volume of Sermons. Crown 8vo. Cloth, price 5*s.*

ALBERT (Mary).
Holland and her Heroes to the year 1585. An Adaptation from Motley's "Rise of the Dutch Republic." Small crown 8vo. Cloth, price, 4*s.* 6*d.*

ALLEN (Rev. R.), M.A.
Abraham ; his Life, Times, and Travels, 3,800 years ago. Second Edition. With Map. Post 8vo. Cloth, price 6*s.*

ALLEN (Grant), B.A.
Physiological Æsthetics. Large post 8vo. 9*s.*

ALLIES (T. W.), M.A.
Per Crucem ad Lucem. The Result of a Life. 2 vols. Demy 8vo. Cloth, price 25*s.*

A Life's Decision. Crown 8vo. Cloth, price 7*s.* 6*d.*

AMATEUR.
A Few Lyrics. Small crown 8vo. Cloth, price 2*s.*

AMOS (Prof. Sheldon).
Science of Law. Fourth Edition. Crown 8vo. Cloth, price 5*s.*

Volume X. of The International Scientific Series.

ANDERSON (Col. R. P.).
Victories and Defeats. An Attempt to explain the Causes which have led to them. An Officer's Manual. Demy 8vo. Cloth, price 14*s.*

ANDERSON (R. C.), C.E.
Tables for Facilitating the Calculation of every Detail in connection with Earthen and Masonry Dams. Royal 8vo. Cloth, price £2 2*s.*

Antiope. A Tragedy. Large crown 8vo. Cloth, price 6*s.*

ARCHER (Thomas).
About my Father's Business. Work amidst the Sick, the Sad, and the Sorrowing. Crown 8vo. Cloth, price 2*s.* 6*d.*

Army of the North German Confederation.
A Brief Description of its Organization, of the Different Branches of the Service and their *rôle* in War, of its Mode of Fighting, &c. &c. Translated from the Corrected Edition, by permission of the Author, by Colonel Edward Newdigate. Demy 8vo. Cloth, price 5*s.*

ARNOLD (Arthur).
Social Politics. Demy 8vo. Cloth, price 14*s.*

Free Land. Crown 8vo. Cloth, price 6*s.*

AUBERTIN (J. J.).

Camoens' Lusiads. Portuguese Text, with Translation by. With Map and Portraits. 2 vols. Demy 8vo. Price 30*s*.

Aunt Mary's Bran Pie.

By the author of "St. Olave's." Illustrated. Cloth, price 3*s*. 6*d*.

AVIA.

The Odyssey of Homer Done into English Verse. Fcap. 4to. Cloth, price 15*s*.

BAGEHOT (Walter).

Physics and Politics; or, Thoughts on the Application of the Principles of "Natural Selection" and "Inheritance" to Political Society. Fifth Edition. Crown 8vo. Cloth, price 4*s*.

Volume II. of The International Scientific Series.

Some Articles on the Depreciation of Silver, and Topics connected with it. Demy 8vo. Price 5*s*.

The English Constitution. A New Edition, Revised and Corrected, with an Introductory Dissertation on Recent Changes and Events. Crown 8vo. Cloth, price 7*s*. 6*d*.

Lombard Street. A Description of the Money Market. Seventh Edition. Crown 8vo. Cloth, price 7*s*. 6*d*.

BAGOT (Alan).

Accidents in Mines: their Causes and Prevention. Crown 8vo. Cloth, price 6*s*.

BAIN (Alexander), LL.D.

Mind and Body: the Theories of their relation. Seventh Edition. Crown 8vo. Cloth, price 4*s*.

Volume IV. of The International Scientific Series.

Education as a Science. Crown 8vo. Third Edition. Cloth, price 5*s*.

Volume XXV. of The International Scientific Series.

BAKER (Sir Sherston, Bart.).

Halleck's International Law; or Rules Regulating the Intercourse of States in Peace and War. A New Edition, Revised, with Notes and Cases. 2 vols. Demy 8vo. Cloth, price 38*s*.

The Laws relating to Quarantine. Crown 8vo. Cloth, price 12*s*. 6*d*.

BALDWIN (Capt. J. H.), F.Z.S.

The Large and Small Game of Bengal and the North-Western Provinces of India. 4to. With numerous Illustrations. Second Edition. Cloth, price 21*s*.

BANKS (Mrs. G. L.).

God's Providence House. New Edition. Crown 8vo. Cloth, price 3*s*. 6*d*.

Ripples and Breakers. Poems. Square 8vo. Cloth, price 5*s*.

BARLEE (Ellen).

Locked Out: a Tale of the Strike. With a Frontispiece. Royal 16mo. Cloth, price 1*s*. 6*d*.

BARNES (William).

An Outline of English Speechcraft. Crown 8vo. Cloth, price 4*s*.

Poems of Rural Life, in the Dorset Dialect. New Edition. complete in 1 vol. Crown 8vo. Cloth, price 8*s*. 6*d*.

Outlines of Redecraft (Logic). With English Wording. Crown 8vo. Cloth, price 3*s*.

BARTLEY (George C. T.).

Domestic Economy: Thrift in Every Day Life. Taught in Dialogues suitable for Children of all ages. Small crown 8vo. Cloth, limp, 2*s*.

BASTIAN (H. Charlton), M.D.

The Brain as an Organ of Mind. With numerous Illustrations. Second Edition. Crown 8vo. Cloth, price 5*s*.

Volume XXIX. of the International Scientific Series.

BAUR (Ferdinand), Dr. Ph.
A Philological Introduction to Greek and Latin for Students. Translated and adapted from the German of. By C. KEGAN PAUL, M.A. Oxon., and the Rev. E. D. STONE, M.A., late Fellow of King's College, Cambridge, and Assistant Master at Eton. Second and revised edition. Crown 8vo. Cloth, price 6s.

BAYNES (Rev. Canon R. H.)
At the Communion Time. A Manual for Holy Communion. With a preface by the Right Rev. the Lord Bishop of Derry and Raphoe. Cloth, price 1s. 6d.
*** Can also be had bound in French morocco, price 2s. 6d.; Persian morocco, price 3s.; Calf, or Turkey morocco, price 3s. 6d.
Home Songs for Quiet Hours. Fourth and cheaper Edition. Fcap. 8vo. Cloth, price 2s. 6d.
This may also be had handsomely bound in morocco with gilt edges.

BELLINGHAM (Henry), Barrister-at-Law.
Social Aspects of Catholicism and Protestantism in their Civil Bearing upon Nations. Translated and adapted from the French of M. le Baron de Haulleville. With a Preface by His Eminence Cardinal Manning. Crown 8vo. Cloth, price 6s.

BENNETT (Dr. W. C.).
Narrative Poems & Ballads. Fcap. 8vo. Sewed in Coloured Wrapper, price 1s.
Songs for Sailors. Dedicated by Special Request to H. R. H. the Duke of Edinburgh. With Steel Portrait and Illustrations. Crown 8vo. Cloth, price 3s. 6d.
An Edition in Illustrated Paper Covers, price 1s.
Songs of a Song Writer. Crown 8vo. Cloth, price 6s.

BERNSTEIN (Prof.).
The Five Senses of Man. With 91 Illustrations. Second Edition. Crown 8vo. Cloth, price 5s.
Volume XXI. of The International Scientific Series.

BETHAM - EDWARDS (Miss M.).
Kitty. With a Frontispiece. Crown 8vo. Cloth, price 6s.

BEVINGTON (L. S.).
Key Notes. Small crown 8vo. Cloth, price 5s.

BLASERNA (Prof. Pietro).
The Theory of Sound in its Relation to Music. With numerous Illustrations. Second Edition. Crown 8vo. Cloth, price 5s.
Volume XXII. of The International Scientific Series.

Blue Roses ; or, Helen Mali-nofska's Marriage. By the Author of "Véra." 2 vols. Fifth Edition. Cloth, gilt tops, 12s.
*** Also a Cheaper Edition in 1 vol. With Frontispiece. Crown 8vo. Cloth, price 6s.

BLUME (Major W.).
The Operations of the German Armies in France, from Sedan to the end of the war of 1870-71. With Map. From the Journals of the Head-quarters Staff. Translated by the late E. M. Jones, Maj. 20th Foot, Prof. of Mil. Hist., Sandhurst. Demy 8vo. Cloth, price 9s.

BOGUSLAWSKI (Capt. A. von).
Tactical Deductions from the War of 1870-71. Translated by Colonel Sir Lumley Graham, Bart., late 18th (Royal Irish) Regiment. Third Edition, Revised and Corrected. Demy 8vo. Cloth, price 7s.

BONWICK (J.), F.R.G.S.
Egyptian Belief and Modern Thought. Large post 8vo. Cloth, price 10s. 6d.
Pyramid Facts and Fancies. Crown 8vo. Cloth, price 5s.
The Tasmanian Lily. With Frontispiece. Crown 8vo. Cloth, price 5s.
Mike Howe, the Bushranger of Van Diemen's Land. With Frontispiece. Crown 8vo. Cloth, price 5s.

BOWEN (H. C.), M.A.
English Grammar for Beginners. Fcap. 8vo. Cloth, price 1s.
Studies in English, for the use of Modern Schools. Small crown 8vo. Cloth, price 1s. 6d.
Simple English Poems. English Literature for Junior Classes. In Four Parts. Parts I. and II., price 6d. each, now ready.

BOWRING (Sir John).
Autobiographical Recollections. With Memoir by Lewin B. Bowring. Demy 8vo. Price 14s.

Brave Men's Footsteps.
By the Editor of "Men who have Risen." A Book of Example and Anecdote for Young People. With Four Illustrations by C. Doyle. Sixth Edition. Crown 8vo. Cloth, price 3s. 6d.

BRIALMONT (Col. A.).
Hasty Intrenchments. Translated by Lieut. Charles A. Empson, R.A. With Nine Plates. Demy 8vo. Cloth, price 6s.

BRODRICK (The Hon. G. C.).
Political Studies. Demy 8vo. Cloth, price 14s.

BROOKE (Rev. S. A.), M.A.
The Late Rev. F. W. Robertson, M.A., Life and Letters of. Edited by.
I. Uniform with the Sermons. 2 vols. With Steel Portrait. Price 7s. 6d.
II. Library Edition. 8vo. With Two Steel Portraits. Price 12s.
III. A Popular Edition, in 1 vol. 8vo. Price 6s.
Theology in the English Poets. — COWPER, COLERIDGE, WORDSWORTH, and BURNS. Fourth and Cheaper Edition. Post 8vo. Cloth, price 5s.
Christ in Modern Life. Fourteenth and Cheaper Edition. Crown 8vo. Cloth, price 5s.
Sermons. First Series. Eleventh Edition. Crown 8vo. Cloth, price 6s.
Sermons. Second Series. Third Edition. Crown 8vo. Cloth, price 7s.

BROOKE (Rev. S. A.), M.A.
continued.
The Fight of Faith. Sermons preached on various occasions. Third Edition. Crown 8vo. Cloth, price 7s. 6d.
Frederick Denison Maurice: The Life and Work of. A Memorial Sermon. Crown 8vo. Sewed, price 1s.

BROOKE (W. G.), M.A.
The Public Worship Regulation Act. With a Classified Statement of its Provisions, Notes, and Index. Third Edition, Revised and Corrected. Crown 8vo. Cloth, price 3s. 6d.
Six Privy Council Judgments—1850-1872. Annotated by. Third Edition. Crown 8vo. Cloth, price 9s.

BROUN (J. A.).
Magnetic Observations at Trevandrum and Augustia Malley. Vol. I. 4to. Cloth, price 63s.
The Report from above, separately sewed, price 21s.

BROWN (Rev. J. Baldwin).
The Higher Life. Its Reality, Experience, and Destiny. Fifth and Cheaper Edition. Crown 8vo. Cloth, price 5s.
Doctrine of Annihilation in the Light of the Gospel of Love. Five Discourses. Third Edition. Crown 8vo. Cloth, price 2s. 6d.
The Christian Policy of Life. A Book for Young Men of Business. New and Cheaper Edition. Crown 8vo. Cloth, price 3s. 6d.

BROWN (J. Croumbie), LL.D.
Reboisement in France; or, Records of the Replanting of the Alps, the Cevennes, and the Pyrenees with Trees, Herbage, and Bush. Demy 8vo. Cloth, price 12s. 6d.
The Hydrology of Southern Africa. Demy 8vo. Cloth, price 10s. 6d.

BROWNE (W. R.).
The Inspiration of the New Testament. With a Preface by the Rev. J. P. NORRIS, D.D. Fcap. 8vo. Cloth, price 2s. 6d.

BRYANT (W. C.)
Poems. Red-line Edition.
With 24 Illustrations and Portrait of
the Author. Crown 8vo. Cloth extra,
price 7s. 6d.
A Cheaper Edition, with Frontispiece. Small crown 8vo. Cloth, price
3s. 6d.

BURCKHARDT (Jacob).
**The Civilization of the Pe-
riod of the Renaissance in Italy.**
Authorized translation, by S. G. C.
Middlemore. 2 vols. Demy 8vo.
Cloth, price 24s.

BURTON (Mrs. Richard).
The Inner Life of Syria,
Palestine, and the Holy Land.
With Maps, Photographs, and
Coloured Plates. 2 vols. Second
Edition. Demy 8vo. Cloth, price 24s.
⁎ Also a Cheaper Edition in
one volume. Large post 8vo. Cloth,
price 10s. 6d.

BURTON (Capt. Richard F.).
The Gold Mines of Midian
and the Ruined Midianite
Cities. A Fortnight's Tour in
North Western Arabia. With numerous Illustrations. Second Edition. Demy 8vo. Cloth, price 18s.
**The Land of Midian Re-
visited.** With numerous illustrations on wood and by Chromo-
lithography. 2 vols. Demy 8vo.
Cloth, price 32s.

CALDERON.
Calderon's Dramas: The
Wonder-Working Magician—Life is
a Dream—The Purgatory of St.
Patrick. Translated by Denis
Florence MacCarthy. Post 8vo.
Cloth, price 10s.

CANDLER (H.).
The Groundwork of Belief.
Crown 8vo. Cloth, price 7s.

CARPENTER (W. B.), M.D.
**The Principles of Mental
Physiology.** With their Applica-
tions to the Training and Discipline
of the Mind, and the Study of its
Morbid Conditions. Illustrated.
Fifth Edition. 8vo. Cloth, price 12s.

CARPENTER (Dr. Philip P.).
His Life and Work. Edited
by his brother, Russell Lant Carpenter. With portrait and vignette.
Second Edition. Crown 8vo. Cloth,
price 7s. 6d.

CAVALRY OFFICER.
Notes on Cavalry Tactics,
Organization, &c. With Dia-
grams. Demy 8vo. Cloth, price 12s.

CHAPMAN (Hon. Mrs. E. W.).
A Constant Heart. A Story.
2 vols. Cloth, gilt tops, price 12s.

CHEYNE (Rev. T. K.).
The Prophecies of Isaiah.
Translated, with Critical Notes and
Dissertations by. Two vols., demy
8vo. Cloth. Vol. I., price 12s. 6d.

Children's Toys, and some
Elementary Lessons in General
Knowledge which they teach. Illus-
trated. Crown 8vo. Cloth, price 5s.

**CHRISTOPHERSON (The late
Rev. Henry), M.A.**
Sermons. With an Intro-
duction by John Rae, LL.D., F.S.A.
Second Series. Crown 8vo. Cloth,
price 6s.

CLAYDEN (P. W.).
**England under Lord Bea-
consfield.** The Political History of
the Last Six Years, from the end of
1873 to the beginning of 1880. Second Edition. With Index, and
Continuation to March, 1880. Demy
8vo. Cloth, price 16s.

CLERY (C.), Major.
Minor Tactics. With 26
Maps and Plans. Fourth and Revised
Edition. Demy 8vo. Cloth, price 16s.

CLODD (Edward), F.R.A.S.
**The Childhood of the
World:** a Simple Account of Man
in Early Times. Sixth Edition.
Crown 8vo. Cloth, price 3s.
A Special Edition for Schools.
Price 1s.

**The Childhood of Reli-
gions.** Including a Simple Account
of the Birth and Growth of Myths
and Legends. Third Thousand.
Crown 8vo. Cloth, price 5s.
A Special Edition for Schools.
Price 1s. 6d.

Jesus of Nazareth. With a
brief Sketch of Jewish History to
the Time of His Birth. Small
crown 8vo. Cloth, price 6s.

COLERIDGE (Sara).
Pretty Lessons in Verse for Good Children, with some Lessons in Latin, in Easy Rhyme. A New Edition. Illustrated. Fcap. 8vo. Cloth, price 3s. 6d.
Phantasmion. A Fairy Tale. With an Introductory Preface by the Right Hon. Lord Coleridge, of Ottery St. Mary. A New Edition. Illustrated. Crown 8vo. Cloth, price 7s. 6d.
Memoir and Letters of Sara Coleridge. Edited by her Daughter. Cheap Edition. With one Portrait. Cloth, price 7s. 6d.

COLLINS (Mortimer).
The Secret of Long Life. Small crown 8vo. Cloth, price 3s. 6d.
Inn of Strange Meetings, and other Poems. Crown 8vo. Cloth, price 5s.

COLOMB (Colonel).
The Cardinal Archbishop. A Spanish Legend in twenty-nine Cancions. Small crown 8vo. Cloth, price 5s.

CONWAY (Hugh).
A Life's Idylls. Small crown 8vo. Cloth, price 3s. 6d.

COOKE (M. C.), M.A., LL.D.
Fungi; their Nature, Influences, Uses, &c. Edited by the Rev. M. J. Berkeley, M.A., F.L.S. With Illustrations. Second Edition. Crown 8vo. Cloth, price 5s.
Volume XIV. of The International Scientific Series.

COOKE (Prof. J. P.)
The New Chemistry. With 31 Illustrations. Fifth Edition. Crown 8vo. Cloth, price 5s.
Volume IX. of The International Scientific Series.
Scientific Culture. Crown 8vo. Cloth, price 1s.

COOPER (H. J.).
The Art of Furnishing on Rational and Æsthetic Principles. New and Cheaper Edition. Fcap. 8vo. Cloth, price 1s. 6d.

COPPÉE (François).
L'Exilée. Done into English Verse with the sanction of the Author by I. O. L. Crown 8vo. Vellum, price 5s.

CORFIELD (Prof.), M.D.
Health. Crown 8vo. Cloth, price 6s.

CORY (William).
A Guide to Modern Eng-lish History. Part I. MDCCCXV. —MDCCCXXX. Demy 8vo. Cloth, price 9s.

COURTNEY (W. L.).
The Metaphysics of John Stuart Mill. Crown 8vo. Cloth, price 5s. 6d.

COWAN (Rev. William).
Poems : Chiefly Sacred, in-cluding Translations from some Ancient Latin Hymns. Fcap. 8vo. Cloth, price 5s.

COX (Rev. Sir G. W.), Bart.
A History of Greece from the Earliest Period to the end of the Persian War. New Edition. 2 vols. Demy 8vo. Cloth, price 36s.
The Mythology of the **Aryan Nations.** New Edition. 2 vols. Demy 8vo. Cloth, price 28s.
A General History of Greece from the Earliest Period to the Death of Alexander the Great, with a sketch of the subsequent History to the present time. New Edition. Crown 8vo. Cloth, price 7s. 6d.
Tales of Ancient Greece. New Edition. Small crown 8vo Cloth, price 6s.
School History of Greece. With Maps. New Edition. Fcap 8vo. Cloth, price 3s. 6d.
The Great Persian War from the Histories of Herodotus. New Edition. Fcap. 8vo. Cloth, price 3s. 6d.
A Manual of Mythology in the form of Question and Answer. New Edition. Fcap. 8vo. Cloth, price 3s.

COX (Rev. Sir G. W.), Bart., **M.A., and EUSTACE HIN-**TON JONES.
Popular Romances of the Middle Ages. Second Edition in one volume. Crown 8vo. Cloth, price 6s.

COX (Rev. Samuel).
Salvator Mundi ; or, Is Christ the Saviour of all Men? Sixth Edition. Crown 8vo. Cloth, price 5s.

The Genesis of Evil, and other Sermons, mainly Expository. Second Edition. Crown 8vo. Cloth, price 6s.

CRAUFURD (A. H.).
Seeking for Light : Sermons. Crown 8vo. Cloth, price 5s.

CRAWFURD (Oswald).
Portugal, Old and New. With Illustrations and Maps. Demy 8vo. Cloth, price 16s.

CRESSWELL (Mrs. G.).
The King's Banner. Drama in Four Acts. Five Illustrations. 4to. Cloth, price 10s. 6d.

CROMPTON (Henry).
Industrial Conciliation. Fcap. 8vo. Cloth, price 2s. 6d.

CROZIER (John Beattie), M.B.
The Religion of the Future. Crown 8vo. Cloth, price 6s.

D'ANVERS (N. R.).
Parted. A Tale of Clouds and Sunshine. With 4 Illustrations. Extra Fcap. 8vo. Cloth, price 3s. 6d.

Little Minnie's Troubles. An Every-day Chronicle. With Four Illustrations by W. H. Hughes. Fcap. Cloth, price 3s. 6d.

Pixie's Adventures ; or, the Tale of a Terrier. With 21 Illustrations. 16mo. Cloth, price 4s. 6d.

Nanny's Adventures ; or, the Tale of a Goat. With 12 Illustrations. 16mo. Cloth, price 4s. 6d.

DAVIDSON (Rev. Samuel), D.D., LL.D.
The New Testament, trans- lated from the Latest Greek Text of Tischendorf. A New and thoroughly Revised Edition. Post 8vo. Cloth, price 10s. 6d.

DAVIDSON (Rev. Samuel), D.D., LL.D.—*continued.*
Canon of the Bible : Its Formation, History, and Fluctuations. Third Edition, revised and enlarged. Small crown 8vo. Cloth, price 5s.

DAVIES (G. Christopher).
Rambles and Adventures of Our School Field Club. With Four Illustrations. Crown 8vo. Cloth, price 5s.

DAVIES (Rev. J. L.), M.A.
Theology and Morality. Essays on Questions of Belief and Practice. Crown 8vo. Cloth, price 7s. 6d.

DAVIES (T. Hart.).
Catullus. Translated into English Verse. Crown 8vo. Cloth, price 6s.

DAWSON (George), M.A.
Prayers, with a Discourse on Prayer. Edited by his Wife. Fifth Edition. Crown 8vo. Price 6s.

Sermons on Disputed Points and Special Occasions. Edited by his Wife. Third Edition. Crown 8vo. Cloth, price 6s.

Sermons on Daily Life and Duty. Edited by his Wife. Second Edition. Crown 8vo. Cloth, price 6s.

DE L'HOSTE (Col. E. P.).
The Desert Pastor, Jean Jarousseau. Translated from the French of Eugène Pelletan. With a Frontispiece. New Edition. Fcap. 8vo. Cloth, price 3s. 6d.

DENNIS (J.).
English Sonnets. Collected and Arranged. Elegantly bound. Fcap. 8vo. Cloth, price 3s. 6d.

DE REDCLIFFE (Viscount Stratford), P.C., K.G., G.C.B.
Why am I a Christian ? Fifth Edition. Crown 8vo. Cloth, price 3s.

DESPREZ (Philip S.).
Daniel and John ; or, the Apocalypse of the Old and that of the New Testament. Demy 8vo. Cloth, price 12s.

DE TOCQUEVILLE (A.).
Correspondence and Conversations of, with Nassau William Senior, from 1834 to 1859. Edited by M. C. M. Simpson. 2 vols. Post 8vo. Cloth, price 21s.

DE VERE (Aubrey).
Legends of the Saxon Saints. Small crown 8vo. Cloth, price 6s.

Alexander the Great. A Dramatic Poem. Small crown 8vo. Cloth, price 5s.

The Infant Bridal, and other Poems. A New and Enlarged Edition. Fcap. 8vo. Cloth, price 7s. 6d.

The Legends of St. Patrick, and other Poems. Small crown 8vo. Cloth, price 5s.

St. Thomas of Canterbury. A Dramatic Poem. Large fcap. 8vo. Cloth, price 5s.

Antar and Zara : an Eastern Romance. INISFAIL, and other Poems, Meditative and Lyrical. Fcap. 8vo. Price 6s.

The Fall of Rora, the Search after Proserpine, and other Poems, Meditative and Lyrical. Fcap. 8vo. Price 6s.

DOBSON (Austin).
Vignettes in Rhyme and Vers de Société. Third Edition. Fcap. 8vo. Cloth, price 5s.

Proverbs in Porcelain. By the Author of "Vignettes in Rhyme." Second Edition. Crown 8vo. 6s.

DOWDEN (Edward), LL.D.
Shakspere : a Critical Study of his Mind and Art. Fifth Edition. Large post 8vo. Cloth, price 12s.

Studies in Literature, 1789-1877. Large post 8vo. Cloth, price 12s.

Poems. Second Edition. Fcap. 8vo. Cloth, price 5s.

DOWNTON (Rev. H.), M.A.
Hymns and Verses. Original and Translated. Small crown 8vo. Cloth, price 3s. 6d.

DRAPER (J. W.), M.D., LL.D.
History of the Conflict between Religion and Science. Fourteenth Edition. Crown 8vo. Cloth, price 5s.
Volume XIII. of The International Scientific Series.

DREW (Rev. G. S.), M.A.
Scripture Lands in connection with their History. Second Edition. 8vo. Cloth, price 10s. 6d.

Nazareth : Its Life and Lessons. Third Edition. Crown 8vo. Cloth, price 5s.

The Divine Kingdom on Earth as it is in Heaven. 8vo. Cloth, price 10s. 6d.

The Son of Man : His Life and Ministry. Crown 8vo. Cloth, price 7s. 6d.

DREWRY (G. O.), M.D.
The Common-Sense Management of the Stomach. Fifth Edition. Fcap. 8vo. Cloth, price 2s. 6d.

DREWRY (G. O.), M.D., and BARTLETT (H. C.), Ph.D., F.C.S.
Cup and Platter : or, Notes on Food and its Effects. New and cheaper Edition. Small 8vo. Cloth, price 1s. 6d.

DRUMMOND (Miss).
Tripps Buildings. A Study from Life, with Frontispiece. Small crown 8vo. Cloth, price 3s. 6d.

DU MONCEL (Count).
The Telephone, the Microphone, and the Phonograph. With 74 Illustrations. Small crown 8vo. Cloth, price 5s.

DU VERNOIS (Col. von Verdy).
Studies in leading Troops. An authorized and accurate Translation by Lieutenant H. J. T. Hildyard, 71st Foot. Parts I. and II. Demy 8vo. Cloth, price 7s.

EDEN (Frederick).
The Nile without a Dragoman. Second Edition. Crown 8vo. Cloth, price 7s. 6d.

EDMONDS (Herbert).

Well Spent Lives : a Series of Modern Biographies. Crown 8vo. Price 5s.

Educational Code of the Prussian Nation, in its Present Form. In accordance with the Decisions of the Common Provincial Law, and with those of Recent Legislation. Crown 8vo. Cloth, price 2s. 6d.

EDWARDS (Rev. Basil).

Minor Chords; or, Songs for the Suffering: a Volume of Verse. Fcap. 8vo. Cloth, price 3s. 6d. ; paper, price 2s. 6d.

ELLIOT (Lady Charlotte).

Medusa and other Poems. Crown 8vo. Cloth, price 6s.

ELLIOTT (Ebenezer), The Corn- Law Rhymer.

Poems. Edited by his Son, the Rev. Edwin Elliott, of St. John's, Antigua. 2 vols. Crown 8vo. Cloth, price 18s.

ELSDALE (Henry).

Studies in Tennyson's Idylls. Crown 8vo. Cloth, price 5s.

Epic of Hades (The). By the author of "Songs of Two Worlds." Tenth and finally revised Edition. Fcap. 8vo. Cloth, price 7s. 6d. **** Also an Illustrated Edition with seventeen full-page designs in photo-mezzotint by GEORGE R. CHAPMAN. 4to. Cloth, extra gilt leaves, price 25s.

EVANS (Mark).

The Gospel of Home Life. Crown 8vo. Cloth, price 4s. 6d.

The Story of our Father's Love, told to Children. Fourth and Cheaper Edition. With Four Illustrations. Fcap. 8vo. Cloth, price 1s. 6d.

A Book of Common Prayer and Worship for Household Use, compiled exclusively from the Holy Scriptures. New and Cheaper Edition. Fcap. 8vo. Cloth, price 1s.

EVANS (Mark)—*continued.*

The King's Story Book. In three parts. Fcap. 8vo. Cloth, price 1s. 6d. each. **** Part I., with four illustrations and Picture Map, now ready.

EX-CIVILIAN.

Life in the Mofussil; or, Civilian Life in Lower Bengal. 2 vols. Large post 8vo. Price 14s.

FARQUHARSON (M.).

I. **Elsie Dinsmore.** Crown 8vo. Cloth, price 3s. 6d.

II. **Elsie's Girlhood.** Crown 8vo. Cloth, price 3s. 6d.

III. **Elsie's Holidays at** Roselands. Crown 8vo. Cloth, price 3s. 6d.

FIELD (Horace), B.A. Lond.

The Ultimate Triumph of Christianity. Small crown 8vo. Cloth, price 3s. 6d.

FINN (the late James), M.R.A.S.

Stirring Times ; or, Records from Jerusalem Consular Chronicles of 1853 to 1856. Edited and Compiled by his Widow. With a Preface by the Viscountess STRANGFORD. 2 vols. Demy 8vo. Price 30s.

Folkestone Ritual Case (The). The Argument, Proceedings, Judgment, and Report, revised by the several Counsel engaged. Demy 8vo. Cloth, price 25s.

FORMBY (Rev. Henry).

Ancient Rome and its Con- nection with the Christian Religion : an Outline of the History of the City from its First Foundation down to the Erection of the Chair of St. Peter, A.D. 42-47. With numerous Illustrations of Ancient Monuments, Sculpture, and Coinage, and of the Antiquities of the Christian Catacombs. Royal 4to. Cloth extra, price 50s. Roxburgh, half-morocco, price 52s. 6d.

FOWLE (Rev. Edmund).

Latin Primer Rules made Easy. Crown 8vo. Cloth, price 3s.

FOWLE (Rev. T. W.), M.A.
The Reconciliation of Religion and Science. Being Essays on Immortality, Inspiration, Miracles, and the Being of Christ. Demy 8vo. Cloth, price 10s. 6d.

The Divine Legation of Christ. Crown 8vo. Cloth, price 7s.

FRASER (Donald).
Exchange Tables of Sterling and Indian Rupee Currency, upon a new and extended system, embracing Values from One Farthing to One Hundred Thousand Pounds, and at Rates progressing, in Sixteenths of a Penny, from 1s. 9d. to 2s. 3d. per Rupee. Royal 8vo. Cloth, price 10s. 6d.

FRISWELL (J. Hain).
The Better Self. Essays for Home Life. Crown 8vo. Cloth, price 6s.

One of Two; or, A Left-Handed Bride. With a Frontispiece. Crown 8vo. Cloth, price 3s. 6d.

GARDNER (J.), M.D.
Longevity: The Means of Prolonging Life after Middle Age. Fourth Edition, Revised and Enlarged. Small crown 8vo. Cloth, price 4s.

GARRETT (E.).
By Still Waters. A Story for Quiet Hours. With Seven Illustrations. Crown 8vo. Cloth, price 6s.

GEBLER (Karl Von).
Galileo Galilei and the Roman Curia, from Authentic Sources. Translated with the sanction of the Author, by Mrs. GEORGE STURGE. Demy 8vo. Cloth, price 12s.

GEDDES (James).
History of the Administration of John de Witt, Grand Pensionary of Holland. Vol. I. 1623—1654. Demy 8vo., with Portrait. Cloth, price 15s.

G. H. T.
Verses, mostly written in India. Crown 8vo. Cloth, price 6s.

GILBERT (Mrs.).
Autobiography and other Memorials. Edited by Josiah Gilbert. Third Edition. With Portrait and several Wood Engravings. Crown 8vo. Cloth, price 7s. 6d.

GILL (Rev. W. W.), B.A.
Myths and Songs from the South Pacific. With a Preface by F. Max Müller, M.A., Professor of Comparative Philology at Oxford. Post 8vo. Cloth, price 9s.

Ginevra and The Duke of Guise. Two Tragedies. Crown 8vo. Cloth, price 6s.

GLOVER (F.), M.A.
Exempla Latina. A First Construing Book with Short Notes, Lexicon, and an Introduction to the Analysis of Sentences. Fcap. 8vo. Cloth, price 2s.

GODWIN (William).
William Godwin: His Friends and Contemporaries. With Portraits and Facsimiles of the handwriting of Godwin and his Wife. By C. Kegan Paul. 2 vols. Demy 8vo. Cloth, price 28s.

The Genius of Christianity Unveiled. Being Essays never before published. Edited, with a Preface, by C. Kegan Paul. Crown 8vo. Cloth, price 7s. 6d.

GOETZE (Capt. A. von).
Operations of the German Engineers during the War of 1870-1871. Published by Authority, and in accordance with Official Documents. Translated from the German by Colonel G. Graham, V.C., C.B., R.E. With 6 large Maps. Demy 8vo. Cloth, price 21s.

GOLDSMID (Sir Francis Henry).
Memoir of. With Portrait. Crown 8vo. Cloth, price 5s.

GOODENOUGH (Commodore J. G.), R.N., C.B., C.M.G.
Memoir of, with Extracts from his Letters and Journals. Edited by his Widow. With Steel Engraved Portrait. Square 8vo. Cloth, 5s.

*** Also a Library Edition with Maps, Woodcuts, and Steel Engraved Portrait. Square post 8vo. Cloth, price 14s.

GOSSE (Edmund W.).
Studies in the Literature of Northern Europe. With a Frontispiece designed and etched by Alma Tadema. Large post 8vo. Cloth, price 12s.
New Poems. Crown 8vo. Cloth, price 7s. 6d.

GOULD (Rev. S. Baring), M.A.
Germany, Present and Past. 2 Vols. Demy 8vo. Cloth, price 21s.
The Vicar of Morwenstow: a Memoir of the Rev. R. S. Hawker. With Portrait. Third Edition, revised. Square post 8vo. Cloth, 10s. 6d.

GREENOUGH (Mrs. Richard).
Mary Magdalene: A Poem. Large post 8vo. Parchment antique, price 6s.

GREY (John), of Dilston.
John Grey (of Dilston): Memoirs. By Josephine E. Butler. New and Revised Edition. Crown 8vo. Cloth, price 3s. 6d.

GRIMLEY (Rev. H. N.), M.A.
Tremadoc Sermons, chiefly on the SPIRITUAL BODY, the UNSEEN WORLD, and the DIVINE HUMANITY. Second Edition. Crown 8vo. Cloth, price 6s.

GRÜNER (M. L.).
Studies of Blast Furnace Phenomena. Translated by L. D. B. Gordon, F.R.S.E., F.G.S. Demy 8vo. Cloth, price 7s. 6d.

GURNEY (Rev. Archer).
Words of Faith and Cheer. A Mission of Instruction and Suggestion. Crown 8vo. Cloth, price 6s.

Gwen: A Drama in Monologue. By the Author of the "Epic of Hades." Second Edition. Fcap. 8vo. Cloth, price 5s.

HAECKEL (Prof. Ernst).
The History of Creation. Translation revised by Professor E. Ray Lankester, M.A., F.R.S. With Coloured Plates and Genealogical Trees of the various groups of both plants and animals. 2 vols. Second Edition. Post 8vo. Cloth, price 32s.
The History of the Evolution of Man. With numerous Illustrations. 2 vols. Large post 8vo. Cloth, price 32s.

HAECKEL (Prof. Ernst.)—continued.
Freedom in Science and Teaching. From the German of Ernst Haeckel, with a Prefatory Note by T. H. Huxley, F.R.S. Crown 8vo. Cloth, price 5s.

HAKE (A. Egmont).
Paris Originals, with twenty etchings, by Léon Richeton. Large post 8vo. Cloth, price 14s.

Halleck's International Law; or, Rules Regulating the Intercourse of States in Peace and War. A New Edition, revised, with Notes and Cases. By Sir Sherston Baker, Bart. 2 vols. Demy 8vo. Cloth, price 38s.

HARDY (Thomas).
A Pair of Blue Eyes. New Edition. With Frontispiece. Crown 8vo. Cloth, price 6s.
The Return of the Native. New Edition. With Frontispiece. Crown 8vo. Cloth, price 6s.

HARRISON (Lieut.-Col. R.).
The Officer's Memorandum Book for Peace and War. Second Edition. Oblong 32mo. roan, elastic band and pencil, price 3s. 6d.; russia, 5s.

HARTINGTON (The Right Hon. the Marquis of), M.P.
Election Speeches in 1879 and 1880. With Address to the Electors of North-East Lancashire. Crown 8vo. Cloth, price 3s. 6d.

HAWEIS (Rev. H. R.), M.A.
Arrows in the Air. Crown 8vo. Second Edition. Cloth, price 6s.
Current Coin. Materialism—The Devil—Crime—Drunkenness—Pauperism—Emotion—Recreation—The Sabbath. Third Edition. Crown 8vo. Cloth, price 6s.
Speech in Season. Fourth Edition. Crown 8vo. Cloth, price 9s.
Thoughts for the Times. Eleventh Edition. Crown 8vo. Cloth, price 7s. 6d.
Unsectarian Family Prayers. New and Cheaper Edition. Fcap. 8vo. Cloth, price 1s. 6d.

HAWKER (Robert Stephen).
The Poetical Works of.
Now first collected and arranged with a prefatory notice by J. G. Godwin. With Portrait. Crown 8vo. Cloth, price 12s.

HAWTREY (Edward M.).
Corydalis. A Story of the Sicilian Expedition. Small crown 8vo. Cloth, price 3s. 6d.

HEIDENHAIN (Rudolf), M.D.
Animal Magnetism. Physiological Observations. Translated from the Fourth German Edition, by L. C. Wooldridge. With a Preface by G. R. Romanes, F.R.S. Crown 8vo. Cloth, price 2s. 6d.

HELLWALD (Baron F. von).
The Russians in Central Asia. A Critical Examination, down to the present time, of the Geography and History of Central Asia. Translated by Lieut.-Col. Theodore Wirgman, LL.B. Large post 8vo. With Map. Cloth, price 12s.

HELVIG (Major H.).
The Operations of the Bavarian Army Corps. Translated by Captain G. S. Schwabe. With Five large Maps. In 2 vols. Demy 8vo. Cloth, price 24s.
Tactical Examples: Vol. I. The Battalion, price 15s. Vol. II. The Regiment and Brigade, price 10s. 6d. Translated from the German by Col. Sir Lumley Graham. With numerous Diagrams. Demy 8vo. Cloth.

HERFORD (Brooke).
The Story of Religion in England. A Book for Young Folk. Crown 8vo. Cloth, price 5s.

HINTON (James).
Life and Letters of. Edited by Ellice Hopkins, with an Introduction by Sir W. W. Gull, Bart., and Portrait engraved on Steel by C. H. Jeens. Second Edition. Crown 8vo. Cloth, 8s. 6d.
Chapters on the Art of Thinking, and other Essays. With an Introduction by Shadworth Hodgson. Edited by C. H. Hinton. Crown 8vo. Cloth, price 8s. 6d.

HINTON (James)—*continued.*
The Place of the Physician. To which is added ESSAYS ON THE LAW OF HUMAN LIFE, AND ON THE RELATION BETWEEN ORGANIC AND INORGANIC WORLDS. Second Edition. Crown 8vo. Cloth, price 3s. 6d.
Physiology for Practical Use. By various Writers. With 50 Illustrations. 2 vols. Second Edition. Crown 8vo. Cloth, price 12s. 6d.
An Atlas of Diseases of the Membrana Tympani. With Descriptive Text. Post 8vo. Price £6 6s.
The Questions of Aural Surgery. With Illustrations. 2 vols. Post 8vo. Cloth, price 12s. 6d.
The Mystery of Pain. New Edition. Fcap. 8vo. Cloth limp, 1s.

HOCKLEY (W. B.).
Tales of the Zenana; or, A Nuwab's Leisure Hours. By the Author of "Pandurang Hari." With a Preface by Lord Stanley of Alderley. 2 vols. Crown 8vo. Cloth, price 21s.
Pandurang Hari; or, Memoirs of a Hindoo. A Tale of Mahratta Life sixty years ago. With a Preface by Sir H. Bartle E. Frere, G. C. S. I., &c. New and Cheaper Edition. Crown 8vo. Cloth, price 6s.

HOFFBAUER (Capt.).
The German Artillery in the Battles near Metz. Based on the official reports of the German Artillery. Translated by Capt. E. O. Hollist. With Map and Plans. Demy 8vo. Cloth, price 21s.

HOLMES (E. G. A.).
Poems. First and Second Series. Fcap. 8vo. Cloth, price 5s. each.

HOLROYD (Major W. R. M.).
Tas-hil ul Kālām; or, Hindustani made Easy. Crown 8vo. Cloth, price 5s.

HOOPER (Mary).
Little Dinners: How to Serve them with Elegance and Economy. Thirteenth Edition. Crown 8vo. Cloth, price 5s.

HOOPER (Mary)—*continued*.

Cookery for Invalids, Per-sons of Delicate Digestion, and Children. Crown 8vo. Cloth, price 3*s*. 6*d*.

Every - Day Meals. Being Economical and Wholesome Recipes for Breakfast, Luncheon, and Sup-per. Second Edition. Crown 8vo. Cloth, price 5*s*.

HOOPER (Mrs. G.).

The House of Raby. With a Frontispiece. Crown 8vo. Cloth, price 3*s*. 6*d*.

HOPKINS (Ellice).

Life and Letters of James Hinton, with an Introduction by Sir W. W. Gull, Bart., and Portrait en-graved on Steel by C. H. Jeens. Second Edition. Crown 8vo. Cloth price 8*s*. 6*d*.

HOPKINS (M.).

The Port of Refuge; or, Counsel and Aid to Shipmasters in Difficulty, Doubt, or Distress. Crown 8vo. Second and Revised Edition. Cloth, price 6*s*.

HORNER (The Misses).

Walks in Florence. A New and thoroughly Revised Edition. 2 vols. Crown 8vo. Cloth limp. With Illustrations.

Vol. I.—Churches, Streets, and Palaces. 10*s*. 6*d*. Vol. II.—Public Galleries and Museums. 5*s*.

HULL (Edmund C. P.).

The European in India. With a MEDICAL GUIDE FOR ANGLO-INDIANS. By R. R. S. Mair, M.D., F.R.C.S.E. Third Edition, Revised and Corrected. Post 8vo. Cloth, price 6*s*.

HUTCHISON (Lieut.-Col. F. J.), and Capt. G. H. MACGREGOR.

Military Sketching and Re-connaissance. With Fifteen Plates. Small 8vo. Cloth, price 6*s*.

The first Volume of Military Hand-books for Regimental Officers. Edited by Lieut.-Col. C. B. BRACKENBURY, R.A., A.A.G.

HUTTON (Arthur), M.A.

The Anglican Ministry. Its Nature and Value in relation to the Catholic Priesthood. With a Pre-face by his Eminence Cardinal New-man. Demy 8vo. Cloth, price 14*s*.

HUXLEY (Prof.)

The Crayfish: An Intro-duction to the Study of Zoology. With Eighty-two Illustrations. Crown 8vo. Cloth, price 5*s*.

Volume XXVIII. of the Interna-tional Scientific Scientific Series.

INCHBOLD (J. W.).

Annus Amoris. Sonnets. Fcap. 8vo. Cloth, price 4*s*. 6*d*.

INGELOW (Jean).

Off the Skelligs. A Novel. With Frontispiece. Second Edition. Crown 8vo. Cloth, price 6*s*.

The Little Wonder-horn. A Second Series of " Stories Told to a Child." With Fifteen Illustrations. Small 8vo. Cloth, price 2*s*. 6*d*.

Indian Bishoprics. By an Indian Churchman. Demy 8vo. 6*d*.

International Scientific Series (The).

I. **Forms of Water: A Fami-**liar Exposition of the Origin and Phenomena of Glaciers. By J. Tyndall, LL.D., F.R.S. With 25 Illustrations. Seventh Edition. Crown 8vo. Cloth, price 5*s*.

II. **Physics and Politics;** or, Thoughts on the Application of the Principles of " Natural Selection " and " Inheritance " to Political So-ciety. By Walter Bagehot. Fifth Edition. Crown 8vo. Cloth, price 4*s*.

III. **Foods.** By Edward Smith, M.D., &c. With numerous Illus-trations. Sixth Edition. Crown 8vo. Cloth, price 5*s*.

IV. **Mind and Body: The Theo-**ries of their Relation. By Alexander Bain, LL.D. With Four Illustra-tions. Seventh Edition. Crown 8vo. Cloth, price 4*s*.

V. **The Study of Sociology.** By Herbert Spencer. Eighth Edition. Crown 8vo. Cloth, price 5*s*.

International Scientific Series (The)—*continued.*

VI. **On the Conservation of Energy.** By Balfour Stewart, LL.D., &c. With 14 Illustrations. Fifth Edition. Crown 8vo. Cloth, price 5s.

VII. **Animal Locomotion;** or, Walking, Swimming, and Flying. By J. B. Pettigrew, M.D., &c. With 130 Illustrations. Second Edition. Crown 8vo. Cloth, price 5s.

VIII. **Responsibility in Mental Disease.** By Henry Maudsley, M.D. Third Edition. Crown 8vo. Cloth, price 5s.

IX. **The New Chemistry.** By Professor J. P. Cooke. With 31 Illustrations. Fifth Edition. Crown 8vo. Cloth, price 5s.

X. **The Science of Law.** By Prof. Sheldon Amos. Fourth Edition. Crown 8vo. Cloth, price 5s.

XI. **Animal Mechanism.** A Treatise on Terrestrial and Aerial Locomotion. By Prof. E. J. Marey. With 117 Illustrations. Second Edition. Crown 8vo. Cloth, price 5s.

XII. **The Doctrine of Descent and Darwinism.** By Prof. Osca Schmidt. With 26 Illustrations. Third Edition. Crown 8vo. Cloth, price 5s.

XIII. **The History of the Conflict between Religion and Science.** By J. W. Draper, M.D., LL.D. Fourteenth Edition. Crown 8vo. Cloth, price 5s.

XIV. **Fungi;** their Nature, Influences, Uses, &c. By M. C. Cooke, LL.D. Edited by the Rev. M. J. Berkeley, F.L.S. With numerous Illustrations. Second Edition. Crown 8vo. Cloth, price 5s.

XV. **The Chemical Effects of Light and Photography.** By Dr. Hermann Vogel. With 100 Illustrations. Third and Revised Edition. Crown 8vo. Cloth, price 5s.

XVI. **The Life and Growth of Language.** By Prof. William Dwight Whitney. Second Edition. Crown 8vo. Cloth, price 5s.

XVII. **Money and the Mechanism of Exchange.** By W. Stanley Jevons, F.R.S. Fourth Edition. Crown 8vo. Cloth, price 5s.

International Scientific Series (The)—*continued.*

XVIII. **The Nature of Light:** With a General Account of Physical Optics. By Dr. Eugene Lommel. With 188 Illustrations and a table of Spectra in Chromo-lithography. Third Edition. Crown 8vo. Cloth, price 5s.

XIX. **Animal Parasites and Messmates.** By M. Van Beneden. With 83 Illustrations. Second Edition. Crown 8vo. Cloth, price 5s.

XX. **Fermentation.** By Prof. Schützenberger. With 28 Illustrations. Second Edition. Crown 8vo. Cloth, price 5s.

XXI. **The Five Senses of Man.** By Prof. Berostein. With 91 Illustrations. Second Edition. Crown 8vo. Cloth, price 5s.

XXII. **The Theory of Sound in its Relation to Music.** By Prof. Pietro Blaserna. With numerous Illustrations. Second Edition. Crown 8vo. Cloth, price 5s.

XXIII. **Studies in Spectrum Analysis.** By J. Norman Lockyer. F.R.S. With six photographic Illustrations of Spectra, and numerous engravings on wood. Crown 8vo. Second Edition. Cloth, price 6s. 6d.

XXIV. **A History of the Growth of the Steam Engine.** By Prof. R. H. Thurston. With numerous Illustrations. Second Edition. Crown 8vo. Cloth, price 6s. 6d.

XXV. **Education as a Science.** By Alexander Bain, LL.D. Third Edition. Crown 8vo. Cloth, price 5s.

XXVI. **The Human Species.** By Prof. A. de Quatrefages. Second Edition. Crown 8vo. Cloth, price 5s.

XXVII. **Modern Chromatics.** With Applications to Art and Industry, by Ogden N. Rood. With 130 original Illustrations. Crown 8vo. Cloth, price 5s.

XXVIII. **The Crayfish:** an Introduction to the Study of Zoology. By Prof. T. H. Huxley. With eighty-two Illustrations. Crown 8vo. Cloth, price 5s.

XXIX. **The Brain as an Organ of Mind.** By H. Charlton Bastian, M.D. With numerous Illustrations. Second Edition. Crown 8vo. Cloth, price 5s.

International Scientific Series (The)—*continued.*

XXX. The Atomic Theory. By Prof. Ad. Wurtz. Translated by E. Clemin-Shaw. Crown 8vo. Cloth, price 5s.

Forthcoming Volumes.

Prof. W. KINGDON CLIFFORD, M.A. The First Principles of the Exact Sciences explained to the Non-mathematical.

Sir JOHN LUBBOCK, Bart., F.R.S. On Ants and Bees.

Prof. W. T. THISELTON DYER, B.A., B.Sc. Form and Habit in Flowering Plants.

Prof. MICHAEL FOSTER, M.D. Protoplasm and the Cell Theory.

Prof. A. C. RAMSAY, LL.D., F.R.S. Earth Sculpture: Hills, Valleys, Mountains, Plains, Rivers, Lakes; how they were Produced, and how they have been Destroyed.

P. BERT (Professor of Physiology, Paris). Forms of Life and other Cosmical Conditions.

HERMANN VON MEYER. The Organs of Speech.

Prof. E. MORSELLI. Suicide: an Essay in Comparative Moral Statistics.

The REV. A SECCHI, D.J., late Director of the Observatory at Rome. The Stars.

Prof. J. ROSENTHAL, of the University of Erlangen. General Physiology of Muscles and Nerves.

J. W. JUDD, F.R.S. The Laws of Volcanic Action.

Prof. F. N. BALFOUR. The Embryonic Phases of Animal Life.

J. LUYS, Physician to the Hospice de la Salpétrière. The Brain and its Functions. With Illustrations.

Dr. CARL SEMPER. Animals and their Conditions of Existence.

GEORGE J. ROMANES, F.L.S. Animal Intelligence.

ALFRED W. BENNETT. A Handbook of Cryptogamic Botany.

JENKINS (Rev. Canon).
The Girdle Legend of Prato. Small crown 8vo. Cloth, price 2s.

JENKINS (E.) and RAYMOND (J.), Esqs.
A Legal Handbook for Architects, Builders, and Building Owners. Second Edition Revised. Crown 8vo. Cloth, price 6s.

JENKINS (Rev. R. C.), M.A.
The Privilege of Peter and the Claims of the Roman Church confronted with the Scriptures, the Councils, and the Testimony of the Popes themselves. Fcap. 8vo. Cloth, price 3s. 6d.

JENNINGS (Mrs. Vaughan).
Rahel: Her Life and Letters. With a Portrait from the Painting by Daffinger. Square post 8vo. Cloth, price 7s. 6d.

Jeroveam's Wife and other Poems. Fcap. 8vo. Cloth, price 3s. 6d.

JEVONS (W. Stanley), M.A., F.R.S.
Money and the Mechanism of Exchange. Fourth Edition. Crown 8vo. Cloth, price 5s.
Volume XVII. of The International Scientific Series.

JOEL (L.).
A Consul's Manual and Shipowner's and Shipmaster's Practical Guide in their Transactions Abroad. With Definitions of Nautical, Mercantile, and Legal Terms; a Glossary of Mercantile Terms in English, French, German, Italian, and Spanish. Tables of the Money, Weights, and Measures of the Principal Commercial Nations and their Equivalents in British Standards; and Forms of Consular and Notarial Acts. Demy 8vo. Cloth, price 12s.

JOHNSTONE (C. F.), M.A.
Historical Abstracts. Being Outlines of the History of some of the less-known States of Europe. Crown 8vo. Cloth, price 7s. 6d.

JONES (Lucy).
Puddings and Sweets. Being Three Hundred and Sixty-Five Receipts approved by Experience. Crown 8vo., price 2s. 6d.

JOYCE (P. W.), LL.D., &c.
Old Celtic Romances.
Translated from the Gaelic by.
Crown 8vo. Cloth, price 7s. 6d.

KAUFMANN (Rev. M.), B.A.
Utopias; or, Schemes of Social Improvement, from Sir Thomas More to Karl Marx. Crown 8vo. Cloth, price 5s.
Socialism : Its Nature, its Dangers, and its Remedies considered. Crown 8vo. Cloth, price 7s. 6d.

KAY (Joseph), M.A., Q.C.
Free Trade in Land.
Edited by his Widow. With Preface by the Right Hon. John Bright, M. P. Third Edition. Crown 8vo. Cloth, price 5s.

KENT (Carolo).
Carona Catholica ad Petri successoris Pedes Oblata. De Summi Pontificis Leonis XIII. Assumptione Epiggramma. In Quinquaginta Linguis. Fcap. 4to. Cloth, price 15s.

KER (David).
The Boy Slave in Bokhara.
A Tale of Central Asia. With Illustrations. Crown 8vo. Cloth, price 3s. 6d.
The Wild Horseman of the Pampas. Illustrated. Crown 8vo. Cloth, price 3s. 6d.

KERNER (Dr. A.), Professor of Botany in the University of Innsbruck.
Flowers and their Unbidden Guests. Translation edited by W. Ogle, M.A., M.D., and a prefatory letter by C. Darwin, F.R.S. With Illustrations. Sq. 8vo. Cloth, price 9s.

KIDD (Joseph), M.D.
The Laws of Therapeutics, or, the Science and Art of Medicine. Crown 8vo. Cloth, price 6s.

KINAHAN (G. Henry), M.R.I.A., &c., of her Majesty's Geological Survey.
Manual of the Geology of Ireland. With 8 Plates, 26 Woodcuts, and a Map of Ireland, geologically coloured. Square 8vo. Cloth, price 15s.

KING (Mrs. Hamilton).
The Disciples. A Poem.
Fourth Edition, with some Notes. Crown 8vo. Cloth, price 7s. 6d.
Aspromonte, and other Poems. Second Edition. Fcap. 8vo. Cloth, price 4s. 6d.

KING (Edward).
Echoes from the Orient.
With Miscellaneous Poems. Small crown 8vo. Cloth, price 3s. 6d.

KINGSLEY (Charles), M.A.
Letters and Memories of his Life. Edited by his Wife. With 2 Steel engraved Portraits and numerous Illustrations on Wood, and a Facsimile of his Handwriting. Thirteenth Edition. 2 vols. Demy 8vo. Cloth, price 36s.
. Also a Cabinet Edition in 2 vols. Crown 8vo. Cloth, price 12s.
All Saints' Day and other Sermons. Second Edition. Crown 8vo. Cloth, 7s. 6d.
True Words for Brave Men: a Book for Soldiers' and Sailors' Libraries. Fifth Edition. Crown 8vo. Cloth, price 2s. 6d.

KNIGHT (Professor W.).
Studies in Philosophy and Literature. Large post 8vo. Cloth, price 7s. 6d.

LACORDAIRE (Rev. Père).
Life : Conferences delivered at Toulouse. A New and Cheaper Edition. Crown 8vo. Cloth, price 3s. 6d.

LAIRD-CLOWES (W.).
Love's Rebellion : a Poem.
Fcap. 8vo. Cloth, price 3s. 6d.

LAMONT (Martha MacDonald).
The Gladiator : A Life under the Roman Empire in the beginning of the Third Century. With four Illustrations by H. M. Paget. Extra fcap. 8vo. Cloth, price 3s. 6d.

LANG (A.).
XXII Ballades in Blue China. Elzevir. 8vo. Parchment, price 3s. 6d.

LAYMANN (Capt.).
The Frontal Attack of Infantry. Translated by Colonel Edward Newdigate. Crown 8vo. Cloth, price 2s. 6d.

LEANDER (Richard).
Fantastic Stories. Translated from the German by Paulina B. Granville. With Eight full-page Illustrations by M. E. Fraser-Tytler. Crown 8vo. Cloth, price 5s.

LEE (Rev. F. G.), D.C.L.
The Other World; or, Glimpses of the Supernatural. 2 vols. A New Edition. Crown 8vo. Cloth, price 15s.

LEE (Holme).
Her Title of Honour. A Book for Girls. New Edition. With a Frontispiece. Crown 8vo. Cloth, price 5s.

LEWIS (Edward Dillon).
A Draft Code of Criminal Law and Procedure. Demy 8vo. Cloth, price 21s.

LEWIS (Mary A.).
A Rat with Three Tales. With Four Illustrations by Catherine F. Frere. Crown 8vo. Cloth, price 5s.

LINDSAY (W. Lauder), M.D., &c.
Mind in the Lower Animals in Health and Disease. 2 vols. Demy 8vo. Cloth, price 32s.

LLOYD (Francis) and Charles Tebbitt.
Extension of Empire Weakness? Deficits Ruin? With a Practical Scheme for the Reconstruction of Asiatic Turkey. Small crown 8vo. Cloth, price 3s. 6d.

LOCKER (F.).
London Lyrics. A New and Revised Edition, with Additions and a Portrait of the Author. Crown 8vo. Cloth, elegant, price 6s.
Also, a Cheaper Edition. Fcap 8vo. Cloth, price 2s. 6d.

LOCKYER (J. Norman), F.R.S.
Studies in Spectrum Analysis; with six photographic illustrations of Spectra, and numerous engravings on wood. Second Edition. Crown 8vo. Cloth, price 6s. 6d.
Vol. XXIII. of The International Scientific Series.

LOKI.
The New Werther. Small crown 8vo. Cloth, price 2s. 6d.

LOMMEL (Dr. E.).
The Nature of Light: With a General Account of Physical Optics. Second Edition. With 188 Illustrations and a Table of Spectra in Chromo-lithography. Third Edition. Crown 8vo. Cloth, price 5s.
Volume XVIII. of The International Scientific Series.

LONSDALE (Margaret).
Sister Dora. A Biography, with Portrait engraved on steel by C. H. Jeens, and one illustration. Twelfth edition. Crown 8vo. Cloth, price 6s.

LORIMER (Peter), D.D.
John Knox and the Church of England: His Work in her Pulpit, and his Influence upon her Liturgy, Articles, and Parties. Demy 8vo. Cloth, price 12s.

John Wiclif and his English Precursors, by Gerhard Victor Lechler. Translated from the German, with additional Notes. 2 vols. Demy 8vo. Cloth, price 21s.

Love's Gamut and other Poems. Small crown 8vo. Cloth, price 3s. 6d.

LOWNDES (Henry).
Poems and Translations. Crown 8vo. Cloth, price 6s.

MAC CLINTOCK (L.).
Sir Spangle and the Dingy Hen. Illustrated. Square crown 8vo., price 2s. 6d.

MACDONALD (G.).
Malcolm. With Portrait of the Author engraved on Steel. Fourth Edition. Crown 8vo. Price 6s.

The Marquis of Lossie. Second Edition. Crown 8vo. Cloth, price 6s.

St. George and St. Michael. Second Edition. Crown 8vo. Cloth, 6s.

MACKENNA (S. J.).
Plucky Fellows. A Book for Boys. With Six Illustrations. Fourth Edition. Crown 8vo. Cloth, price 3s. 6d.

At School with an Old Dragoon. With Six Illustrations. Second Edition. Crown 8vo. Cloth, price 5s.

MACLACHLAN (Mrs.).
Notes and Extracts on Everlasting Punishment and Eternal Life, according to Literal Interpretation. Small crown 8vo. Cloth, price 3s. 6d.

MACNAUGHT (Rev. John).
Cœna Domini: An Essay on the Lord's Supper, its Primitive Institution, Apostolic Uses, and Subsequent History. Demy 8vo. Cloth, price 14s.

MAGNUSSON (Eirikr), M.A., and PALMER (E.H.), M.A.
Johan Ludvig Runeberg's Lyrical Songs, Idylls and Epigrams. Fcap. 8vo. Cloth, price 5s.

MAIR (R. S.), M.D., F.R.C.S.E.
The Medical Guide for Anglo-Indians. Being a Compendium of Advice to Europeans in India, relating to the Preservation and Regulation of Health. With a Supplement on the Management of Children in India. Second Edition. Crown 8vo. Limp cloth, price 3s. 6d.

MALDEN (H. E. and E. E.)
Princes and Princesses. Illustrated. Small crown 8vo. Cloth, price 2s. 6d.

MANNING (His Eminence Cardinal).
Essays on Religion and Literature. By various Writers. Third Series. Demy 8vo. Cloth, price 10s. 6d.

The Independence of the Holy See, with an Appendix containing the Papal Allocution and a translation. Cr. 8vo. Cloth, price 5s.

The True Story of the Vatican Council. Crown 8vo. Cloth, price 5s.

MAREY (E. J.).
Animal Mechanics. A Treatise on Terrestrial and Aerial Locomotion. With 117 Illustrations. Second Edition. Crown 8vo. Cloth, price 5s.
Volume XI. of The International Scientific Series.

Marie Antoinette: a Drama. Small crown 8vo. Cloth, price 5s.

MARKHAM (Capt. Albert Hastings), R.N.
The Great Frozen Sea. A Personal Narrative of the Voyage of the "Alert" during the Arctic Expedition of 1875-6. With six full-page Illustrations, two Maps, and twenty-seven Woodcuts. Fourth and cheaper edition. Crown 8vo. Cloth, price 6s.

Master Bobby : a Tale. By the Author of "Christina North." With Illustrations by E. H. Bell. Extra fcap. 8vo. Cloth, price 3s.6d.

MASTERMAN (J.).
Half-a-dozen Daughters. With a Frontispiece. Crown 8vo. Cloth, price 3s. 6d.

MAUDSLEY (Dr. H.).
Responsibility in Mental Disease. Third Edition. Crown 8vo. Cloth, price 5s.
Volume VIII. of The International Scientific Series.

MEREDITH (George).
The Egoist. A Comedy in Narrative. 3 vols. Crown 8vo. Cloth.
*** Also a Cheaper Edition, with Frontispiece. Crown 8vo. Cloth, price 6s.

The Ordeal of Richard Feverel. A History of Father and Son. In one vol. with Frontispiece. Crown 8vo. Cloth, price 6s.

MERRITT (Henry).
Art - Criticism and Romance. With Recollections, and Twenty-three Illustrations in *eau-forte*, by Anna Lea Merritt. Two vols. Large post 8vo. Cloth, 25s.

MIDDLETON (The Lady).
Ballads. Square 16mo. Cloth, price 3s. 6d.

MILLER (Edward).
The History and Doctrines of Irvingism ; or, the so-called Catholic and Apostolic Church. 2 vols. Large post 8vo. Cloth, price 25s.

The Church in Relation to the State. Crown 8vo. Cloth, price 7s. 6d.

MILNE (James).
Tables of Exchange for the
Conversion of Sterling Money into
Indian and Ceylon Currency, at
Rates from 1s. 8d. to 2s. 3d. per
Rupee. Second Edition. Demy
8vo. Cloth, price £2 2s.

MINCHIN (J. G.).
Bulgaria since the War.
Notes of a Tour in the Autumn of
1879. Small crown 8vo. Cloth,
price 3s. 6d.

MIVART (St. George), F.R.S.
Contemporary Evolution :
An Essay on some recent Social
Changes. Post 8vo. Cloth, price
7s. 6d.

MOCKLER (E.).
A Grammar of the Baloo-
chee Language, as it is spoken in
Makran (Ancient Gedrosia), in the
Persia-Arabic and Roman characters.
Fcap. 8vo. Cloth, price 5s.

MOFFAT (Robert Scott).
The Economy of Consump-
tion; an Omitted Chapter in Political
Economy, with special reference to
the Questions of Commercial Crises
and the Policy of Trades Unions; and
with Reviews of the Theories of Adam
Smith, Ricardo, J. S. Mill, Fawcett,
&c. Demy 8vo. Cloth, price 18s.

The Principles of a Time
Policy : being an Exposition of a
Method of Settling Disputes between
Employers and Employed in regard
to Time and Wages, by a simple Pro-
cess of Mercantile Barter, without
recourse to Strikes or Locks-out.
Reprinted from "The Economy of
Consumption," with a Preface and
Appendix containing Observations on
some Reviews of that book, and a Re-
criticism of the Theories of Ricardo
and J. S. Mill on Rent, Value, and
Cost of Production. Demy 8vo.
Cloth, price 3s. 6d.

MOLTKE (Field-Marshal Von).
Letters from Russia.
Translated by Robina Napier.
Crown 8vo. Cloth, price 6s.

Notes of Travel. Being Extracts from the Journals of. Crown
8vo. Cloth, price 6s.

Monmouth : A Drama, of which
the Outline is Historical. Dedicated
by permission to Mr. Henry Irving.
Small crown 8vo. Cloth, price 5s.

MORELL (J. R.).
Euclid Simplified in Me-
thod and Language. Being a
Manual of Geometry. Compiled from
the most important French Works,
approved by the University of Paris
and the Minister of Public Instruction. Fcap. 8vo. Cloth, price 2s. 6d.

MORICE (Rev. F. D.), M.A.
The Olympian and Pythian
Odes of Pindar. A New Transla-
tion in English Verse. Crown 8vo.
Cloth, price 7s. 6d.

MORSE (E. S.), Ph.D.
First Book of Zoology.
With numerous Illustrations. Crown
8vo. Cloth, price 5s.

MORSHEAD (E. D. A.)
The Agamemnon of Æs-
chylus. Translated into English
verse. With an Introductory Essay.
Crown 8vo. Cloth, price 5s.

MORTERRA (Felix).
The Legend of Allandale,
and other Poems. Small crown 8vo.
Cloth, price 6s.

NAAKE (J. T.).
Slavonic Fairy Tales.
From Russian, Servian, Polish, and
Bohemian Sources. With Four Illus-
trations. Crown 8vo. Cloth, price 5s.

NEWMAN (J. H.), D.D.
Characteristics from the
Writings of. Being Selections
from his various Works. Arranged
with the Author's personal approval.
Third Edition. With Portrait.
Crown 8vo. Cloth, price 6s.
** A Portrait of the Rev. Dr. J. H.
Newman, mounted for framing, can
be had, price 2s. 6d.

NICHOLAS (Thomas), Ph.D.,
F.G.S.
The Pedigree of the English
People: an Argument, Historical
and Scientific, on the Formation and
Growth of the Nation, tracing Race-
admixture in Britain from the earliest
times, with especial reference to the
incorporation of the Celtic Abori-
gines. Fifth Edition. Demy 8vo.
Cloth, price 16s.

NICHOLSON (Edward Byron).

The Christ Child, and other Poems. Crown 8vo. Cloth, price 4s. 6d.

The Rights of an Animal. Crown 8vo. Cloth, price 3s. 6d.

The Gospel according to the Hebrews. Its Fragments translated and annotated, with a critical Analysis of the External and Internal Evidence relating to it. Demy 8vo. Cloth, price 9s. 6d.

NICOLS (Arthur), F.G.S., F.R.G.S.

Chapters from the Physical History of the Earth. An Introduction to Geology and Palæontology, with numerous illustrations. Crown 8vo. Cloth, price 5s.

NOAKE (Major R. Compton).

The Bivouac ; or, Martial Lyrist, with an Appendix—Advice to the Soldier. Fcap. 8vo. Price 5s. 6d.

NORMAN PEOPLE (The).

The Norman People, and their Existing Descendants in the British Dominions and the United States of America. Demy 8vo. Cloth, price 21s.

NORRIS (Rev. Alfred).

The Inner and Outer Life Poems. Fcap. 8vo. Cloth, price 6s.

Notes on Cavalry Tactics, Organization, &c. By a Cavalry Officer. With Diagrams. Demy 8vo. Cloth, price 12s.

Nuces : Exercises on the Syntax of the Public School Latin Primer. New Edition in Three Parts. Crown 8vo. Each 1s.
*** The Three Parts can also be had bound together in cloth, price 3s.

O'BRIEN (Charlotte G.).

Light and Shade. 2 vols. Crown 8vo. Cloth, gilt tops, price 12s.

Ode of Life (The).

Third Edition. Fcap. 8vo. Cloth, price 5s.

O'HAGAN (John).

The Song of Roland. Translated into English Verse. Large post 8vo. Parchment antique, price 10s. 6d.

O'MEARA (Kathleen).

Frederic Ozanam, Professor of the Sorbonne ; His Life and Works. Second Edition. Crown 8vo. Cloth, price 7s. 6d.

Oriental Sporting Magazine (The).

A Reprint of the first 5 Volumes, in 2 Volumes. Demy 8vo. Cloth, price 28s.

OWEN (F. M.).

John Keats. A Study. Crown 8vo. Cloth, price 6s.

OWEN (Rev. Robert), B.D.

Sanctorale Catholicum ; or Book of Saints. With Notes, Critical, Exegetical, and Historical. Demy 8vo. Cloth, price 18s.

Palace and Prison and Fair Geraldine. Two Tragedies, by the Author of "Ginevra" and the "Duke of Guise." Crown 8vo. Cloth, 6s.

PALGRAVE (W. Gifford).

Hermann Agha ; An Eastern Narrative. Third and Cheaper Edition. Crown 8vo. Cloth, price 6s.

PALMER (Charles Walter).

The Weed : a Poem. Small crown 8vo. Cloth, price 3s.

PANDURANG HARI ;

Or, Memoirs of a Hindoo. With an Introductory Preface by Sir H. Bartle E. Frere, G.C.S.I., C.B. Crown 8vo. Price 6s.

PARKER (Joseph), D.D.

The Paraclete : An Essay on the Personality and Ministry of the Holy Ghost, with some reference to current discussions. Second Edition. Demy 8vo. Cloth, price 12s.

PARR (Capt. H. Hallam).

A Sketch of the Kafir and Zulu Wars : Guadana to Isandhlwana, with Maps. Small crown 8vo. Cloth, price 5s.

PARSLOE (Joseph).

Our Railways : Sketches, Historical and Descriptive. With Practical Information as to Fares, Rates, &c., and a Chapter on Railway Reform. Crown 8vo. Cloth, price 6s.

PATTISON (Mrs. Mark).

The Renaissance of Art in France. With Nineteen Steel Engravings. 2 vols. Demy 8vo. Cloth, price 32s.

PAUL (C. Kegan).

Mary Wollstonecraft. Letters to Imlay. With Prefatory Memoir by, and Two Portraits in *eau forte*, by Anna Lea Merritt. Crown 8vo. Cloth, price 6s.

Goethe's Faust. A New Translation in Rime. Crown 8vo. Cloth, price 6s.

William Godwin: His Friends and Contemporaries. With Portraits and Facsimiles of the Handwriting of Godwin and his Wife. 2 vols. Square post 8vo. Cloth, price 28s.

The Genius of Christianity Unveiled. Being Essays by William Godwin never before published. Edited, with a Preface, by C. Kegan Paul. Crown 8vo. Cloth, price 7s. 6d.

PAUL (Margaret Agnes).

Gentle and Simple : A Story. 2 vols. Crown 8vo. Cloth, gilt tops, price 12s.

*** Also a Cheaper Edition in one vol. with Frontispiece. Crown 8vo. Cloth, price 6s.

PAYNE (John).

Songs of Life and Death. Crown 8vo. Cloth, price 5s.

PAYNE (Prof. J. F.).

Lectures on Education. Price 6d.

II. Fröbel and the Kindergarten system. Second Edition.

PAYNE (Prof. J. F.)—*continued*.

A Visit to German Schools: Elementary Schools in Germany. Notes of a Professional Tour to inspect some of the Kindergartens, Primary Schools, Public Girls' Schools, and Schools for Technical Instruction in Hamburgh, Berlin, Dresden, Weimar, Gotha, Eisenach, in the autumn of 1874. With Critical Discussions of the General Principles and Practice of Kindergartens and other Schemes of Elementary Education. Crown 8vo. Cloth, price 4s. 6d.

PELLETAN (E.).

The Desert Pastor, Jean Jarousseau. Translated from the French. By Colonel E. P. De L'Hoste. With a Frontispiece. New Edition. Fcap. 8vo. Cloth, price 3s. 6d.

PENNELL (H. Cholmondeley).

Pegasus Resaddled. By the Author of "Puck on Pegasus," &c. &c. With Ten Full-page Illustrations by George Du Maurier. Second Edition. Fcap. 4to. Cloth elegant, price 12s. 6d.

PENRICE (Maj. J.), B.A.

A Dictionary and Glossary of the Ko-ran. With copious Grammatical References and Explanations of the Text. 4to. Cloth, price 21s.

PESCHEL (Dr. Oscar).

The Races of Man and their Geographical Distribution. Large crown 8vo. Cloth, price 9s.

PETTIGREW (J. Bell), M.D., F.R.S.

Animal Locomotion; or, Walking, Swimming, and Flying. With 130 Illustrations. Second Edition. Crown 8vo. Cloth, price 5s. Volume VII. of The International Scientific Series.

PFEIFFER (Emily).

Quarterman's Grace, and other Poems. Crown 8vo. Cloth, price 5s.

Glan Alarch: His Silence and Song. A Poem. Second Edition. Crown 8vo. price 6s.

PFEIFFER (Emily)—*continued.*
Gerard's Monument, and other Poems. Second Edition. Crown 8vo. Cloth, price 6*s.*

Poems. Second Edition. Crown 8vo. Cloth, price 6*s.*

Sonnets and Songs. New Edition. 16mo, handsomely printed and bound in cloth, gilt edges, price 5*s.*

PINCHES (Thomas), M.A.
Samuel Wilberforce: Faith —Service—Recompense. Three Sermons. With a Portrait of Bishop Wilberforce (after a Photograph by Charles Watkins). Crown 8vo. Cloth, price 4*s.* 6*d.*

PLAYFAIR (Lieut.-Col.), Her Britannic Majesty's Consul-General in Algiers.

Travels in the Footsteps of Bruce in Algeria and Tunis. Illustrated by facsimiles of Bruce's original Drawings, Photographs, Maps, &c. Royal 4to. Cloth, bevelled boards, gilt leaves, price £3 3*s.*

POLLOCK (W. H.).
Lectures on French Poets. Delivered at the Royal Institution. Small crown 8vo. Cloth, price 5*s.*

POUSHKIN (A. S.).
Russian Romance. Translated from the Tales of Belkin, &c. By Mrs. J. Buchan Telfer (*née* Mouravieff). Crown 8vo. Cloth, price 3*s.* 6*d.*

PRESBYTER.
Unfoldings of Christian Hope. An Essay showing that the Doctrine contained in the Damnatory Clauses of the Creed commonly called Athanasian is unscriptural. Small crown 8vo. Cloth, price 4*s.* 6*d.*

PRICE (Prof. Bonamy).
Currency and Banking. Crown 8vo. Cloth, price 6*s.*

Chapters on Practical Political Economy. Being the Substance of Lectures delivered before the University of Oxford. Large post 8vo. Cloth, price 12*s.*

Proteus and Amadeus. A Correspondence. Edited by Aubrey De Vere. Crown 8vo. Cloth, price 5*s.*

PUBLIC SCHOOLBOY.
The Volunteer, the Militiaman, and the Regular Soldier. Crown 8vo. Cloth, price 5*s.*

PULPIT COMMENTARY (The). Edited by the Rev. J. S. EXELL and the Rev. Canon H. D. M. SPENCE.

Ezra, Nehemiah, and Esther. By Rev. Canon G. Rawlinson, M.A.; with Homilies by Rev. Prof. J. R. Thomson, M.A., Rev. Prof. R. A. Redford, LL.B., M.A., Rev. W. S. Lewis, M.A., Rev. J. A. Macdonald, Rev. A. Mackennal, B.A., Rev. W. Clarkson, B.A., Rev. F. Hastings, Rev. W. Dinwiddie, LL.B., Rev. Prof. Rowlands, B.A., Rev. G. Wood, B.A., Rev. Prof. P. C. Barker, LL.B., M.A., and Rev. J. S. Exell. Second Edition. One Vol., price 12*s.* 6*d.*

1 Samuel. By the Very Rev. R. P. Smith, D.D. With Homilies by the Rev. Donald Fraser, D.D., Rev. Prof. Chapman, and Rev. B. Dale. Price 15*s.*

Punjaub (The) and North Western Frontier of India. By an old Punjaubee. Crown 8vo. Cloth, price 5*s.*

QUATREFAGES (Prof. A. de).
The Human Species. Second Edition. Crown 8vo. Cloth, price 5*s.*
Vol. XXVI. of The International Scientific Series.

RAVENSHAW (John Henry), B.C.S.
Gaur: Its Ruins and Inscriptions. Edited with considerable additions and alterations by his Widow. With forty-four photographic illustrations and twenty-five fac-similes of Inscriptions. Super royal 4to. Cloth, 3*l.* 13*s.* 6*d.*

READ (Carveth).
On the Theory of Logic: An Essay. Crown 8vo. Cloth, price 6*s.*

Realities of the Future Life. Small crown 8vo. Cloth, price 1*s.* 6*d.*

REANEY (Mrs. G. S.).
Blessing and Blessed; a Sketch of Girl Life. With a frontispiece. Crown 8vo. Cloth, price 5*s*.

Waking and Working; or, from Girlhood to·Womanhood. With a Frontispiece. Crown 8vo. Cloth, price 5*s*.

English Girls: their Place and Power. With a Preface by R. W. Dale, M.A., of Birmingham. Second Edition. Fcap. 8vo. Cloth, price 2*s*. 6*d*.

Just Anyone, and other Stories. Three Illustrations. Royal 16mo. Cloth, price 1*s*. 6*d*.

Sunshine Jenny and other Stories. Three Illustrations. Royal 16mo. Cloth, price 1*s*. 6*d*.

Sunbeam Willie, and other Stories. Three Illustrations. Royal 16mo. Cloth, price 1*s*. 6*d*.

REYNOLDS (Rev. J. W.).
The Supernatural in Na-ture. A Verification by Free Use of Science. Second Edition, revised and enlarged. Demy 8vo. Cloth, price 14*s*.

Mystery of Miracles, The. By the Author of "The Supernatural in Nature." Crown 8vo. Cloth, price 6*s*.

RIBOT (Prof. Th.).
English Psychology. Second Edition. A Revised and Corrected Translation from the latest French Edition. Large post 8vo. Cloth, price 9*s*.

Heredity: A Psychological Study on its Phenomena, its Laws, its Causes, and its Consequences. Large crown 8vo. Cloth, price 9*s*.

RINK (Chevalier Dr. Henry).
Greenland: Its People and its Products. By the Chevalier Dr. Henry Rink, President of the Greenland Board of Trade. With sixteen Illustrations, drawn by the Eskimo, and a Map. Edited by Dr. Robert Brown. Crown 8vo. Price 10*s*. 6*d*.

ROBERTSON (The Late Rev. F. W.), M.A., of Brighton.
Notes on Genesis. New and cheaper Edition. Crown 8vo., price 3*s*. 6*d*.

Sermons. Four Series. Small crown 8vo. Cloth, price 3*s*. 6*d*. each.

Expository Lectures on St. Paul's Epistles to the Corinthians. A New Edition. Small crown 8vo. Cloth, price 5*s*.

Lectures and Addresses, with other literary remains. A New Edition. Crown 8vo. Cloth, price 5*s*.

An Analysis of Mr. Tenny-son's "In Memoriam." (Dedicated by Permission to the Poet-Laureate.) Fcap. 8vo. Cloth, price 2*s*.

The Education of the Human Race. Translated from the German of Gotthold Ephraim Lessing. Fcap. 8vo. Cloth, price 2*s*. 6*d*.

Life and Letters. Edited by the Rev. Stopford Brooke, M.A., Chaplain in Ordinary to the Queen.

I. 2 vols., uniform with the Sermons. With Steel Portrait. Crown 8vo. Cloth, price 7*s*. 6*d*.

II. Library Edition, in Demy 8vo., with Two Steel Portraits. Cloth, price 12*s*.

III. A Popular Edition, in one vol. Crown 8vo. Cloth, price 6*s*.

The above Works can also be had half-bound in morocco.

*** A Portrait of the late Rev. F. W. Robertson, mounted for framing, can be had, price 2*s*. 6*d*.

ROBINSON (A. Mary F.).
A Handful of Honey-suckle. Fcap. 8vo. Cloth, price 3*s*. 6*d*.

RODWELL (G. F.), F.R.A.S., F.C.S.
Etna: a History of the Mountain and its Eruptions. With Maps and Illustrations. Square 8vo. Cloth, price 9*s*.

ROOD (Ogden N.).
Modern Chromatics, with
Applications to Art and Industry. With 130 Original Illustrations. Crown 8vo. Cloth, price 5s.
Vol. XXVII. of The International Scientific Series.

ROSS (Mrs. E.), ("Nelsie Brook").
Daddy's Pet. A Sketch
from Humble Life. With Six Illustrations. Royal 16mo. Cloth, price 1s.

ROSS (Alexander), D.D.
Memoir of Alexander
Ewing, Bishop of Argyll and the Isles. Second and Cheaper Edition. Demy 8vo. Cloth, price 10s. 6d.

SADLER (S. W.), R.N.
The African Cruiser. A
Midshipman's Adventures on the West Coast. With Three Illustrations. Second Edition. Crown 8vo. Cloth, price 3s. 6d.

SALTS (Rev. Alfred), LL.D.
Godparents at Confirmation. With a Preface by the Bishop of Manchester. Small crown 8vo. Cloth, limp, price 2s.

SAUNDERS (Katherine).
Gideon's Rock, and other
Stories. Crown 8vo. Cloth, price 6s.
Joan Merryweather, and other
Stories. Crown 8vo. Cloth, price 6s.
Margaret and Elizabeth.
A Story of the Sea. Crown 8vo. Cloth, price 6s.

SAUNDERS (John).
Israel Mort, Overman : A
Story of the Mine. Cr. 8vo. Price 6s.
Hirell. With Frontispiece.
Crown 8vo. Cloth, price 3s. 6d.
Abel Drake's Wife. With
Frontispiece. Crown 8vo. Cloth, price 3s. 6d.

SAYCE (Rev. Archibald Henry).
Introduction to the Science
of Language. Two vols., large post 8vo. Cloth, price 25s.

SCHELL (Maj. von).
The Operations of the
First Army under Gen. von Goeben. Translated by Col. C. H. von Wright. Four Maps. Demy 8vo. Cloth, price 9s.

SCHELL (Maj. von)—*continued.*
The Operations of the
First Army under Gen. von Steinmetz. Translated by Captain E. O. Hollist. Demy 8vo. Cloth, price 10s. 6d.

SCHELLENDORF (Maj.-Gen. B. von).
The Duties of the General
Staff. Translated from the German by Lieutenant Hare. Vol. I. Demy 8vo. Cloth, 10s. 6d.

SCHERFF (Maj. W. von).
Studies in the New Infantry Tactics. Parts I. and II. Translated from the German by Colonel Lumley Graham. Demy 8vo. Cloth, price 7s. 6d.

SCHMIDT (Prof. Oscar).
The Doctrine of Descent
and Darwinism. With 26 Illustrations. Third Edition. Crown 8vo. Cloth, price 5s.
Volume XII. of The International Scientific Series.

SCHÜTZENBERGER (Prof. F.).
Fermentation. With Numerous Illustrations. Second Edition. Crown 8vo. Cloth, price 5s.
Volume XX. of The International Scientific Series.

Scientific Layman. The New
Truth and the Old Faith : are they Incompatible? Demy 8vo. Cloth, price 10s. 6d.

SCOONES (W. Baptiste).
Four Centuries of English
Letters. A Selection of 350 Letters by 150 Writers from the period of the Paston Letters to the Present Time. Edited and arranged by. Large crown 8vo. Cloth, price 9s.

SCOTT (Leader).
A Nook in the Apennines:
A Summer beneath the Chestnuts. With Frontispiece, and 27 Illustrations in the Text, chiefly from Original Sketches. Crown 8vo. Cloth, price 7s. 6d.

SCOTT (Robert H.).
Weather Charts and Storm
Warnings. Illustrated. Second Edition. Crown 8vo. Cloth, price 3s. 6d.

Seeking his Fortune, and
other Stories. With Four Illustrations. Crown 8vo. Cloth, price 3s. 6d.

SENIOR (N. W.).

Alexis De Tocqueville. Correspondence and Conversations with Nassau W. Senior, from 1833 to 1859. Edited by M. C. M. Simpson. 2 vols. Large post 8vo. Cloth, price 21s.

Sermons to Naval Cadets. Preached on board H.M.S. "Britannia." Small crown 8vo. Cloth, price 3s. 6d.

Seven Autumn Leaves from Fairyland. Illustrated with Nine Etchings. Square crown 8vo. Cloth, price 3s. 6d.

SHADWELL (Maj.-Gen.), C.B.

Mountain Warfare. Illustrated by the Campaign of 1799 in Switzerland. Being a Translation of the Swiss Narrative compiled from the Works of the Archduke Charles, Jomini, and others. Also of Notes by General H. Dufour on the Campaign of the Valtelline in 1635. With Appendix, Maps, and Introductory Remarks. Demy 8vo. Cloth, price 16s.

SHAKSPEARE (Charles).

Saint Paul at Athens: Spiritual Christianity in Relation to some Aspects of Modern Thought. Nine Sermons preached at St. Stephen's Church, Westbourne Park. With Preface by the Rev. Canon FARRAR. Crown 8vo. Cloth, price 5s.

SHAW (Major Wilkinson).

The Elements of Modern Tactics. Practically applied to English Formations. With Twenty-five Plates and Maps. Small crown 8vo. Cloth, price 12s.

*** The Second Volume of "Military Handbooks for Officers and Non-commissioned Officers." Edited by Lieut.-Col. C. B. Brackenbury, R.A., A.A.G.

SHAW (Flora L.).

Castle Blair: a Story of Youthful Lives. 2 vols. Crown 8vo. Cloth, gilt tops, price 12s. Also, an edition in one vol. Crown 8vo. 6s.

SHELLEY (Lady).

Shelley Memorials from Authentic Sources. With (now first printed) an Essay on Christianity by Percy Bysshe Shelley. With Portrait. Third Edition. Crown 8vo. Cloth, price 5s.

SHELLEY (Percy Bysshe).

Poems selected from. Dedi-cated to Lady Shelley. With Preface by Richard Garnett. Printed on hand-made paper. With miniature frontispiece. Elzevir. 8vo., limp parchment antique. Price 6s., vellum 7s. 6d.

SHERMAN (Gen. W. T.).

Memoirs of General W. T. Sherman, Commander of the Federal Forces in the American Civil War. By Himself. 2 vols. With Map. Demy 8vo. Cloth, price 24s. *Copyright English Edition.*

SHILLITO (Rev. Joseph).

Womanhood: its Duties, Temptations, and Privileges. A Book for Young Women. Second Edition. Crown 8vo. Price 3s. 6d.

SHIPLEY (Rev. Orby), M.A.

Principles of the Faith in Relation to Sin. Topics for Thought in Times of Retreat. Eleven Addresses. With an Introduction on the neglect of Dogmatic Theology in the Church of England, and a Postscript on his leaving the Church of England. Demy 8vo. Cloth, price 12s.

Church Tracts, or Studies in Modern Problems. By various Writers. 2 vols. Crown 8vo. Cloth, price 5s. each.

SMITH (Edward), M.D., LL.B., F.R.S.

Health and Disease, as In-fluenced by the Daily, Seasonal, and other Cyclical Changes in the Human System. A New Edition. Post 8vo. Cloth, price 7s. 6d.

Foods. Profusely Illustrated. Sixth Edition. Crown 8vo. Cloth, price 5s.

Volume III. of The International Scientific Series.

SMITH (Edward), M.D., LL.B., F.R.S.—*continued.*

Practical Dietary for Families, Schools, and the Labouring Classes. A New Edition. Post 8vo. Cloth, price 3s. 6d.

Tubercular Consumption in its Early and Remediable Stages. Second Edition. Crown 8vo. Cloth, price 6s.

Songs of Two Worlds. By the Author of "The Epic of Hades." Fifth Edition. Complete in one Volume, with Portrait. Fcap. 8vo. Cloth, price 7s. 6d.

Songs for Music.
By Four Friends. Square crown 8vo. Cloth, price 5s.
Containing songs by Reginald A. Gatty, Stephen H. Gatty, Greville J. Chester, and Juliana Ewing.

SPEDDING (James).
Reviews and Discussions, Literary, Political, and Historical, not relating to Bacon. Demy 8vo. Cloth, price 12s. 6d.

SPENCER (Herbert).
The Study of Sociology. Eighth Edition. Crown 8vo. Cloth, price 5s.
Volume V. of The International Scientific Series.

STEDMAN (Edmund Clarence).
Lyrics and Idylls. With other Poems. Crown 8vo. Cloth, price 7s. 6d.

STEPHENS (Archibald John), LL.D.
The Folkestone Ritual Case. The Substance of the Argument delivered before the Judicial Committee of the Privy Council. On behalf of the Respondents. Demy 8vo. Cloth, price 6s.

STEVENS (William).
The Truce of God, and other Poems. Small crown 8vo. Cloth, price 3s. 6d.

STEVENSON (Robert Louis).
An Inland Voyage. With Frontispiece by Walter Crane. Crown 8vo. Cloth, price 7s. 6d.

STEVENSON (Robert Louis)—*continued.*
Travels with a Donkey in the Cevennes. With Frontispiece by Walter Crane. Crown 8vo. Cloth, price 7s. 6d.

STEVENSON (Rev. W. F.).
Hymns for the Church and Home. Selected and Edited by the Rev. W. Fleming Stevenson.
The most complete Hymn Book published.
The Hymn Book consists of Three Parts:—I. For Public Worship.—II. For Family and Private Worship.—III. For Children.
** *Published in various forms and prices, the latter ranging from 8d. to 6s. Lists and full particulars will be furnished on application to the Publishers.*

STEWART (Prof. Balfour), M.A., LL.D., F.R.S.
On the Conservation of Energy. Fifth Edition. With Fourteen Engravings. Crown 8vo. Cloth, price 5s.
Volume VI. of The International Scientific Series.

STORR (Francis), and TURNER Hawes).
Canterbury Chimes; or, Chaucer Tales retold to Children. With Illustrations from the Ellesmere MS. Extra Fcap. 8vo. Cloth, price 3s. 6d.

STRETTON (Hesba).
David Lloyd's Last Will. With Four Illustrations. Royal 16mo., price 2s. 6d.
The Wonderful Life. Thirteenth Thousand. Fcap. 8vo. Cloth, price 2s. 6d.
Through a Needle's Eye : a Story. 2 vols. Crown 8vo. Cloth, gilt top, price 12s.
** Also a Cheaper Edition in one volume, with Frontispiece. Crown 8vo. Cloth, price 6s.

STUBBS (Lieut.-Colonel F. W.)
The Regiment of Bengal Artillery. The History of its Organization, Equipment, and War Services. Compiled from Published Works, Official Records, and various Private Sources. With numerous Maps and Illustrations. 2 vols. Demy 8vo. Cloth, price 32s.

STUMM (Lieut. Hugo), German Military Attaché to the Khivan Expedition.

Russia's advance Eastward. Based on the Official Reports of. Translated by Capt. C. E. H. VINCENT. With Map. Crown 8vo. Cloth, price 6s.

SULLY (James), M.A.
Sensation and Intuition. Demy 8vo. Cloth, price 10s. 6d.

Pessimism : a History and a Criticism. Demy 8vo. Price 14s.

Sunnyland Stories.
By the Author of "Aunt Mary's Bran Pie." Illustrated. Small 8vo. Cloth, price 3s. 6d.

Sweet Silvery Sayings of Shakespeare. Crown 8vo. Cloth gilt, price 7s. 6d.

SYME (David).
Outlines of an Industrial Science. Second Edition. Crown 8vo. Cloth, price 6s.

Tales from Ariosto. Retold for Children, by a Lady. With three illustrations. Crown 8vo. Cloth, price 4s. 6d.

TAYLOR (Algernon).
Guienne. Notes of an Autumn Tour. Crown 8vo. Cloth, price 4s. 6d.

TAYLOR (Sir H.).
Works Complete. Author's Edition, in 5 vols. Crown 8vo. Cloth, price 6s. each.

Vols. I. to III. containing the Poetical Works, Vols. IV. and V. the Prose Works.

TAYLOR (Col. Meadows), C.S.I., M.R.I.A.
A Noble Queen : a Romance of Indian History. Crown 8vo. Cloth. Price 6s.

Seeta. 3 vols. Crown 8vo. Cloth.

Tippoo Sultaun : a Tale of the Mysore War. New Edition with Frontispiece. Crown 8vo. Cloth, price 6s.

TAYLOR (Col. Meadows), C.S.I., M.R.I.A.—*continued.*
Ralph Darnell. New and Cheaper Edition. With Frontispiece. Crown 8vo. Cloth, price 6s.

The Confessions of a Thug. New Edition. Crown 8vo. Cloth, price 6s.

Tara : a Mahratta Tale. New Edition. Crown 8vo. Cloth, price 6s.

TEBBITT (Charles) and Francis Lloyd.
Extension of Empire Weak- ness ? Deficits Ruin ? With a Practical Scheme for the Reconstruction of Asiatic Turkey. Small crown 8vo. Cloth, price 3s. 6d.

TENNYSON (Alfred).
The Imperial Library Edi- tion. Complete in 7 vols. Demy 8vo. Cloth, price £3 13s. 6d. ; in Roxburgh binding, £4 7s. 6d.

Author's Edition. Complete in 6 Volumes. Post 8vo. Cloth gilt ; or half-morocco, Roxburgh style :—

VOL. I. **Early Poems, and** English Idylls. Price 6s. ; Roxburgh, 7s. 6d.

VOL. II. **Locksley Hall,** Lucretius, and other Poems. Price 6s. ; Roxburgh, 7s. 6d.

VOL. III. **The Idylls of** the King (*Complete*). Price 7s. 6d.; Roxburgh, 9s.

VOL. IV. **The Princess, and** Maud. Price 6s.; Roxburgh, 7s. 6d.

VOL. V. **Enoch Arden,** and In Memoriam. Price 6s. ; Roxburgh, 7s. 6d.

VOL. VI. **Dramas.** Price 7s. ; Roxburgh, 8s. 6d.

Cabinet Edition. 12 vols. Each with Frontispiece. Fcap. 8vo. Cloth, price 2s. 6d. each.
CABINET EDITION. 12 vols. Complete in handsome Ornamental Case. 32s.

Pocket Volume Edition. 13 vols. In neat case, 36s. Ditto, ditto. Extra cloth gilt, in case, 42s.

TENNYSON (Alfred)—*continued.*

The Royal Edition. Complete in one vol. Cloth, 16s. Cloth extra, 18s. Roxburgh, half morocco, price 20s.

The Guinea Edition. Complete in 12 vols., neatly bound and enclosed in box. Cloth, price 21s. French morocco, price 31s. 6d.

The Shilling Edition of the Poetical and Dramatic Works, in 12 vols., pocket size. Price 1s. each.

The Crown Edition. Complete in one vol., strongly bound in cloth, price 6s. Cloth, extra gilt leaves, price 7s. 6d. Roxburgh, half morocco, price 8s. 6d.

*** Can also be had in a variety of other bindings.

Original Editions:

The Lover's Tale. (Now for the first time published.) Fcap. 8vo. Cloth, 3s. 6d.

Poems. Small 8vo. Cloth, price 6s.

Maud, and other **Poems.** Small 8vo. Cloth, price 3s. 6d.

The Princess. Small 8vo. Cloth, price 3s. 6d.

Idylls of the King. Small 8vo. Cloth, price 5s.

Idylls of the King. Complete. Small 8vo. Cloth, price 6s.

The Holy Grail, and other Poems. Small 8vo. Cloth, price 4s. 6d.

Gareth and Lynette. Small 8vo. Cloth, price 3s.

Enoch Arden, &c. Small 8vo. Cloth, price 3s. 6d.

In Memoriam. Small 8vo. Cloth, price 4s.

Queen Mary. A Drama. New Edition. Crown 8vo. Cloth, price 6s.

Harold. A Drama. Crown 8vo. Cloth, price 6s.

Selections from Tenny- son's Works. Super royal 16mo. Cloth, price 3s. 6d. Cloth gilt extra, price 4s.

TENNYSON (Alfred)—*continued.*

Songs from Tennyson's Works. Super royal 16mo. Cloth extra, price 3s. 6d.
Also a cheap edition. 16mo. Cloth, price 2s. 6d.

Idylls of the King, and other Poems. Illustrated by Julia Margaret Cameron. 2 vols. Folio. Half-bound morocco, cloth sides, price £6 6s. each.

Tennyson for the Young and for Recitation. Specially arranged. Fcap. 8vo. Price 1s. 6d.

Tennyson Birthday Book. Edited by Emily Shakespear. 32mo. Cloth limp, 2s.; cloth extra, 3s.
*** A superior edition, printed in red and black, on antique paper, specially prepared. Small crown 8vo. Cloth extra, gilt leaves, price 5s.; and in various calf and morocco bindings.

In Memoriam. A new Edition, choicely printed on hand-made paper, with a Miniature Portrait in *eau forte* by Le Rat, after a photograph by the late Mrs. Cameron. Bound in limp parchment, antique, price 6s., vellum 7s. 6d.

The Princess. A Medley. Choicely printed on hand-made paper, with a miniature frontispiece by H. M. Paget and a tail-piece in outline by Gordon Browne. Limp parchment, antique, price 6s., vellum, price 7s.

Songs Set to Music, by various Composers. Edited by W. G. Cusins. Dedicated by express permission to Her Majesty the Queen. Royal 4to. Cloth extra, gilt leaves, price 21s., or in half-morocco, price 25s.

THOMAS (Moy).
A Fight for Life. With Frontispiece. Crown 8vo. Cloth, price 3s. 6d.

THOMPSON (Alice C.).
Preludes. A Volume of Poems. Illustrated by Elizabeth Thompson (Painter of "The Roll Call"). 8vo. Cloth, price 7s. 6d.

THOMSON (J. Turnbull).
Social Problems; or, an Inquiry into the Law of Influences. With Diagrams. Demy 8vo. Cloth, price 10s. 6d.

THRING (Rev. Godfrey), B.A.
Hymns and Sacred Lyrics. Fcap. 8vo. Cloth, price 3s. 6d.

THURSTON (Prof. R. H.).
A History of the Growth of the Steam Engine. With numerous Illustrations. Second Edition. Crown 8vo. Cloth, price 6s. 6d.

TODHUNTER (Dr. J.)
A Study of Shelley. Crown 8vo. Cloth, price 7s.

Alcestis: A Dramatic Poem. Extra fcap. 8vo. Cloth, price 5s.

Laurella; and other Poems. Crown 8vo. Cloth, price 6s. 6d.

TOLINGSBY (Frere).
Elnora. An Indian Mythological Poem. Fcap. 8vo. Cloth, price 6s.

Translations from Dante, Petrarch, Michael Angelo, and Vittoria Colonna. Fcap. 8vo. Cloth, price 7s. 6d.

TURNER (Rev. C. Tennyson).
Sonnets, Lyrics, and Translations. Crown 8vo. Cloth, price 4s. 6d.

TWINING (Louisa).
Recollections of Workhouse Visiting and Management during twenty-five years. Small crown 8vo. Cloth, price 3s. 6d.

TYNDALL (John), LL.D., F.R.S
Forms of Water. A Familiar Exposition of the Origin and Phenomena of Glaciers. With Twenty-five Illustrations. Seventh Edition. Crown 8vo. Cloth, price 5s.
Volume I. of The International Scientific Series.

VAN BENEDEN (Mons.).
Animal Parasites and Messmates. With 83 Illustrations. Second Edition. Cloth, price 5s.
Volume XIX of The International Scientific Series.

VAUGHAN (H. Halford), sometime Regius Professor of Modern History in Oxford University.
New Readings and Renderings of Shakespeare's Tragedies. Vol. I. Demy 8vo. Cloth, price 15s.

VILLARI (Prof.).
Niccolo Machiavelli and His Times. Translated by Linda Villari. 2 vols. Large post 8vo. Cloth, price 24s.

VINCENT (Capt. C. E. H.).
Elementary Military Geography, Reconnoitring, and Sketching. Compiled for Non-Commissioned Officers and Soldiers of all Arms. Square crown 8vo. Cloth, price 2s. 6d.

VOGEL (Dr. Hermann).
The Chemical Effects of Light and Photography, in their application to Art, Science, and Industry. The translation thoroughly revised. With 100 Illustrations, including some beautiful specimens of Photography. Third Edition. Crown 8vo. Cloth, price 5s.
Volume XV. of The International Scientific Series.

VYNER (Lady Mary).
Every day a Portion. Adapted from the Bible and the Prayer Book, for the Private Devotions of those living in Widowhood. Collected and edited by Lady Mary Vyner. Square crown 8vo. Cloth extra, price 5s.

WALDSTEIN (Charles), Ph. D.
The Balance of Emotion and Intellect: An Essay Introductory to the Study of Philosophy. Crown 8vo. Cloth, price 6s.

WALLER (Rev. C. B.)
The Apocalypse, Reviewed under the Light of the Doctrine of the Unfolding Ages and the Restitution of all Things. Demy 8vo. Cloth, price 12s.

WALTERS (Sophia Lydia).
The Brook: A Poem. Small crown 8vo. Cloth, price 3s. 6d.

WALTERS (Sophia Lydia)—*continued.*
A Dreamer's Sketch Book.
With Twenty-one Illustrations by Percival Skelton, R. P. Leitch, W. H. J. Boot, and T. R. Pritchett. Engraved by J. D. Cooper. Fcap. 4to. Cloth, price 12s. 6d.

WARTENSLEBEN (Count H. von).
The Operations of the South Army in January and February, 1871. Compiled from the Official War Documents of the Head-quarters of the Southern Army. Translated by Colonel C. H. von Wright. With Maps. Demy 8vo. Cloth, price 6s.

The Operations of the First Army under Gen. von Manteuffel. Translated by Colonel C. H. von Wright. Uniform with the above. Demy 8vo. Cloth, price 9s.

WATERFIELD, W.
Hymns for Holy Days and Seasons. 32mo. Cloth, price 1s. 6d.

WATSON (William).
The Prince's Quest and other Poems. Crown 8vo. Cloth, price 5s.

WATSON (Sir Thomas), Bart., M.D.
The Abolition of Zymotic Diseases, and of other similar enemies of Mankind. Small crown 8vo. Cloth, price 3s. 6d.

WAY (A.), M.A.
The Odes of Horace Lite- rally Translated in Metre. Fcap. 8vo. Cloth, price 2s.

WEBSTER (Augusta).
Disguises. A Drama. Small crown 8vo. Cloth, price 5s.

WEDMORE (Frederick).
The Masters of Genre Painting. With sixteen illustrations. Crown 8vo. Cloth, price 7s. 6d

WELLS (Capt. John C.), R.N.
Spitzbergen—The Gate- way to the Polynia; or, A Voyage to Spitzbergen. With numerous Illustrations by Whymper and others, and Map. New and Cheaper Edition. Demy 8vo. Cloth, price 6s.

Wet Days, by a Farmer.
Small crown 8vo. Cloth, price 6s.

WETMORE (W. S.).
Commercial Telegraphic Code. Second Edition. Post 4to. Boards, price 42s.

WHITAKER (Florence).
Christy's Inheritance. A London Story. Illustrated. Royal 16mo. Cloth, price 1s. 6d.

WHITE (A. D.), LL.D.
Warfare of Science. With Prefatory Note by Professor Tyndall. Second Edition. Crown 8vo. Cloth, price 3s. 6d.

WHITNEY (Prof. W. D.)
The Life and Growth of Language. Second Edition. Crown 8vo. Cloth, price 5s. *Copyright Edition.*
Volume XVI. of The International Scientific Series.

Essentials of English Grammar for the Use of Schools. Crown 8vo. Cloth, price 3s. 6d.

WICKHAM (Capt. E. H., R.A.)
Influence of Firearms upon Tactics : Historical and Critical Investigations. By an OFFICER OF SUPERIOR RANK (in the German Army). Translated by Captain E. H. Wickham, R.A. Demy 8vo. Cloth, price 7s. 6d.

WICKSTEED (P. H.).
Dante : Six Sermons. Crown 8vo. Cloth, price 5s.

WILLIAMS (Rowland), D.D.
Life and Letters of, with Extracts from his Note-Books. Edited by Mrs. Rowland Williams. With a Photographic Portrait. 2 vols. Large post 8vo. Cloth, price 24s.

Stray Thoughts from the Note-Books of the Late Rowland Williams, D.D. Edited by his Widow. Crown 8vo. Cloth, price 3s. 6d.

Psalms, Litanies, Coun- sels and Collects for Devout Persons. Edited by his Widow. New and Popular Edition. Crown 8vo. Cloth, price 3s. 6d.

WILLIS (R.), M.D.
Servetus and Calvin : a Study of an Important Epoch in the Early History of the Reformation. 8vo. Cloth, price 16s.

William Harvey. A History of the Discovery of the Circulation of the Blood. With a Portrait of Harvey, after Faithorne. Demy 8vo. Cloth, price 14s.

WILLOUGHBY (The Hon. Mrs.).
On the North Wind — **Thistledown.** A Volume of Poems. Elegantly bound. Small crown 8vo. Cloth, price 7s. 6d.

WILSON (H. Schütz).
The Tower and Scaffold. A Miniature Monograph. Large fcap. 8vo. Price 1s.

Within Sound of the Sea. By the Author of "Blue Roses," "Vera," &c. Third Edition. 2 vols. Crown 8vo. Cloth, gilt tops, price 12s.
     **** Also a cheaper edition in one Vol. with frontispiece. Crown 8vo. Cloth, price 6s.

WOINOVITS (Capt. I.).
Austrian Cavalry Exercise. Translated by Captain W. S. Cooke. Crown 8vo. Cloth, price 7s.

WOLLSTONECRAFT (Mary).
Letters to Imlay. With a Preparatory Memoir by C. Kegan Paul, and two Portraits in *eau forte* by Anna Lea Merritt. Crown 8vo. Cloth, price 6s.

WOLTMANN (Dr. Alfred), and WOERMANN (Dr. Karl).
History of Painting. Edited by Sidney Colvin. With numerous illustrations. Medium 8vo. Vol. I. Painting in Antiquity and the Middle Ages. Cloth, price 28s. ; cloth, bevelled boards, gilt leaves, price 30s.

WOOD (Major-General J. Creighton).
Doubling the Consonant. Small crown 8vo. Cloth, price 1s. 6d.

WOODS (James Chapman).
A Child of the People, and other poems. Small crown 8vo. Cloth, price 5s.

WRIGHT (Rev. David), M.A.
Waiting for the Light, and other Sermons. Crown 8vo. Cloth, price 6s.

WURTZ (Professor).
The Atomic Theory. Translated by E. Cleminshaw, F.C.S. Crown 8vo. Cloth, price 5s.
     Vol. XXX. of The International Scientific Series.

YOUMANS (Eliza A.).
An Essay on the Culture of the Observing Powers of Children, especially in connection with the Study of Botany. Edited, with Notes and a Supplement, by Joseph Payne, F.C.P., Author of "Lectures on the Science and Art of Education," &c. Crown 8vo. Cloth, price 2s. 6d.

First Book of Botany. Designed to Cultivate the Observing Powers of Children. With 300 Engravings. New and Cheaper Edition. Crown 8vo. Cloth, price 2s. 6d.

YOUMANS (Edward L.), M.D.
A Class Book of Chemistry, on the Basis of the New System. With 200 Illustrations. Crown 8vo. Cloth, price 5s.

YOUNG (William).
Gottlob, etcetera.   Small crown 8vo. Cloth, price 3s. 6d.

ZIMMERN (H.).
Stories in Precious Stones. With Six Illustrations. Third Edition. Crown 8vo. Cloth, price 5s.

www.ingramcontent.com/pod-product-compliance
Lightning Source LLC
Chambersburg PA
CBHW021752110726
47902CB00006B/1496